The Pawnbro

Clare Hawkins

First Published in 2022 by
Blossom Spring Publishing
The Pawnbroker's Pledge
Copyright © 2022 Clare Hawkins
ISBN 978-1-7397357-3-9
E: admin@blossomspringpublishing.com
W: www.blossomspringpublishing.com
Published in the United Kingdom.

Chapter 1

'Blood sucker, that's what you are,' said the woman to Nathan.

Insults went with his trade, though today the words stung more keenly.

The woman stuck her hand into the pocket of her apron and pulled out a couple of farthings. A small child with matted hair clutched her skirts, staring at Nathan; an imp, a little devil to shame him to pity, as though the woman had trained him for such work.

'I'll take that if it's all you have,' Nathan sighed, averting his eyes from the child's face.

Most who came to him lived from hand to mouth. Why should he show favour to these two? The woman's face softened, her scowl vanishing quickly.

'I'll redeem it next week,' she said.

She eyed him as she handed over the coins, as though he meant to pluck the hand from her arm as forfeit. Nathan entered the payment in his ledger, noting that the woman had pledged this same coat three times previously. A moment later the two were gone.

Filthy profiteer, pedlar of misery, usurer, all these names he'd been called and never denied them. It was fruitless to say that necessity had driven him into this trade, that he too had to live, though these days he would gladly have relinquished even that impulse. He could argue that he was providing a service, and did so according to the regulations. His business was a means whereby people could stay alive, though they might have to strip the clothes from their backs in order to do so.

His cash box was half full when he turned the key on it, preparing to shut the shop for the night. Wearily, Nathan carried out the first wooden shutter to secure it to the shop window outside. On the street, the late shoppers and costermongers were still about. Two regular beggars sat close by his shop on the pavement. A cart laden with horse dung rolled slowly past, pushed by a crook-backed man. Nathan coughed, the smoke catching his throat and looked the other way down the street, before slotting the shutter in place, fastening the metal hook and eye with the first padlock.

'Sir, spare a penny?' croaked one of the beggars half-heartedly, a man with a long, tangled beard.

Nathan took a few steps towards them and tossed two halfpennies. He knew that he shouldn't have started this habit, as he could hardly afford it, but he couldn't break it now. He was about to return for the next shutter when there was a shout from a distance down the street.

'Wait, wait, mister.'

It was a young woman or rather a girl, running towards him along the street. She moved awkwardly, dragging one foot, clutching a bundle of cloth in front of her, dodging past the few other pedestrians. He stopped and watched her coming, a small figure in a dirty white linen cap, bare-footed. He debated whether to ignore her, to finish securing his shop and bolt the door against her. Business was done for the day. He'd had enough. But he didn't move. The sight of her white face, her halting gait and the bundle she was holding made him stay and wait for her.

'I have something here, mister,' she said, gasping with the effort of her urgent pace.

She looked to Nathan around twelve years of age. Her face had the grey pallor of the unwashed, her legs were sticks, one foot a deformed, foreshortened thing and her eyes were large and darkly sunken in their sockets. His own sick daughter had looked at him with eyes like that.

'What have you there?' he asked. 'Do you want to pledge it?'

'A gown sir, yes sir, a fine one too, given by my mistress. She's no more need of it.'

Nathan scrutinised the girl from the grimy cap to her muddy feet. She was no servant. She was probably a thief.

'It's my ma and my brothers and sisters. We've not had bread in days,' she said.

So, what matter if she were a thief? She was poor and hungry. And hadn't he taken many a pilfered silk handkerchief, jewels and trinkets, even silver he knew had been burgled from houses? He'd been forced to it, in those times of sickness when he'd have done anything for money, for doctors and their useless potions. That past was a shame to him. His place wasn't one of these dolly shops, where fences shifted their goods. His was a licensed business in Fleet Street after all, and he'd promised Kate he'd not deal with thieves. Mercifully, she had never known of his broken promises. But now, with this child standing before him, he reasoned that it was possible that she might have come by the gown by other means than theft.

'Come in,' he said to her.

In the shop he took the thing from her and shook it out, holding it up by the shoulders. It was a silk gown, full-skirted, a day dress, not of the very best quality, but a sound fabric, well-made, a Sunday dress for a respectable shop keeper's or apothecary's wife maybe. The stuff was woven in stripes of green and cream, with a velvet collar and lace cuffs. It was crumpled by the handling, but as a faint rose scent wafted from its folds, he fancied that the wearer had not long quitted it. It was not warm, but nor was it chilled and fusty as stored garments frequently are.

'Your mistress gave you this?' he said to the girl, peering at her, searching her face for the trace of a lie.

She fidgeted, dipping from one foot to the other.

'She's no use for it now. She says, "take it, Betty, for it's more than I owes you." So, mister, what'll you give me on it?'

Maybe the girl's story was true, and Nathan, without the will to debate with himself about it, wanted to get rid of her and be done, close the shop, get his supper and a drink.

'Ten shillings,' he said, 'and a half penny a week if you wish to redeem it.'

The girl's eyes widened and she held out her filthy hand.

'Name?' Nathan said, opening the ledger.

The girl stared at him.

'I need to take a note of your details,' Nathan said. 'Your name, address. It's the law.'

'Liza,' she said.

He half-smiled at her poor attempt at a lie.

'I thought you said your name was Betty.'

She wriggled as she stood before him but held her gaze.

'Elizabeth, that's what I was christened. There's some call me Betty and some says Liza Hopkins. Elizabeth Hopkins and I live up Portugal Street, next to the fishmonger.'

Nathan had to admire her quickness and knew that she would never return to redeem the dress. The ten shillings was a fortune to her, as the surprise on her thin face had shown. Ten shillings was too much, he knew. He would make nothing on it, when he had to auction it or sell it at the market after it had lain unclaimed for the statutory fifteen months.

He opened his cash box again and handed the money to the girl. She took the five florins in her palm and stared for a few seconds, before clamping them tight in her grip.

'Your ticket,' Nathan said, as the girl turned to go.

She grabbed the slip of paper from his hand and limped quickly out, without another look or word to him. Nathan laid the gown over the counter of his shop and went to shutter up the

5

other window.

In his small parlour at the back of the shop, after a supper of bread and salt pork, Nathan poured himself a brandy. It was his habitual comfort and gave hope of at least a few hours' sleep, though if he sank too far into its depths, he would dream and wake in a sweat, or with a howl sometimes. On the nights when sleep did not come at all, he lay listening, hoping, dreading the sound of soft footsteps coming near to his bed, of whispering children's voices, a trickle of fingers touching his hand.

Nathan sometimes could not tell the hour, whether it was morning or night. The smoky air or fog made it hard work for the sun to penetrate, so the day and night seemed to him to merge into one. The next morning however, a pale glow lit his window, so he rose to splash chill water on his face and strop his razor. He used no glass; after their deaths he could not look at himself, the sole survivor. He imagined his tough, forbidding countenance, so unwholesome that the disease had fled at one look, preferring the tender flesh of his children and his wife.

A spark of sunlight through the shutters made him hurry his ablutions and he gulped down bread and a brew of tea to break his fast. He stepped out into a morning which smelt less foul than some days, with the blurred sun creeping over the rooftops opposite. He removed the shutters and returned inside the shop. It was then that he noticed the gown, lying where he had placed it, over the counter, after the departure of the girl. The light now caught the green stripes of the silk and Nathan lifted it up once more.

He held it close to his face, smelt the faintest trace of roses and tightened his arms around it, as though the form of the woman were still there and might swell to fill his embrace. He ran his hand down its smooth skirt, felt the thin ridge of a seam and something harder, more resistant at the side. The skirt was gathered tightly for a small waist and at the side he detected a slit in the seam, an artfully concealed pocket. The opening was small, for a lady's hand, but he managed to probe with his fingers and reached inside. He gasped, shocked at what seemed to him almost an act of lewdness, to be exploring with such intimacy. Then his finger touched something, a folded paper in the pocket. Carefully he withdrew it and brought it into the light. He laid the dress down again. Upon the outside was written in a woman's hand: **To Miss Burdett.** The other side of the paper contained a letter, densely black in the same small, neat hand.

The Yard, Dombey Street,
Whitechapel

Dear Miss Burdett,

Forgive me for this intrusion by a person scarce known to you. I bear the name of someone who once served you and your family, for he was my dear husband, now departed this life. I would not have presumed upon your mercy and charity for help, had I other means to preserve myself and my poor child, the only one spared to me.

My husband, James Harding, on leaving your father's service of many years as coachman, groom and stableman, took up the trade of saddlemaker. Sadly his business did not thrive, not through want of diligence on his part, but due to the cruelty of one who claimed to be his partner, and who stole from us all the money we had laid out for the pursuance of the business. So, my husband took low work in the docks and I plain sewing and laundering to keep our children fed, attending school and our rent paid.

Then the cholera came and took my husband and my children, all save one, my youngest daughter of only nine years now. I too am afflicted with sickness and cannot work, so it is with regret that I am begging you to lend me aid. I seek only a loan of such monies as will pay the rent for a room and food for a month when I shall be well enough again to take in work and support my child.

I know you are a bountiful Christian lady and hope that you will answer my plea, in remembrance of the long and faithful service rendered to you and your family by my late husband. I only have one wish that my daughter will live and thrive and will be saved the fate of many unfortunate girls in this city who find themselves orphans, homeless and friendless.

May God bless you and keep you for your kind consideration of my plea.

Your servant,
Selina Harding

Nathan sat down. A tightness gripped his throat and chest. It was some moments before he could chase away the images that flitted behind his closed eyelids, as he failed to blot out the sight of death by cholera. He scanned the letter again. The name of the would-be benefactress, Miss Angela Burdett, seemed somehow familiar to him, though he could not recall where he might have heard it before.

He turned to the letter again, noting the address of the writer. The street in Whitechapel he knew to be a poor place of crowded tenements. The letter was well-written, however, by a person who had been schooled, a little unlikely for the wife of a saddler maybe. Was this letter a genuine plea, or some fraudulent effort to beguile a rich and benevolent lady? It did not seem so to him, though he knew that sometimes his judgement, in weaker moments, was not sound. If she were real, the unfortunate writer was almost certainly dead by now, if the desperation of her need was as great as the letter stated. If so, why had she not pawned the gown or sold it herself? The price would have saved her from destitution at least for a while. The woman said that she was sick, however, and was maybe incapable of rising from her bed. And what of her child, if there was one? The girl who had brought him the gown was almost certainly not this woman's servant, as he had suspected.

He was roused by a knock on the door and saw, by the ancient gold watch he had in his waistcoat, that it was already the hour when he usually opened up. He picked up the letter, slid it into his pocket and went to the door.

A trickle of customers came by during the morning, some to pay their paltry retainers, one even to reclaim a cheap, battered locket that she held in her hand as though it were a jewel from the royal crown itself. Later an Irishman, a gentleman by his manner and speech, came to pledge a wool cloak, a heavy thing of fine quality.

'Richard Dunn, barrister at law,' said the man with an arrogant toss of his head, at Nathan's request for his name and address, 'presently residing at Number 10 Dean's Court.'

'I can give you three pounds on this sir,' said Nathan.

'Dammit,' said the man. 'It's robbery.'

'No, sir,' said Nathan, writing out the ticket. 'Not at all. It is a loan, for you will surely redeem it.'

'In a good way of business, are you, fleecing folk?' he sneered.

Nathan, unable to conceal his irritation, picked up his pen as though intending to strike out the entry in the ledger.

'Sir, you may go elsewhere if you wish,' he

said.

'No, just hand over the money,' said the gentleman, grabbing the pawn ticket and sweeping out of the shop, in a show of disdainful superiority.

As Nathan endured the rest of the morning trade, he found himself troubled more and more by thoughts of the letter writer and her child. He checked his watch at three o'clock in the afternoon and made a decision. He would close up for an hour or two. There was likely little business to be lost in that time.

He set out along Fleet Street to the west, weaving his way through streams of folk that thronged the roadway. He was still unsure of what was driving him to go in search of the woman, as he knew that the chances of tracing her were poor, but he would not question himself any further about it. The letter was in his pocket, the gown hanging in a cupboard in the storeroom, though he'd pondered on whether he should have brought it with him, as an aid to identification.

He walked briskly once he had cleared the crowds on Fleet Street, up Chancery Lane, to reach Gray's Inn Road. It was unaccustomed exercise for him and he felt the pull and wheeze of his chest. He realised that he had not been this far from his shop for many months, nor had he been among so many people. His friend Silas would regularly come by to enquire after him. The widow Simpson too had brought pies, but he found it hard to exchange even a few words about everyday matters: the weather, the smoke or how business was going. He saw now how much he had withdrawn inside his own miserable self.

At the corner of the street a man was scraping out a slow fiddle tune, while a woman at his side sang. Her voice was harsh, its pitch rising and plunging in a plaintive Scots song: ...'til all the seas gang dry, my love, and the rocks melt wi' the sun...

He threw a penny into the hat that lay at the man's feet. Neither acknowledged his passing by; the woman sang with closed eyes.

As he walked, Nathan observed how it was possible in this city to move from the streets of prosperous dwellings to those of doleful poverty in a matter of five minutes. He was now entering a district of the latter state. The houses that lined the streets were mainly brick-built terraces, interspersed with older ones, even some jettied, timber framed shops from centuries past. Soon puddles of dirt appeared on the roadway and the houses became poorer, their brickwork stained and crumbling, the windows opaque with grime.

He turned into Dombey Street, a dark tunnel of terraces at one end, with older tenement buildings at the far one. A cluster of small children was grouped around something on the road, which Nathan saw was a dead rat, which the smallest boy was poking with a stick. A woman sat on a doorstep suckling a baby. Close by, three men engaged in a card game upon an upturned box broke off and stared as he came past. He was on the point of asking them where he could find The Yard, but guessed that it would be within the tenement block, as was typical in many such streets.

A narrow passageway cut in from the street down the side of the tall building and led him to a sordid quadrangle. A cesspit in the centre lay like a suppurating wound. All around rose blackened walls, marked with the dead eyes of windows. Cloths and greying garments hung from window ledges. The stench made Nathan gag and grope for the handkerchief in his pocket to cover his nose and mouth. A sudden screech came from a high window along with the sound of a bawling child. In the entrance to a stairway sat a few women, their heads bent in conversation, while a gaggle of half-naked children tossed small stones to each other nearby.

Nathan's shock was compounded with a realisation of his ignorance of such places. He dealt every day with the poor and the desperate, daily passed humble dwellings, dilapidated houses, but he had had no occasion to frequent such a place as this. He had known poverty, certainly, the draining worry of how to feed his family, the endless penny pinching, when his printing business had failed. But fortunately, he had been taken on by an old neighbour in the pawnbroker's shop, for which he'd managed to secure the lease when the old man died. He'd gone without food himself, too, when he'd had to pay for medicines. He knew well what it was to be gnawed by despair, but had never had to live like this, in a place unfit for pigs.

He thought of the letter writer, Mrs Harding, driven to this hellish place, maybe dying here too before she could deliver her letter. But what of the child? Nathan approached one of the men who lay half asleep near a doorway. He cleared his throat audibly and when the man made no movement, he addressed him.

'Excuse me, can you help me?' he said.

Nathan wondered for a brief moment if the man were still living. He moved closer, reaching out a tentative hand just as two youths, in dripping wet rags appeared in the yard. One, with a bloody foot, limped along yelping and hopped his way behind his companion.

'Lost yer way, mister?' called the uninjured one of the two to Nathan. 'I'll get you back on yer way for a penny.'

'I'm looking for someone,' Nathan replied, recoiling from the moribund figure of the man. His eye was drawn instead to the sight of the limping boy who was now half crawling along the ground, his injured foot trailing behind him. 'What happened to your friend?' he said.

The first youth glanced at the injured one. 'Got a nail in his foot, in the river. Went right in.'

Nathan saw now that the foot in question had a rusty spike protruding from the sole. Nathan winced.

'That needs to come out,' he said, taking a step towards the boy.

'Stay away from me, mister,' the youth

growled and Nathan saw the pain bleaching his face.

An injured animal, Nathan thought, ready to slink away to its lair to suffer and maybe die there alone.

'Who you looking for, then?' said the first boy, a lad of around fourteen, a loose shirt in rags dangling from a skinny body.

The dozing, half-dead man suddenly roused himself and snorted, while above, the child's cries were slowly weakening. A sheet of liquid, aimed at the cesspit, splashed down from a window above.

'A woman by the name of Mrs Harding and her daughter,' Nathan said to the boy.

He shook his head. 'Never heard of her. That her real name, is it?'

Nathan nodded. 'Selina Harding, a widow. Is there anyone else who might know of her?'

The boy shrugged. 'Maybe, there's folks come and go. Old Ma Salter. She's been here years.'

'And where might I find her?'

The youth nodded towards an upper window on the first floor over on the opposite side of the yard. The injured boy was now cradling his foot, balancing it over his knee and peering at the nail.

'Go to a surgeon,' Nathan said.

He reached into his pocket and found a shilling, which he handed to the wounded boy, who looked back with an expression somewhere between shock and disbelief. Nathan turned to the boy's companion.

'Take him, will you, or it will poison and go bad.'

The two said nothing, staring at him as he started across the yard to the doorway leading to the upper storey. The stairway was thick with filth and the stink of urine. On the first landing were two doors and Nathan chose the side which he thought the boy had indicated, then knocked. A woman's voice sounded inside, which he took as an invitation to enter.

It was a small dark room, containing a bed piled with tousled bedclothes in the midst of which sat two small silent children. At a fireplace with the ash of a dead fire, sat a squat woman in a black shawl and dirty lace cap. She was holding an infant of around a year old in her arms, asleep, mouth agape, emitting bubbling breaths. A torn straw mattress lay on the floor beside the woman and child. The only other furniture beyond the chair where the woman sat, was a cupboard in the corner containing a few bowls and stone pots.

'Pardon me,' Nathan said, removing his hat. 'Are you Mrs Salter?'

The woman grinned at him, her small eyes curious like a bird's. Her face was plump and white with a simple, open expression.

'Yes, I am and who might you be, sir?' she said.

Nathan told her and briefly explained his mission, that he had come across something belonging to a Mrs Selina Harding and needed to find her to return it. He held back for the moment from mentioning the young girl who had brought him the gown. She might well be here, living among a gang of thieves and pickpockets. Maybe, it occurred to him, that Mrs Salter herself might be a breeder of them. The old woman, however, had something almost homely about her, and in appearance and manner appeared out of place in this vile setting.

To Nathan's surprise, the woman nodded at the mention of the name Selina Harding.

'Yes, poor soul,' she said to Nathan's surprise. 'She came looking for somewhere to stay. She and her little girl; they'd been throwed out. Out of their lodgings, that is. Someone told her, go to Old Ma Salter, for she takes in all sorts. Well, I don't like to turn folk away.'

Nathan glanced at the empty mattress and the small children, who were now playing with some sort of limp rag while watching him from the bed. Could it be that this woman was simply a generous soul?

'I let them bed down here for a bit. She was very sick, poor woman.'

'And they've gone, have they? How long ago?'

The woman frowned, thinking. 'A week past, I reckon, must have been. One morning she rises up, though she's weak and pale as a sheet. Couldn't hardly walk. But anyway, she rises up and puts on her good gown that she has in her bundle. She does up her child as best she can too, hair combed and plaited.'

'Her best gown? What colour?'

Mrs Salter peered at Nathan, puzzled no doubt by his question.

'Green, striped, a pretty thing, but what matter? The poor woman puts it on and says she and her girl must go and seek relief. She thanks me and gives me this.'

The old woman grovelled for a few seconds in the folds of her skirt and pulled out a small lace handkerchief. She handed it to him and he saw the embroidered initials of her name SH.

'Do you know where she intended to go?' Nathan said, wondering if it had been her intention to deliver her letter by hand to Miss Burdett.

Mrs Salter shook her head. 'Workhouse maybe, or could've been the Sisters of Mercy or some such. She said she had no relatives or friends could help her.'

It was then that Nathan decided to describe the young girl who had brought him the gown. He gave her the fullest account of her appearance that he could remember, but the woman said she knew of no girl here that fitted the description. Nathan cast his eyes around the clutter of the room.

'These children?' Nathan said.

'Orphans or foundlings,' she said. 'There's others too, but they're out on the streets or maybe working, mudlarking, street sweeping and the like. Better than the workhouse anyway, or dead in the gutter.'

Nathan agreed. Whatever this Mrs Salter was, she provided a sanctuary, sordid and impoverished but at least without cruelty. He gave her sixpence for the handkerchief and his last shilling for food, at which she nodded and smiled her thanks. This was becoming a costly venture for him. He took his leave of the woman, descended again to the yard and was glad to note that the two boys had disappeared, he hoped, to have the injured one's foot tended.

Away from Dombey Street, he breathed a little more easily and with a small sense of satisfaction about what he had discovered of Selina Harding and her daughter. The mystery remained, however, of how the gown had been given up or stolen and how the girl had acquired it. And what had become of the two? He had little hope of being able to find the girl who had brought the gown to him, to question her.

As he walked, he pondered on the idea that Selina Harding might by now have contacted Miss Burdett by other means than her undelivered letter. But if not, should he not inform this lady of the desperate plight of a former employee's family? If Miss Burdett were a truly benevolent sort, a kindly lady, she would most likely feel it her duty to help. With this new conviction, his next step was to discover the address of this lady in order to convey a message to her.

It occurred to Nathan that a likely source of information might be a public house. Though it had been some time since he had frequented such places, he knew of one, in an alley off

Fleet Street, *The Cheshire Cheese*, where he remembered that the landlord, a garrulous sort, seemed abreast of all the current gossip and was an avid reader of newssheets and pamphlets. The place, so he had heard, was frequented by a few famous men of letters, as well as politicians and journalists, so he reckoned there was a good chance of finding someone there with knowledge of rich ladies in the city.

He entered the low-ceilinged building, into a room thick with smoke, with numerous small snugs and corners beyond, furnished with tables and stools for those who wished to indulge in private or serious talk. In the main parlour, however, was a polished mahogany bar, behind which two white-aproned men were busy drawing tankards of beer and ale for a busy house, full of the rumble of many conversations, punctuated by barks of laughter. Nathan made his way to the bar, where he saw, at the far end a man, who he was sure was the landlord in conversation with another. Nathan ordered a brandy and water and edged his way towards the landlord. The two men, noticing Nathan's approach, broke off.

'Pardon me,' Nathan said, 'but I wonder if you could help me with some information.'

The landlord looked Nathan up and down, with undisguised suspicion.

'Depends,' said the landlord.

His companion had turned to stare. Nathan cleared his throat, full of doubt about his chances of finding an answer to his query, but determined to press on with this reluctant pair.

'I have a letter, an important one that needs to be delivered to a Miss Burdett. She is a wealthy lady, I believe. Have you heard of a lady by that name?'

The landlord snorted and then grinned.

'Miss Burdett, she wouldn't just be the richest woman in the country now, would she?'

'In the whole bloody world,' said the other man with a note of disgruntled admiration.

Nathan saw their satisfaction at his ignorance and their desire to enlighten him. The landlord's plump face slackened. It was clear that he now reckoned that Nathan was an unthreatening presence. The man twisted around and whipped a paper out of a pile he had behind the bar. It appeared to be a newspaper and he rifled through it busily.

'Wait a minute. It's here somewhere,' he said.

'The lady's the heiress of Coutts, you know, the banker. Royalty banks with them and all the quality folk too,' said the landlord's companion helpfully while the search through the paper continued.

'Here,' said the landlord suddenly, thrusting the folded newspaper towards Nathan. 'Get a load of that. You can read, I suppose.'

Nathan scanned the paper and his eye lighted on the relevant item.

MORNING HERALD March 1837

MISS ANGELA BURDETT'S FORTUNE

The late Duchess of St. Albans has left this young lady the sum of £1,800,000. The weight of this enormous sum, in gold, reckoning 60 sovereigns to the pound, is 13 tons, 7cwt, 3 quarters 12 lbs and would require 107 men to carry it, supposing each of them carried 289lbs, being the weight of a sack of coal. Counting at the rate of 60 sovereigns in a minute, for eight hours a day, and six days a week, it would take ten weeks, two days and four hours to accomplish the task! In sovereigns, by the most exact computation, (each measuring in diameter 17 20ths of an inch and placed to touch each other), it would extend to the length of 24 miles and 260 yards.

Nathan tried not to react to the preposterous nature of the article, but he could see why it was a memorable piece.

'Unless it was another Miss Burdett you were after,' said the landlord.

'No, this is likely the lady,' said Nathan, hoping that his next question would be as fruitful as his first. 'Thank you, sir. Would you happen to know where Miss Burdett lives?'

At this the publican let out a loud guffaw.

'What? You mean to press your suit with the lady, eh? Or are you going a-begging?'

Nathan felt a surge of indignation and he replied stiffly.

'My enquiries are on behalf of another person.'

'Well, beg pardon, sir,' said the landlord, his tone larded with sarcasm.

But he looked around the assembled

company of drinkers at the tables nearby and called out loudly, holding up the paper which he'd snatched from Nathan.

'Hoi, any of you know where she lives this Miss Burdett or Miss Coutts or whatever she's called, that one that's rolling in money? Remember, her with millions.'

Three men sitting at a table at the side of the room appeared to confer for a moment.

'Burdett,' one of them called out. 'He's an MP ain't he? Don't he live somewhere in Piccadilly?'

The landlord turned to Nathan.

'That good enough for you?' he said.

That evening, after his supper, Nathan sat down to write a message to Miss Burdett, in the hope that he would be able to locate her precise whereabouts for delivery the next day. It was likely that she was the sister or daughter of the said MP, so enquiries around Piccadilly might yield the information he required.

N Hines Pawnbroker
Fleet Street

Dear Miss Burdett,

I write on behalf of a person whom I believe you may have knowledge of and who, it would appear, is in need of urgent assistance. The enclosed letter was found in the pocket of a garment brought to my shop. I have endeavoured to discover the whereabouts of the writer and her child but have met with no success thus far.

If you choose to verify the identity of the writer and the validity of her request, I would be pleased to render you any service that is within my power.

Respectfully yours
Nathan Hines

The next morning, Nathan went to Piccadilly. After a number of enquiries, he met a messenger boy who thought he had heard of a very rich lady who had recently moved to a house on Stratton Street. Then, in a coffee shop on that street, Nathan was pleased to discover that the proprietor was a fund of information about the Miss Burdett in question. The man was very proud to say that Miss Burdett did in fact live directly opposite his establishment at Number One, along with her lady companion. He saw the two ladies out walking quite frequently.

Glad that he had achieved this goal successfully, Nathan went to the servants' entrance of Miss Burdett's residence to hand in his letter. A maid took it from him and assured him that she would place it with the lady's correspondence for her attention that day.

Chapter 2

'But Miss Burdett, banking and finance, I must say, is not the usual occupation of ladies,' said Mr Marjoribanks.

Angela studied the man's pleasant gaze and knew that his assumption of the role as her guide and adviser was kindly meant. She would not comply with his wishes, however, nor take his advice on this point.

'That may well be,' she replied, 'but I wish to make myself familiar with the workings of this institution. It is my duty to do so. My grandfather and the Duchess must have deemed me capable.'

Mr Marjoribanks smiled, though his mouth twitched slightly at Angela's declaration.

'Do not worry, Mr Marjoribanks,' she said, aware of his embarrassment. 'In seeking to know more of the business of the bank, I have no desire to interfere with its workings. I only seek to understand. I have after all, a half share in it.'

Angela would not betray to the banker that she had little liking for figures, computations and calculations, profit and loss and suchlike. She was driven by the need to mend her ignorance, in this as in many other matters. There were other solemn obligations closer to her heart, however, those that God had placed upon her. This was a burden that she would willingly take up.

'Very well, Miss Burdett,' said Mr Marjoribanks, 'would you care to call here at the bank next week to begin your instruction?'

'Thank you, I will, on Wednesday, if that is convenient to you,' she said. 'And Mr Marjoribanks, I wish to point out that the Duchess's will stipulated that I must take the name of Coutts, in honour of my grandfather.'

'Of course, Miss Coutts,' he said with a gracious bow.

When she arrived home, Angela was glad of Hannah's welcome and her attentive questions about how she had fared at the bank. There was comforting tea and cake in the drawing room, too. Even the old grey parrot, inherited from the Duchess, squawked at her entry, swinging on his perch in his cage in the window. 'What a shocking bad hat!' he squealed, one of his regular utterances. Fan, Angela's little black dog, sniffed at her skirts then leapt onto the sofa beside her.

Angela, relaxed now, stroked the dog's smooth coat and sipped her tea, noting several piles of opened letters on the table next to the window.

'I've made a start on today's correspondence,' Hannah said, getting up and going to the table.

'You are too good,' Angela said, 'thank you.'

Her gratitude was genuine; her need of Hannah's support was greater now than ever. Governess, friend, companion and now secretary, Hannah was as indispensable to Angela as she was loved.

'Only a few letters are worthy of your

attention, I think,' Hannah said, turning round to Angela with a smile on her round face. 'I'm afraid that most are of the usual sort.'

It was inevitable, Angela supposed, once the news of her inheritance was out, that she would be bombarded with such letters. These tiresome and opportunistic men never doubted that marriage was her object in life and it was clear that society at large assumed the same. Goodness knows what a woman with both beauty and fortune would have to endure. Angela knew that she was in possession only of the latter. She also had no desire to be wooed or wed. There were so many far more important matters to attend to. However, the letters had to be dealt with. Amidst the bald offers of marriage, pretended affections of would-be suitors, gentlemen offering financial advice, long-lost relatives or acquaintances of acquaintances, there would be genuine appeals from worthy causes. She would never wish to ignore pleas from decent, righteous people or organisations working for the improvement of the lot of the poor and ignorant. Her riches were ordained by God; her life from now on would be driven by the necessity for practical action, the fulfilment of her duty to do good.

With this sense of her mission, Angela looked up at Hannah who was standing by the table, perusing one of the letters. Angela patted Fan and lifted him off her lap, rising to join Hannah. Angela reached for an opened paper on the top of one of the piles.

'No, not that one,' said Hannah. 'Those ones

are only fit for the fire.'

But Angela had already started scanning the content of the letter.

My Dear Miss Burdett-Coutts,

May I beg your indulgence and favour to consider my sincere declaration to you. Your image, your candid smile, your gesture to me are with me in my waking and my sleeping hours. Since our encounter in Green Park, when I was truly smitten by you, I am incapable of thought or feeling except that which pertains to you. Pardon this outpouring of my heart, but I swear upon my honour that my feelings for you...

'Isn't it outrageous!' said Hannah, snatching the letter from Angela. 'It's from that presumptuous man, that Irishman.'

Angela had no difficulty in remembering the encounter of the previous day when she and Hannah had gone for a walk in Green Park, as the day had turned out to be fair. At the gates of the park stood the tall figure of a gentleman in a top hat and black coat, watching them as they waited for a pause in the passing traffic on Piccadilly. Angela noted that the man maintained his gaze as a carriage and several hansom cabs flitted past them. As they approached the gates, Angela met his eye, but looked away quickly, though she had observed something of his appearance. His features were strong and quite handsome, though there was something about the curl of his mouth, his upper lip, which soured his looks, creating an expression akin to a sneer. He raised his hat and with a sudden bounding step was standing before them.

'I beg your pardon, ladies, but have I the honour of addressing Miss Burdett-Coutts?' he said.

Angela felt Hannah's grip upon her arm with a force that made her recoil a step from him. His mouth had now formed itself into a grin and he bowed.

'Sir, we have not been introduced,' said Hannah in a sharp, teacherly voice, for which Angela was grateful, as she herself was too taken aback by the man's sudden approach to respond.

He, however, seemed not at all perturbed by Hannah's rebuff. He smiled broadly.

'Well then,' he said, in a jocular tone, 'permit me to introduce myself. Richard Dunn, Esquire, barrister at law, late of Dublin town, now resident in this great city of London.'

Hannah reacted with a forbidding stare.

'We must go,' she said, tugging Angela's arm.

Angela knew that she was blushing, an unfortunate tendency, which manifested itself when she was excited or embarrassed. On this occasion, her discomfort was caused in part by Hannah's forthright rebuttal of the gentleman, but also by the man's unwavering gaze. The skin on her face felt tight and she longed to be gone, though she seemed to lack the power to move.

'Good day to you, sir,' said Hannah.

Angela responded to Hannah's tightening pressure on her arm as they turned and walked briskly away along the Queen's Walk in the direction of St James's Palace. The pace was a little uncomfortable for Angela, though she was grateful for her friend's swift action in extricating themselves.

'What a dreadful man,' Hannah murmured.

Angela, sharing Hannah's unease, glanced back and saw that he had not moved far from the spot of their encounter and was staring after them. The direct approach of a stranger like this could only signify that he was a rude opportunist. He had spied out Angela's residence with the purpose of meeting with her, as though by chance. Angela breathed deeply to steady her agitation and better manage their pace.

'Are you all right, my dear?' Hannah asked. 'We'll be clear of him soon. Let's go to the fountain.'

Though a gentler speed, accompanied by Hannah's chatter, should have reassured Angela, her discomfort lingered. As they walked, they passed a nursemaid pushing a perambulator, two ladies strolling with parasols and two scampering children under the loose and inattentive charge of a couple walking arm in arm. These scenes in the park, a place of leisure and carefree pastimes, did not have their usual calming effect on Angela, however, as in the distance she caught sight of that same dark-coated figure again. He was sauntering along the walkway on the other side of the small lake, where the path curved around to join their own route to the fountain.

'Let's go back,' said Angela stopping suddenly and Hannah, without enquiry or protest at this suggestion, turned with her and they headed back along the path towards the park gates again.

'Don't worry,' Hannah said. 'He will not follow us to the house. He wouldn't dare.'

Angela's house at 1 Stratton Street was easily accessible from the park and there were two crossing sweepers ready to aid their passage back over Piccadilly. The sense that the man was following burned like a hot brand into Angela's head, though she dared not look back again. She knew that her place of residence was no secret. The newspapers had published accounts of her move from her father's house to set up a home of her own. How she wished that her new life could have remained in a private world, that she could mix only with those whose company she sought and who valued her for who she was. She had never wished to be prominent, to have to stand up to public scrutiny. Her fortune had thrust celebrity upon her and was the sole cause of all the clamour and attention. She shrank from it, needing only the satisfaction of seeing the beneficial outcomes of her work, no more. She longed to be unknown.

So, the arrival of a letter from this Richard Dunn was for Angela more troubling than all the others she had received, because he had confronted her directly, had presumed that she would be willing to entertain his attentions. She was filled with a desire to run away from it all, to go to the country, to a place where she could once again be an unremarkable lady engaged in her own private pursuits.

Hannah, with a flourish, tossed Richard Dunn's and the other unwanted letters from would be suitors onto the fire. Angela watched her thrusting them deeply into the coals with the poker. The parrot, meanwhile, shifting from foot to foot on his perch, chirruped, 'More blooming letters, more blooming letters,' in the voice of one of the servants. Hannah and Angela embraced, laughing with relief.

'Let's leave the remaining correspondence,' Hannah said turning to Angela. 'It can wait until tomorrow. You look tired, my dear.'

Angela looked at the pile of unopened letters on the desk and sighed. It was true, she was tired, with the strain of settling into this house and starting on her new duties. She sank down on her favourite chaise longue by the fire.

Hannah, suddenly, with a bright expression that signalled a momentary inspiration, sat down at her side.

'I think we need to go away for a spell, out of London, to the country. What do you think?'

Angela frowned. Hannah must see weakness in her, a cowardly response to the encounter in the park the day before.

'We could go to Yorkshire, to Harrogate. It will be very pleasant at this time of the year,'

Hannah persisted.

'But I have so much to do here,' Angela said. 'There is the meeting at the bank. I promised Mr Majoribanks – and I have to meet the architect for the new church and also Mr Dickens has a new project to discuss – and my father's library – I promised I would help him re-catalogue some of his books.'

'Hush,' said Hannah, reaching for her hand and squeezing it. 'You can carry on your correspondence while you're in Yorkshire, but at a distance. It will be good for you. Taking the waters in Harrogate would be most beneficial.'

Hannah's suggestion struck home.

'Harrogate it is then,' said Angela, feeling a release of tension from her body, in relief and gratitude to her friend. 'Let us leave as soon as we can arrange it.'

That evening Angela went to her small library, to select some books to take with her on their trip. The shutters lay open and the window glass glowed faintly yellow from the street lamps below. She moved to the window and glanced out. A lone cab passed by, and she glimpsed the moving shadows of a few pedestrians on the pavement. Directly opposite her window, on the other side of the street, a tiny red dot flitted and Angela peered at it, making out the dark figure of a man, the red light, the tip of his cigar she assumed. His face was not visible until he raised his head, holding an upward gaze directly at her. For a second, she could not move, but then quickly banged the shutter closed.

Chapter 3

'She'll be mine before the year's end,' said Richard Dunn stretching his legs out in front of the fire in the *Ship Inn*.

'You're deluded, man. She'll not go for the likes of you,' said O'Rourke. 'There'll be dukes and princes from all over after her.'

Richard Dunn sat up in his seat. O'Rourke was beginning to get his goat. What did he know about women, after all? He didn't have an inkling about their likes and desires. What's more, he, Richard Dunn, was a professional man, a man of some standing and of a goodish family, if you didn't include his mother's side. He had the vigour needed for sport in the bedroom too. She was a woman after all and she'd be a fool to ignore him, being no beauty herself, a bit on the skinny side, though he could happily get used to the look of her.

O'Rourke, cigar between his teeth, held up his empty glass.

'I'm after another,' he said, 'and it's your turn.'

'Well, that's a pity,' said Dunn getting up. 'I've business to do, in matters of courting you understand. It's a serious undertaking this, requires effort and imagination, but the reward will be there in the end.'

'Reward, aye and how much is the lady worth by your reckoning?'

'She is priceless,' said Dunn adopting a self-righteous tone and a look of pious outrage. It was important, he realised, to practise such arts, if he were to come across as at all convincing. 'Well, as you're asking, they put her near two million pounds.'

O'Rourke raised his eyebrows. 'The odds are not in your favour.'

'We'll see,' said Dunn. 'Are you wanting to put a bet on it?'

'Five guineas says you'll not do it,' said O'Rourke.

'You're on,' said Dunn offering his hand.

'Within six months, say?'

'Och come on, these things take time,' said Dunn. 'Ladies take some wearing down.'

'A year and a half?' said O'Rourke and they shook on it.

Dunn, on parting from his friend, headed back to the room he had rented in a street off Shaftesbury Avenue, to work on the next stage of the operation. Today had gone well. Miss Burdett or Miss Coutts or Miss Burdett-Coutts or however she wished to fashion herself, was modest; that was easy to see, and serious-minded. There was also that clinging companion of hers; she was bound to be an obstacle. If he could just get to see the girl on her own, ply her with a few sweet words. Underneath that grave exterior, that sober gown, beat a heart full of passion. He could release that passionate nature if he could just see her face to face, touch her hand or maybe more than that. He was getting ahead of himself. Step by step, that was the way to do it.

It was a trifle unfortunate that he found

himself a little short of cash, however, which might prove a distinct drawback to success, if he was in this for the long haul. It was just as well he'd found modest lodgings and that he had the remnants of the small legacy from his uncle. There would be expenses incurred in the pursuit of the lady, hiring a horse, for example, to follow her carriage on such occasions when she was driven a distance from her home. He would also need to take rooms closer to her house, as it would make tracking and access to the place easier.

In order to defray some immediate expenses, he'd had to suffer the humiliation of visiting a pawn shop, to hock his cloak, a fine Donegal tweed garment, for which the miserable skinflint of a pawnbroker had only given him three pounds. Still, once he had succeeded in his quest, he'd not want for as many fashionable clothes as took his fancy.

Another potential obstacle to the smooth progress of his plan was the father. Although the heiress was an independent young lady, as could be seen clearly by her setting up home with just her companion, she was still by all accounts in regular contact with her father. Dunn had gleaned this information from reading the gossip columns in various papers and in conversation with a coffee shop proprietor in Stratton Street, who seemed to be particularly well-informed about the very wealthy young lady now residing across the way.

So, it seemed that he would have to make a

foray to the house of the father, Sir Francis Burdett, and beg an audience with him. This illustrious father had apparently been someone in his day, a radical political agitator and currently an MP. That was no reason to be put off, Richard Dunn mused, for he was equal to any man, lord or commoner. Hadn't he proved as much more than once in court? He could present a powerful case for himself as a suitor to Burdett's daughter too. He was glad that he'd had printed some new calling cards; his learned profession as a barrister was bound to impress. This thought bolstered his confidence as he strolled along Piccadilly toward his lodgings.

Two filthy children approached him, holding out some small muddy objects, whining in pathetic voices that here were some bargains to be had.

'Give us a penny, sir, nice bit of joollery here,' one said.

Dunn would have skirted around them had not a hansom cab been clipping along the roadside, threatening to splash into a puddle and soak him.

'Get away,' he said to the beggar children, recoiling from the proffered objects, a bent tin belt buckle, and a couple of links from a chain, no doubt scoured from the stinking cesspit of the Thames at low tide.

The children passed by, blank faced at his rejection, but a few paces further on, he thought of Miss Coutts and her soft merciful heart that was moved to succour the poor, by all accounts. It was said she was planning to do good works for the impoverished wretches that teemed in the city. Maybe, he thought, a more bountiful turn of his heart might come in handy in this wooing game. Here was a chance to practise. Turning back again, he called after the beggar children.

'Come here, my little ones,' he said, in a sickly tone, which he fancied appropriate to the occasion.

The ragamuffins stared for a moment.

'I have something for you,' he called to them, beckoning with a finger to bring them just close enough to toss a couple of farthings their way, with little risk of close contact.

The children paused for only a second longer, then ran off quickly in the opposite direction. Ungrateful creatures that they were, most likely play acting their poverty. Anyway, he had saved a few pennies, which was to be celebrated. The fat landlady wanted another week's rent from him, so he had to oblige, giving her nearly everything he had, and a shilling extra to launder his linen. Good grooming, he knew, was essential, else his cause was lost.

In his room, he removed the jug and basin from the washstand and prepared his pen and paper to compose the next letter. It did not flow with the same ease as the first, however and he was forced to go out for a quick snort of gin to reignite his creative flame. Maybe, he thought on his return, a poem would be more fitting.

Fair Angela, angel in name and nature...'

No good. He dipped his thumb into the ink pot and smeared this out. It would have to be more religious in its tone, as she was deeply committed to God and the church, so he had heard.

Saintly Angela, look upon me as a lost soul...

It was mighty difficult to strike the right note and he didn't have time to wait on a visitation of the Muse. Maybe he'd have one of these scriveners compose him some lines. But that would cost. He'd have to do it by his own effort. What to do, a sonnet or an ode? She was without doubt a woman of culture, who would respond to works of poetry more readily than to the banality of everyday talk. He scribbled again.

Your beatific smile, dear Angela
Reveals a heart of charity so full
That would it spill a little in my way
I would be blest, replete with ardent love
For thee, my angel, who has given me hope
That I may be in your dear presence, presently

It would have to do. She was likely to indulge in scribbling verses herself, as most ladies of her class liked to do, to fill their days. Though he suspected that she might be more of a serious turn of mind, of an intellectual bent, with her solemn face and plain dress. For a woman who was rolling in riches, there was no great outward show of it.

With the poem written out as a fair copy, he fell into a deep and comforting sleep, only to rise the next day at noon. He could not believe that he had slept so long and accounted for it by the dissipation of his energies in the composition of his poem.

He dressed with speed, decided to forgo breakfast, though he was hungry as an ox and set forth for Piccadilly. Arriving at the doorway of her house in Stratton Street, he rang the bell and stood back waiting. Some moments later, a black-suited young manservant, a footman, came to the door.

'I have an appointment with Miss Burdett-Coutts,' Dunn said, in an imperious tone suited to the occasion.

'Miss Coutts is not at home sir,' said the servant, who had a thin face with close-set eyes and a distinctly underfed look.

'May I ask when she is due to return?' Dunn said, annoyed that he had missed her departure by sleeping too late that morning.

The servant shrugged. 'Don't know exactly. Gone up north somewhere.'

Dunn cursed inwardly. What was she doing taking herself off like that? This had beggered his plans. Dunn had to think quickly.

'Well, it's most important that I contact her,' he said. 'She's expecting to hear from me. Would you go and find out for me where she has gone, so that I may write to her?'

The young servant glanced shiftily back over his shoulder.

'Don't know if I can do that, sir,' he said.

Dunn scrutinised him for a brief moment, detecting an opening here for some assistance with his plans.

He poked a finger into his waistcoat pocket and brought out a sixpence.

'And what's your name, young man?' Dunn said.

'George, sir.'

'Well, George, I reckon you're just the fellow to help a gentleman out.'

Chapter 4

The Stray in Harrogate was a delightful wild space with meadows, wooded copses, grassland and several mineral springs. Angela and Hannah were enjoying their daily rambles there in the clean, fresh air. Angela already felt the benefits and taking the waters had also improved her troubled skin. They were staying at the Old Swan Hotel, a very comfortable and well-appointed establishment, managed with efficiency by the Manager, Mr Braithwaite. Their rooms overlooked the pretty rear rose garden, offering peaceful seclusion when needed, though there were also opportunities for conversation with other patrons. One particularly agreeable acquaintance was a Mrs Clara Slingsby, who lived in the nearby countryside and visited the town on a regular basis to take the waters and to dine at the Old Swan Hotel with her husband, after he had attended to business.

Mrs Slingsby was a genteel and humane lady with an active interest in many charitable causes, which immediately endeared her to Angela. She told them of her work raising money for a pauper's hospital and of her plans for a school for the children of her husband's mill workers. Her husband, she confided, had come from a very humble background, but through his application and ambition had risen from becoming an overseer in a textiles mill to management and then ownership of several large ones in the West Riding. His prosperity was evident in the quality of his wife's expensively discreet attire and jewellery.

'And does your husband share your interests?' Angela enquired as the three women sat in the orangery taking coffee one morning.

Mrs Slingsby smiled.

'He does, though he needs a little persuasion. In practice I keep some of my activities out of his sight, as I know he would not approve.'

Angela, intrigued by her need for secrecy from her husband soon discovered why the lady adopted such a judicious approach to her charitable activities. Mr Slingsby joined them for luncheon. He was a well-fed looking man, with the ruddy complexion of a person accustomed to vigorous outdoor exercise and a little too much indulgence in liquor. After his wife's introductions, he greeted Angela and Hannah brusquely but politely and sat down, snapping his fingers at the head waiter and ordering a scotch and water.

'William,' said Clara Slingsby to her husband, 'Miss Coutts has just this moment been telling us about her charitable work in London.'

He looked up and nodded, grunting in acknowledgement of the remark, then went back to studying the menu. Angela exchanged a quick glance with Hannah, surprised at the mismatched nature of this couple. The man was simply rude and obviously disinclined to engage in polite conversation or perhaps found female company tiresome. But as Angela reflected, many women did not have the luxury of choosing a husband to suit their own dispositions, when to most marriage was simply a necessity for survival. Whatever the circumstances of their marriage, Clara Slingsby was, Angela could see, a quietly persistent woman.

'Miss Coutts has marvellous plans to establish a hostel for homeless women,' said Mrs Slingsby, touching her husband lightly on the arm.

William Slingsby looked up and put the menu aside.

'Beggars, do you mean?' he said.

Angela, knowing that she had allies in Hannah and Clara Slingsby, was not intimidated by the man's manner and directness.

'It's true that some girls and women are forced upon the streets to beg, for want of food, shelter and employment. Many do not have the protection of husbands,' she said calmly.

'Beggars. I've no time for them. There's always work for those who've a mind to it,' he said. 'No excuse for beggary in my book.'

'I do not think that many paupers would choose to live on the streets if there were other options open to them,' Angela said.

'I agree, Miss Coutts,' said Clara Slingsby eagerly. 'It is not only the feckless and lazy who are poor.'

The man leaned back in his seat, eyeing Angela then his wife with a slight smile on his lips.

'You think not, eh?'

'I believe that many of the poor, if they can be given the skills to earn a living, would prefer to support themselves, and to take pride in their ability to do so,' Angela said.

'So, you think folk from the gutter can be reformed, do you?' he said, his face brightening, clearly beginning to enjoy this opportunity for an argument, which he seemed convinced he would win.

'I do,' said Angela decisively, 'I believe in the power of education and religious faith to restore those who are lost. There are many charitable institutions that have shown this to be the case.'

'Well, in my experience, there are some wretches that would lie like pigs in their filth and be happy,' he said.

'William, please,' Clara Slingsby said.

Hannah, Angela noted, was fidgeting with her napkin in frustration.

'Mr Slingsby,' she said. 'Perhaps you and your wife would care to come to London and visit Miss Coutts's hostel and the church she is having built in Westminster, with a school and welfare centre for the poor. Then you may judge for yourself whether reform and redemption of the poor and destitute is possible.'

The man smiled and it seemed, this time, with pleasure rather than ridicule or disapproval.

'Now that's a mighty fine suggestion,' he said.

Angela, feeling the confidence of her rightness, continued, 'When hunger gnaws at a homeless beggar, he can hardly be expected to live a good life. When his soul is starved of the nourishment of the love of God, how can he be respectable?'

'Miss Coutts and Miss Meredith,' said William Slingsby, with a grin. 'You are two very dangerous ladies. You will put ideas into my wife's head, with your do-gooding.'

Angela smiled, exchanging a glance with Clara Slingsby.

'I think Mrs Slingsby has plenty of ideas of her own.'

They all laughed and any tension between them was quickly dissipated. The Slingsbys suggested that Angela and Hannah might wish to join Clara on a trip to Fountains Abbey during their stay, to which they agreed with enthusiasm.

Later, Angela withdrew to the reading room at the back of the hotel, to write a letter to her friend and soon-to-be associate Charles Dickens, about his latest proposals for the hostel for homeless girls. The man was tireless, it seemed, in his efforts to provide better lives for the poor. He had already instigated a Ragged School for pauper children in one of the most wretched districts in the East End. Angela had intended to write to him, to lend her support for these two projects, before departing from London. The haste of their preparations, however, had resulted in the neglect of this and her remaining correspondence. With an urgency driven in part by guilt, she set to work.

As she wrote, she became aware of the fading light in the early dusk of a cloudy day. She looked up, thinking that she should ring for a servant to come and light the lamps. Through the window, she could see the garden and a white-haired gentleman rising from the bench where he had been reading. He was making his way slowly across the lawn towards a porch at the rear of the building. Then something beyond the elderly figure caught her eye, on the top of the wall that encircled the garden. The wall was above six feet in height, but there, at the top, a man's head appeared, then his upper body, swinging over, followed by long legs. A whole black-coated figure descended smoothly on to the grass at the foot of the wall.

Angela jumped up from the chair and withdrew quickly from the window. Numbed by her surprise, doubting the reliability of her sight in the failing light, she peered at the figure, which was standing up now, pausing, looking around. It could not be a servant or gardener, entering in such a strange and suspicious manner. She edged towards the door of the room, deciding that she must report this immediately to the manager. The man must surely be a thief or a burglar.

With her hand on the door knob, she turned back to glance at the window once more. Perhaps her work at the desk had strained her eyes to such an extent that they were inventing shadows where none existed. But at that moment a white face at the glass slid into view: the staring black eyes, the curled mouth of a man she recognised. Shock struck her like a blow to the chest and she tugged at the handle of the door. It flew open and Angela ran as fast as she could to Hannah's room.

'It's him,' Angela said, bursting in.

'Who?' Hannah said, rising from her dressing table. 'My dear, what's wrong?'

'Richard Dunn, that awful man.'

'But it can't be. Here in Harrogate?' said Hannah.

Angela was conscious of Hannah's arm in hers, guiding her to a chair.

'Are you sure?' her companion said, in the tone of one indulging a nervous child.

'I am not mistaken,' Angela said, hearing the querulous anger in her voice that Hannah should disbelieve her.

'Well,' Hannah said, 'We must go straight to the manager.'

Together they hurried to the main reception hall and Hannah rang the bell on the hall table. A young man, a clerk, appeared almost immediately from a side door and Hannah reported what Angela had witnessed, demanding that something be done immediately.

The young man, looking suitably alert, rang the bell vigorously again.

'Don't worry,' he said. 'We'll check the grounds. If there's anyone here who shouldn't be, we will find him.'

'But the man is known to us,' Angela said, thinking that there was little point in concealing this fact.

Mr Braithwaite the Manager appeared a few moments later, walking swiftly from the end of a passage that led into the reception hall and greeted Angela and Hannah. The clerk explained quickly what had arisen.

'Get Morris and Fielding. Search everywhere,' Mr Braithwaite told the clerk, then turned to Angela and Hannah.

'Ladies, please do not distress yourselves. Come and sit down.'

He ushered them into a discreet corner of the small adjoining lounge.

'Now, Miss Coutts, please tell me exactly what you saw,' said Mr Braithwaite. 'A description of the person would be helpful.'

Angela described Dunn and explained briefly about his past unwanted attentions.

'It's vital not to let this man into the hotel while we are staying here,' Hannah broke in. 'Would you please give us that assurance? This man must not be allowed to accost Miss Coutts.'

The manager nodded. 'Of course, madam. I will ensure that this does not happen. I will inform the magistrate if necessary and enlist the help of a constable. All my staff and servants will be alerted to look out for any strangers, or persons without the authority to be on the premises.'

Mr Braithwaite was most reassuring about securing the hotel against any attempt by

Dunn to enter it. Later that day, he was able to report to Angela and Hannah that a thorough search had been undertaken and had yielded only some footprints on a rose bed in the garden and a sighting by a maid of a gentleman in a black frock coat passing quickly by the front door.

The next few days passed without further alarm and with the added distraction of several pleasant outings to places of interest, with Mr and Mrs Slingsby, who were excellent guides and hospitable hosts. Angela had almost managed to dismiss all thoughts of Richard Dunn, until their post was brought to them when they were taking refreshments in Angela's room. There were six letters in all, which they shared between them. But when Angela opened the first, she felt her body go cold with shock.

'That man again. I can't believe it,' Angela said, scanning the letter then holding out the paper to Hannah. 'Will he not leave me alone?'

Most Esteemed Miss Coutts,

Forgive a man who writes to you with the purest of hearts. I know it is imprudent to have followed you north, but I was drawn by a force so strong as to be overwhelming, my love and adoration of you. How could I, knowing that you were so distant, bear such separation? So I came, forgive me, dearest Miss Coutts, and sought out your room, so that I could gaze...

'What on earth shall I do?' Angela said, as Hannah read it quickly.

Hannah's response was unconcealed rage.

'I shall put a stop to this, once and for all,' she said. 'I shall go to Mr Braithwaite immediately and ask him to report this dreadful pestering to the magistrate. We shall have him arrested, locked up.'

Angela frowned and fingered the sleeve of her gown anxiously, alarmed by the vehemence of Hannah's response.

'Is that not a little too harsh?' she said, hesitating. 'The man must surely have lost his wits. Perhaps he is to be pitied. He needs a firm refusal, though perhaps not a cruel one. I just want him to stop.'

'My dear, you can't be sorry for him. He is a rogue,' said Hannah. 'He needs to be dismissed finally and for ever. He must be made to accept the fact that you will never, under any circumstances, receive him or his advances.'

Angela knew that Hannah was right but doubted that he would accept a rebuff unless it was uttered by herself. She must make her declaration to his face in front of witnesses.

'Hannah,' she said. 'Let me see him and tell him that he must cease this behaviour at once. I will of course threaten to go to the law, if he takes no heed, but he must hear it from me.'

Hannah looked doubtful but Angela was determined not be deflected from her decision. She must not use other people as intermediaries. She must have the courage to command her own affairs, even those of an unpleasant nature. In the end, Hannah complied with Angela's wishes. They instructed Mr Braithwaite to take a message to Dunn's lodgings and request that he should come to the hotel the next day.

In the corner of the reception hall, Angela, Hannah and Mr Braithwaite awaited the arrival of their unwanted guest. Angela felt her stomach knotting painfully, but hoped she was managing to conceal her discomfort. Shortly before the appointed time, a clerk ushered Dunn to them. On seeing them, Dunn smiled broadly with an intrusive gaze, which lingered too long on Angela. His cloying and forward manner made him appear repulsive to her.

'Miss Coutts, Miss Meredith,' he said, approaching. 'What a pleasure to see you again.'

Angela did not offer her hand, recoiling from him slightly. She introduced Mr Braithwaite and felt a tight pulsing in her head as she spoke. She was ready with her carefully rehearsed statement.

The man was beaming at her, in spite of her cold reception.

'I trust that the country air is agreeable to you, Miss Coutts and may I say how charming you look today, positively blooming,' said Dunn.

Angela saw Hannah's furious fidgeting with her handkerchief before she burst in.

'Stop this, sir. Will you just listen to what Miss Coutts has to say and then be gone? We have no more need or desire for your company!'

This outburst was effective in producing a short pause, enabling Angela to speak.

'I must tell you Mr Dunn, that I reject entirely your attentions to me,' she said in an effort to maintain her steady tone. 'I have never given you cause to imagine that I had any interest in you. I am sorry for being so blunt, but that is my feeling and I demand that you desist in your pursuit of me.'

Angela felt light-headed, having hardly drawn breath during her speech to the man, who persisted in staring at her nodding, with a smile curling on his lips. Dunn said nothing in response. He simply shook his head and bowed it slightly, looking at his boots. Mr Braithwaite cleared his throat loudly.

'Sir, I think that Miss Coutts has made her feelings and instructions quite clear. So, I would ask you to leave now and not return, under any circumstances. If you do not comply, it will be a matter for the law. You must not bother Miss Coutts whether here or abroad in the town. If you do, I shall be forced to inform the magistrate of your unwelcome and unlawful behaviour.'

Dunn raised his head and looked at Angela with the staring eyes that so perturbed her.

'You may control my movements about the town, but you cannot control the movements of my heart,' he said in the wistful tone of a second-rate actor.

Mr Braithwaite's response to this was to call for the clerk who entered swiftly with another man.

'Jones, Thomas, escort this gentleman out of the hotel. Our business is finished. He is not to be allowed here again under any pretext.'

Angela watched as the men took Dunn firmly by his arms and led him out.

That evening at dusk, when a man was seen creeping behind some shrubs in the back garden, Mr Braithwaite sent a message to the magistrate. The next morning, the manager calmly reported to Angela and Hannah at breakfast that Mr Dunn had been arrested and was being held in custody.

Chapter 5

Although it was early in the morning, only the day after their return from Yorkshire, Angela was already at her desk in the library writing a letter. She had started on the neglected correspondence, which had lain in a pile during her time away. She broke off when Hannah came in to bid her good morning.

'I simply had to ask Mr Dickens to report on the progress of his Ragged School,' she said. 'It is a most worthwhile project, though to read his account of his visit would make you weep with pity for the wretched state of the children. They need a larger schoolroom and public baths. Another master is required too, so I shall provide for another teacher's salary and the new buildings. What do you think?'

'I entirely approve,' said Hannah. 'Mr Dickens is energetic for his causes. It will be gratifying for you to be involved.'

Angela felt refreshed by the prospect of seeing Charles Dickens again, to discuss the matter. He was a provocative but charming man, who enjoyed goading and teasing them, particularly Hannah, with arguments on topics as various as the church, politics and the state of the drains. His charitable works were as ardent as his writing, which both Angela and Hannah devoured. There was much to admire in the man.

Angela handed Hannah Charles Dickens's letter, which contained a sad but amusing description of his encounter with the bold pauper boys in the sordid school and she read on.

'...*some of the fashionable philanthropists would deem this too humble a cause, but you my dear Miss Coutts, are different and I know will be touched by such a desperate need...*'

'Yes, it is very worthy work, though the business of educating the poor should not be left solely in the hands of the benevolent,' Hannah said.

'I agree,' said Angela, 'but until the government sees fit to fund and set up a national system of education, we must do the best we can.'

Together Angela and Hannah worked through the considerable pile of correspondence, containing the usual range of begging letters. They had returned to London from Harrogate, relieved that the situation with the persistent and objectionable Richard Dunn had been resolved. He had been charged with causing a nuisance and harassment, brought before the magistrate and given a custodial sentence in York Castle. It troubled Angela, however, that the man's foolish attentions had led to such extreme action, but the whole business had caused her so much anguish, that relief overrode her compunction. This measure must surely have taught him the dire consequences of his offensive and unwanted behaviour, and would end his fruitless pursuits for ever.

Angela unfolded the last paper from the pile, one which had been delivered by hand. It was a letter in which another was enclosed. She had to read both twice to absorb their content and significance.

'This is a very sad case,' Angela said to Hannah. 'This letter has been forwarded by a well-meaning man, a pawnbroker, would you believe. It relates to a former servant of ours, a James Harding. I remember him well. He was our coachman and stableman for many years until he left my father's service a few years ago. My father thought very highly of him. He was a hard-working, honest and reliable man. This letter is from his widow.'

Angela handed both letters to Hannah who perused them carefully for some minutes.

'But what can you do about this? What does this man expect of you?' she said, looking up.

Angela too was at a loss as to what action could be taken about the matter. She thought for a moment, taking the letters back from Hannah.

'I wonder if we should perhaps send for this Mr Hines,' Angela said, 'and question him further about the poor woman and her child. It may be that he has more information about their whereabouts by now. It has been some weeks since he delivered the message, after all.'

'But he's a pawnbroker,' said Hannah. 'Should you really entertain such a person? There are those that would ban such trade, exchanging possessions for money. Some say it encourages drunkenness and criminal behaviour amongst the lower classes and interferes with church going.'

Angela nodded. 'Yes, I agree it is not a wholesome occupation - a business that profits from misery and poverty. But this man clearly shows compassion for poor Mrs Harding's circumstances.'

It was not only the plight of the unfortunate widow and her child that had touched Angela. There was also something about the letter that excited her curiosity as to the nature of the writer. Should such a person be dismissed and judged so critically simply because of his profession?

'We have to be careful,' said Hannah. 'As you well know, there are many unscrupulous people who seek to take advantage of generosity such as yours.'

'All the more reason to see the man for ourselves,' Angela said, her mind made up, 'so that we may judge his character. Would you write a note to him please, dear?'

When the pawnbroker presented himself to them, Angela found it hard to conceal her surprise at his appearance and manner. Although his letter was written in a good hand and was literate and correct, she had imagined a man of his sort to be old, unkempt, uncouth or possibly of a ruthless and criminal disposition. Mr Nathan Hines was none of these things. He was soberly dressed, in his Sunday coat, no doubt. He was tall with an upright bearing, a good-looking, clean-shaven, though somewhat haggard face, and thick, well-tamed dark hair. He held his hat in his hand, a thoroughly respectable looking figure. It was his eyes, however, that Angela noticed most of all. They were dark and with the most mournful expression she had ever seen. He had called at the tradesmen's entrance at the appointed time. Coleman the butler had brought him to them in the small parlour. Angela could see the hint of surprise in Hannah's observation of their visitor too.

'Good afternoon, Mr Hines. Thank you for coming,' Angela said.

The man bowed to them both as Angela introduced herself and Hannah. When offered the chair placed opposite them, he sat down looking ill at ease. His expression was strained and he clutched the brim of his hat tightly in one fist.

'You did right to contact me, Mr Hines,' Angela said. 'The widow Selina Harding's husband was indeed our family's coachman for many years. I met Mrs Harding once or twice myself and saw some of her children. I am most upset to hear of her hardships and I would willingly provide for both her and her daughter, if they could be found. But as you suggest this may be difficult. Have you discovered anything else that might lead us to her whereabouts?'

Nathan Hines shook his head. He told them how he had come upon the letter and about a visit he had made to the address given upon it. Here he had encountered an old woman who had provided the two with a roof over their heads for a while, until their departure in search of relief. She did not know where they had gone. He produced a handkerchief given to him by the old woman with Selina Harding's initials upon it.

'I fear that the gown was likely stolen from Mrs Harding,' the pawnbroker said. 'But I gave the girl who brought it ten shillings, as she looked hungry and in need. She told me that she had to feed her brothers and sisters. Then, when I found the letter, I knew I must act. I thought the gown and the handkerchief could be useful in tracking down the woman and her child. But though I've enquired in the places where desperate folk seek help - the workhouse, religious houses too - I've found no one with knowledge of the two.'

Angela studied him closely as he spoke. She was impressed by the candour and honesty of the man, in spite of his undesirable occupation.

'I shall make it my business to speak to my father's secretary. He may have knowledge of family or friends of the Hardings,' Angela said. 'I shall also contact the charitable bodies who rescue women from the streets. Perhaps someone will have knowledge of the poor woman and her child. And maybe Mr Hines, your wife could help by visiting such hostels and homes for women in your locality.'

Nathan Hines shook his head and looked down at his boots.

'I regret that I have no wife,' he said.

Angela blushed, embarrassed by her false

assumption and Hannah, noting this, spoke for her.

'You are not married, Mr Hines?' said.

'My wife died last year, of the cholera,' he said.

'We are so sorry to hear that, Mr Hines,' Hannah said. 'But do you have children?'

'They were taken too,' he said, without raising his head, 'my son and my daughter both.'

There was a heavy moment's pause, in which Angela, struck by the revelation of this tragedy, could say nothing beyond a silent prayer for those lost souls and for this man who was so completely bereft. He looked up at them, acknowledging their sympathy and in control of himself again.

'I will continue to search wherever I can,' he said. 'Perhaps the child has survived and is alone and in need, but the mother was very sick, so the old woman told me.'

'Your compassion does you credit, Mr Hines,' Angela said, realising the strangeness of the encounter.

This man, if he had been of her class, would have been someone she might have valued as a friend and fellow campaigner for the very causes which were close to her heart.

'Please let me know if you require remuneration in your search. You have a shop, I assume, and imagine that you cannot leave it untended.'

'My lady,' he said, 'I have a friend who will come to mind the shop for a while, if need be and I lock up at midday for an hour. Thank you for your generosity, but it will cost me nothing to walk the streets and enquire of people I see.'

Angela reflected that this man must be the only person she had ever encountered who had refused a donation of money. As he took his leave, she was aware also of a vague feeling of unfinished business, of the need to follow up this meeting with the surprising Mr Hines.

That night, sleep would not come to Angela. It was not worry or anxiety that was the cause, but rather the action of her thoughts in formulating a plan which excited her with its possibilities and benefits. She wished to discuss it with Hannah and was impatient that she would have to wait until the next day. However, when the morning arrived, her mind was already resolved to set her proposal in motion.

'Mr Hines, the pawnbroker, seems to be an honest man. I should like to help him.'

'Help him?' said Hannah frowning, as she poured tea for Angela at breakfast.

'Yes,' said Angela. 'He has suffered so and still he tries to help others.'

Hannah sighed.

'My dear, the poor man is bereaved. Generosity will not bring back his wife and children. What kind of help can you give? He doesn't appear to be in need of money.'

Angela smiled. 'I'll tell you of my idea, on our way to Mr Hines's shop.'

Hannah's eyes widened.

'You mean to go to his pawnbroker's shop? Are you sure that's wise? What scheme are you hatching?'

Angela ignored Hannah's protests, insisting that she herself ought to discover more of the lives of others, particularly those in hardship, such as the customers of Mr Hines's shop. She was also concerned to test the accuracy of her judgement as to the man's good character, and to see the nature of his business. Her experiences so far had made her much more aware of those who would trick, flatter or bully their way into her favour. It struck her that this Mr Hines was someone who possessed none of these unsavoury traits or tendencies. And she wanted to see things for herself, as she did with her other projects. Some benefactors gave their money to certain causes without seeing the circumstances, nor even following up the consequences of their donations. Angela was not satisfied with that role. She needed to see the evidence of God's work through human endeavour.

Hannah had Coleman secure a hansom cab to take them to Fleet Street and they set off along Piccadilly at a good pace. Soon, however, they were slowed in the flow of heavy traffic. This gave Angela the chance to explain her plan, to which she found Hannah reluctantly agreeable.

'But would Mr Dickens approve of such an idea?' she said.

'I think so,' said Angela, with a swift little

smile to herself, as she imagined the conversation with her friend and collaborator. 'If not, I'll bring him around to my view.'

The cab driver steered his horse with some difficulty past a number of stationary waggons and carts in the bustle of Fleet Street, where crowds were clustering around shop windows, swarming along the pavements or weaving their way through the traffic on the roadway. The cab drew up at the corner of Bell Yard, a narrow, cobbled street off Fleet Street itself, where Angela caught sight of the pawnbroker's shop. It had a clean, green-painted shop front with its sign of three brass balls hanging above the door. Discreet gold lettering bore the proprietor's name and the bow-fronted window was filled with a clutter of goods.

They alighted and Angela paused for a moment or two to examine the contents of the window. Through the glass, she could see items of pottery and china, small piles of trinkets, ornaments, jewellery, kitchen implements, medals, shoes, carpenter's tools, a trumpet, two violins and some jackets and coats slung up above them. It was hardly a display, Angela reflected, more of a jumble. Hannah too peered with interest, curiosity overcoming her disapproval. Then she took the lead, opened the door and held it for Angela to enter.

A bell rang as they stepped into the shop. The floor was cleanly scrubbed and a wooden counter ran almost the length of the small room. Behind were many shelves, stacked with boxes, marked with various labels. On the counter were several large ledgers. Suddenly, Mr Hines appeared, from an area at the back of the shop and when he saw them, he was unable to conceal his surprise. His face flushed and he greeted them with a hesitant welcome.

'Miss Coutts, Miss Meredith, good day to you both.'

'Mr Hines,' said Angela, 'I am sorry that we have arrived unannounced but I need to beg a moment of your time. I have a proposal to make to you.'

'A proposal?' he said, frowning in his puzzlement, but quickly in command of himself again.

'Allow me to close the shop, Miss Coutts, so that we may talk without interruption.'

'If that will not harm your business,' said Hannah. 'It would be most convenient.'

The man came from behind the counter and quickly turned his closed sign to the door, then locked it.

'Please, come. This way,' he said, indicating a narrow passage behind the counter leading to the back of the shop.

Angela and Hannah entered a small parlour, with a fireplace and two stuffed easy chairs of worn appearance. Though modestly appointed with shabby furniture, the place was clean but cold. The pawnbroker bade them take a seat while he stood awkwardly in front of the empty fireplace.

'Forgive me,' the man said. 'I have not lit the fire. I have few guests. I -. Would you care for some refreshment - tea?'

'Please do not trouble yourself, Mr Hines,' Angela said. 'We will not inconvenience you for long. She added quickly, 'Mr Hines, are you happy in your work?'

He coloured again, looking at her with a questioning expression.

'I'm not sure of your meaning, my lady,' he said, faltering. 'The shop? It's not what I would have chosen to do, but I had to support my family, so the chance came to take on the business. I gain little pleasure from it but I go by the rule of the law on a pawnbroker's trade. I charge the least interest I can. I try not to...'

'And what would you choose as your profession, if such a choice were available to you?' Angela persisted.

She could see that her interrogation was causing him some unease.

'I don't know, precisely,' he said. 'I was a printer by trade, so it might be that I'd return to that.'

He paused, frowning as he thought, then looked at her.

'But my choice of occupation? I suppose it would be to work to help others. That would be my wish. Something that might lessen the want, give succour to despairing souls.'

Angela nodded. The air seemed almost palpable between them, as though their aspirations had collided. Maybe, she thought her proposal might take hold.

'I have an idea,' said Angela, 'but you must not take it up if you have no wish. How would it be for you to become a teacher in a Ragged School? Have you heard of such a thing?'

He stared back at her as though he had not heard correctly. Angela knew that this was rash on her part. Hannah had said as much. To make such an offer to a stranger, a man of unknown education, a man involved in a dubious trade, was a rather risky venture.

'You have some education, Mr Hines,' Angela continued, feeling a swell of excitement in her boldness. 'You write a good, scholarly hand and a fluent letter. And you are presumably proficient with things arithmetical as well, in your trade.'

He nodded. 'I attended school until the age of twelve and then taught myself more through reading. I think I am competent but not learned,' he said.

'Then would you consider taking a position as a master in the Ragged School in Field Lane? Mr Charles Dickens has promoted this project to teach poor children elementary reading, writing and computation. And now an excellent couple, Mr and Mrs Greaves, are holding classes there. It has proved so popular that another master is needed. Such a venture will give these children a chance of bettering themselves and to read the Bible, of course. Could you consider such a thing?'

The man was clearly astonished at her suggestion, hesitating as he tried to reply.

'I can see you're surprised,' Angela said, then, smiling, she turned to Hannah. 'Should we ask Miss Meredith's opinion about your suitability if you doubt it yourself? She has knowledge and experience of teaching children.'

'I'm afraid,' Hannah said, with a slight laugh, 'my teaching has been limited to small groups and individuals. Miss Coutts knows - she was one of my pupils. But it seems to me, Mr Hines, that you have sympathy for others, you wish to improve the lot of the poor and have skills that would equip you well for such work. May we suggest that you visit the school first to see for yourself?'

'Yes,' Angela said. 'You could see the children and talk to the master in charge.'

He looked back at them and Angela fancied that his eyes had lost something of their tragic gaze.

'I am very grateful that you should think me capable,' he said.

'Good,' said Angela briskly, to conceal her satisfaction with the success of her plan so far. 'I will write you a letter of introduction and Hannah will give you details of the place and of the master in charge, so that you may arrange to visit the school.'

At this point, Angela and Hannah were startled by a loud knocking on the door.

'You must see to your customers, Mr Hines,' said Hannah rising from her seat.

'Yes, of course, you must,' Angela said. 'I will send a messenger with your letter tomorrow.'

Chapter 6

Although Mr Bezer Blundell had been summoned without warning to appear before the Board of Management on a serious and confidential matter, he was not overly concerned. Whatever it was, he could handle it easily enough. The evidence, if they had any, was scanty and he was sure anything incriminating would be too insubstantial to stand up to scrutiny. Larkin, the clerk, ushered him into the meeting room where he was surprised to find the table replete with many of the members.

They were not a welcoming sight. Bezer Blundell experienced an unpleasant tightness around his waistline where the trouserband had been digging into his stomach of late. The Reverend James Rudge was wearing his funeral face and the others, eight of them, sat with expressions unyielding as stone.

'Pray, take a seat, Mr Blundell,' said the Reverend.

Bezer tried to smile in an effort to reassure himself of the fellow feeling that must surely still exist beneath these cold gazes.

'It is my regrettable duty,' Reverend Rudge intoned, 'to dismiss you from your position as Assistant Secretary of the Society, with immediate effect.'

This statement took a few seconds to register fully in Bezer's brain, but when it did, it activated both his outrage and his powers of speech.

'But – it's well – unbelievable,' he spluttered. 'I demand an explanation. I will take this to a higher authority, to Lord –.'

'Enough!'

The Reverend Rudge slapped his hand on the table.

'I warn you, Mr Blundell. Be aware that your misdemeanours could become a police matter. It is the decision of this board, however, to dismiss you summarily without any public show, for the reputation of the Society. It must be protected from those who would bring it into disrepute.'

Bezer watched the Reverend's face colouring as he spoke. It occurred to him at that moment that these accusations could well be a bluff. He eyed the two gentlemen, both of whom had been happy to drink brandy in his company only the other day. That fellow Jack Hume was a different story, however. He had always been stand-offish and superior and now stared with pitiless eyes as though Bezer were some unsavoury creature that had crawled out of the river mud. Well, they might try to gang up against him if they wished, but he would refute their accusations, demand that they provide incontrovertible evidence of his wrongdoing. He was not prepared to cave in. They had underestimated Mr Bezer Blundell.

'I have been a loyal servant to this charitable cause,' he said with admirable hauteur, adding a note of hurt, thinking that a measure of humility might be wise in the circumstances.

Reverend Rudge's eyes appeared to darken.

'You have violated our highest principles. The London Society for the Suppression of Mendicity works for the benefit of the poor and needy of this city and you, charged with a duty to carry out this work, have stolen from this very Society for your own gain. We have received complaints from several people who paid lifetime subscriptions of £10 and who have never been invited to take up their positions as governors, nor have had notification of membership.'

Bezer let out his breath. Was this all they had against him? He felt the tension slip from his body.

'But my dear sirs, this is a mere oversight on my part, I assure you,' he said. 'In fact, I was on the point of writing to the new subscribers and inviting them to attend our next charitable event.'

'Some of these complaints relate to ladies and gentlemen who subscribed more than a year ago.'

'Ah well, I admit there may have been some oversights, probably, and I hesitate to point the finger, but Larkin has not been himself these last months. He may have been remiss in carrying out my instructions.'

Someone cleared his throat and Reverend Rudge's face took on a strangely murderous look.

'We have spoken to Mr Larkin and he assures us that he received no instructions from you on this matter. He has recorded all tasks assigned by you. He keeps meticulous records.'

Bezer was aware of perspiration forming on his brow, but he resisted the desire to take out his pocket handkerchief to swab it.

'Gentlemen,' he said, assuming a comradely tone, 'please remember the excellent service I have rendered to the Society. I must have rallied more than one hundred new subscribers last year alone,' he said.

'Fifty one in the last two years,' said Hector Blain, a pernickety, nit-picking fellow, who Bezer observed was consulting a ledger, which lay open in front of him. 'And that includes those for which we have received no monies. £100 from these subscriptions has never been paid into the Society's account. That is what you owe.'

'Really? Then there has been some kind of mistake, clearly,' said Bezer, shaking his head in puzzlement. 'But I can tell you I will work night and day to rectify this clerical error.'

His collar felt uncomfortably sticky, but it was just a question of holding his nerve and maintaining a smiling demeanour. Hector Blain flicked over to the next page of the ledger.

'And there is the matter of the counterfeit tickets,' said the Reverend, holding up a small clump of the tickets that the Society sold to benevolent folk to give to beggars on the street. The presentation of a ticket to Bezer, as Assistant Secretary, allowed street beggars and other undesirables to seek relief in the form or money, food or clothes.

Bezer, with some difficulty managed to maintain his look of benign surprise. 'Counterfeit tickets?' he said. 'I know nothing of such things.'

'Surprising, since some have been found in your desk. We know they are fake, as the numbers had already been assigned and used,' said Reverend Rudge, whose voice has become an ugly growl.

'Falsehood! This is simply untrue,' Bezer spluttered. 'Someone must have placed the objects in my private drawer. Who would perpetrate such an act of subterfuge?'

Bezer was making quite a good show of outrage, fired by his genuine fury at the sneak who had been searching among his private papers.

The Reverend Rudge was pointing a finger at him now, jabbing as though he wished to inflict a wound.

'Have you no conscience, no morals before God, if not in your duty to this charitable society? You have cheated the very people you were supposed to be helping. The false tickets could not be used, so you sent these poor people away.'

'I deny it!' said Bezer, feeling a horrible quivering in his belly.

'Deny it all you wish, Blundell, but it is the decision of the board. There will be no further argument.'

Bezer had to get out of the room. He hoped to leave, haughty, proud and undiminished by this merciless encounter, but instead it was a shuffling exit from the room, to the low murmurs of the occupants.

At the front door, the porter handed him his hat and cane. Was there a smirk on the man's face? Bezer had the urge to crack him on the head, but with the bubble of his rage burst, he stomped down the steps, cursing the place and all those in it. On the pavement, he looked up at the sky, raised his cane and petitioned the Almighty to send a thunderbolt to blast to hell the Reverend Rudge and the whole Society for the Suppression of Mendicity, along with all the stinking beggars who clustered there hoping for handouts.

To fortify himself before returning home, he took a brandy and water in the *Dog and Duck* on Gray's Inn Road. He had to have another when he thought about his wife and how she would react to his news. But it was her doing after all, insisting that they move to more expensive apartments and hire a servant girl. It had stretched his salary to the limit. In spite of his creative measures to boost his income, with the cost of brandy and his recent bad luck at the card table, he was in an uncomfortable financial state. Now he had no income and those skinflints at the Society were demanding back the subscription monies. He ordered another brandy to further soothe his anger. Those men would happily hand out money to the scum of the earth, but they would hound one of their own out of employment, he who had been such a diligent worker on behalf of the Society.

With a heavy head and unsteady step, Bezer Blundell made his way home to his wife, Susan, to break the unfortunate news. He pondered on the likelihood that they would have to move to a cheaper place like one of those on Percy Street not far from their own address. It was bad enough to have to walk along it, past the houses where the Irish had moved in and a collection of vagrants would gather to buy cheap beer and gin from a woman's front room. Bezer felt a gloomy mood descending upon him like a damp cloak. How could they hold their heads up now? He climbed the stairs, groping for the banister rail to steady himself, head throbbing now.

'Home my dear one,' he called in a strangled falsetto as he came in the door.

Susan appeared, wearing a large white apron, her hands caked with flour, her face puckered in a frown.

'That stupid girl,' she said with no greeting to Bezer. 'She didn't turn up today. I've had to do everything. I'm worn out.'

Bezer took off his hat, aimed his cane at the umbrella stand and missed. Susan was going to have to get used to doing all household work from now on. They would have to let the maid go, if she hadn't already decided to quit. Susan was scrutinising him as he stood in the hallway, wishing that he could simply collapse on his bed and sleep away the rest of the evening, to wake tomorrow and discover that it had all been an unpleasant dream. He excused himself saying that he needed a rest.

'Go then, don't worry about me,' she snapped, flouncing off into the kitchen.

Supper when it arrived some hours later, revived Bezer somewhat, though he knew that he could not for much longer evade the truth of his situation. He swallowed the last piece of stewed lamb and pushed his plate aside.

'My dear, I have some unfortunate news to convey,' he said.

Susan's eyes narrowed. 'I thought there was something amiss; the smell of brandy and all this "my dearest love" business. I thought "he's in trouble, I can tell",' she said with a snort of satisfaction.

When he told her, she gave remarkably little outward show of anger for the injustice of others and for his suffering at their hands. But he could tell she was raging in her silent way.

'You're an utter fool,' she said as he finished the first instalment of his tale of the treachery and ingratitude of others towards him. 'I told you the forging of the tickets would be discovered. Paupers aren't that stupid when there's money in it for them. One of these ragamuffins probably reported being turned away. Deception only works when there's little chance of detection.'

Bezer ran his fingers through his mop of straw-coloured hair, feeling dishevelled in every part of his being. Why could she not be sympathetic? A wife was supposed to support and stand by her husband, boost his pride in himself, be his servant and helpmeet.

'At least they didn't notice the loan I took

from the funds and have only asked for the payment of the missing subscriptions,' he said sulkily.

'How much?'

'A hundred pounds.'

Susan's mouth tightened to a thin line.

'It could have been worse, my dear one,' Bezer said, hanging his head. Playing the naughty child might surely evoke some kind of pity.

She said nothing, clashing the dishes together as she cleared the table, and Bezer retired to bed, pulling the coverlet over his head to shut out the world.

A hard thump on the leg brought Bezer back to half-consciousness. The room was in darkness but he heard Susan striking a match to light the lamp on her bedside cabinet.

'Wake up, will you' she whispered sharply in his ear, tugging at his arm.

'Let me alone. Let me sleep.'

Another kick and he knew that resistance was pointless.

'I have a plan,' she said, gripping him with sharp fingers.

He elbowed his way up the bed and found her face close to his, her mob cap askew in her excitement.

'Yes, my dear one?' he said.

'How do street beggars, vagrants and other creatures of the gutter get money?' she said.

He was appalled. 'You don't mean that we should beg on the streets, do you?'

'No, you numbskull. We're respectable, whatever else we are. We'd never demean ourselves in such a way. Listen, you know of plenty of these do-gooders, fine folk with so much money they can scarce think of what to spend it on, dizzy-headed gentry, Christian folk who would do God's work, benevolent souls who wish to relieve suffering and hardship. There are many would be willing to give to needy causes.'

Bezer saw that she was so fired up with her idea that he dared not interrupt by casting doubt on their status as a needy cause, particularly in the light of his recent exposure.

'All we have to do is to write letters, respectful, polite, genteel from unfortunate folks who are down on their luck, ill, cheated out of money, that sort of thing, even fallen into poverty and being on the parish, through no fault of their own.'

He grasped her hand. She certainly had the core of a workable plan here. It would require some investigation of course, but she was right, he had much of the necessary knowledge and expertise. He also had, he was proud to admit, a certain skill at creative composition, a fine turn of phrase and Susan herself could write a passable hand. He embraced his stout wife around what used to be her waist and gave her a grateful wet kiss.

Two weeks later, Bezer, toiling at his third or fourth letter, was finding the business exceedingly tiresome. He broke off writing, put down his pen and turned to Susan who was sitting by the fire, scanning the advertisements in a newspaper.

'Haven't you finished that yet?' she said, looking up.

'It isn't easy, you know, inventing these stories,' he said, taking up his unfinished letter. 'I'm at a loss about how to proceed.'

He cleared his throat and read her his effort thus far.

c/o The Grapes Inne, Shoreditch

Most Honourable Lord,

Your noble reputation as a gentleman replete with the Christian virtues of mercy and generosity, has persuaded me to appeal to you. I, Archibald Bracewell, former minister of the church, but now advanced in years and in a sad state of health, find myself in dire distress. My fear is that I shall die a pauper and my poor dear wife also, for she suffers with me...

Susan let out an impatient sigh, weary with the burden of an inadequate husband.

'Why don't you say you were burgled of all your worldly goods, that you couldn't pay your rent and your poor wife is gravely sick and so on and so forth?' she said.

'But that's what I wrote in the one to the Earl of Chichester and even something similar to Lord Calthorpe. I can't always be some ancient, burgled vicar every time. Word will get around. These fine folk are always exchanging news with each other.'

Bezer was beginning to tire of this letter writing and Susan didn't really seem to be doing her part, for all she professed to be looking for inspiration in the newspaper. So far, their appeals to a number of likely benefactors had produced quite swift but unhelpful responses: one straight refusal and another letter returned unanswered. Susan had thought it advisable to use a number of different addresses from which to send their letters, so that it was easier to conceal their real identities. They stated their own address on a few, but the other letters gave the return addresses of a number of public houses in different parts of town, where they paid the landlords a small fee to collect post on behalf of the individuals they were purporting to be.

'Use your imagination,' said Susan pettishly. 'You could be an old soldier, lost your leg at the Battle of Waterloo, made your living selling pies on the street, got run over by a cart, hand crushed, can't work, that sort of thing.'

Bezer smiled at his wife.

'Your mind is a treasure house, my dearest,' he said. 'That will be my next, yes, an old soldier. But would be you be an angel and write one or two yourself?'

She pursed her lips. 'Yes, if I must, but if I'm to write as an old soldier, I will have to take on a more manly style.'

Bezer sighed. This was the hardest work he had ever undertaken in many years and his head ached with it. He was gasping for a drink, a measure of brandy, but there was only a thimbleful remaining in the bottle and he knew that Susan would chide him for taking it all and depriving her. They had no money for drink, their last reserves being for the purchase of paper and ink and some bread and cheese. If they did not have any success from their letters soon, they were liable to starve, Bezer thought in a moment of panic. He had no choice but to persevere, a process quite alien to him. He thought with a certain fondness of those times when he had had a regular salary from the Society, as well as the chance of some supplementary funds. This reminded him of the other less comforting aspect of this memory, the need to pay back the money he owed. Reverend Rudge had agreed to let him pay this back in instalments over the months and years. This was a deeply dispiriting thought.

He took his place again at the table and resumed where he had left off, as the elderly vicar. Susan sat down at his side and took a new sheet from their diminishing supply. They had been at work, amidst much sighing from Bezer, for about another hour when there was a sharp knock on their door. Bezer answered it, discovering a boy there holding an envelope.

'Is there a Mrs Norris here?' said the boy.

'Yes, I'll give it to her,' said Bezer snatching the letter, and slamming the door on the boy, who shouted a few curses and kicked it in anger at a man who would not give him a penny for his trouble. Bezer hurried back to Susan, waving the envelope in front of her face.

'Well open it, you numbskull,' she said, putting down her pen.

'I have a good feeling about this one, my dearest,' Bezer said, fingers quivering as he opened the letter.

2 Belgrave Square,
Grosvenor Estate

Dear Mrs Norris,

Lady Dartmouth received your letter last week and has given your request very serious consideration. She is most moved to hear of the condition of your daughter and notes that she requires urgent medical assistance. To that end Lady Dartmouth has requested that her own physician, Dr William Semple, should call upon you to examine the child and provide whatever medicaments he recommends to relieve her suffering. The costs incurred will be met by Lady Dartmouth and a small donation will be delivered by Dr Semple too, to assist you in your immediate need. Please send a note to me at the above address indicating when Dr Semple may call.

Yours
Samuel R Taylor
(Secretary to Lady Dartmouth)

'Damn and blast!' said Bezer. 'What are we

going to do?'

Susan rose from the table and paced up and down the room in furious thought, her hefty stomping shaking the floorboards. After a few moments she stopped suddenly.

'I have it. We'll have to write back and say the child is dead. We can't have some doctor coming round here.'

This triggered something unexpected in Bezer's head, an inspired idea.

'Dear one, couldn't Mrs Norris, in her grief and distress request money for the funeral of the unfortunate child?'

Susan looked at him for a second or two, frowning in thought.

'Not a bad notion, Bezer,' she said, which he knew was the highest praise he was likely to get.

'Right, I'll get writing, but we'll have to be quick. You finish the vicar's letter and I'll take it to the General Post Office. You can go to Belgrave Square with the note for Lady Dartmouth.

Susan set to with a scrap of spare paper to write the letter from poor Mrs Norris, now overwhelmed with grief and sorrow.

Dear Mr Taylor,

My heart bleeds with sorrow and gratitude for the generosity of Lady Dartmouth, but I fear that her offer comes too late. My child is dead, passed away in agony last night in my arms. She now lies lifeless on the bed and I with no means to give my darling a fitting Christian burial. If her Ladyship would grant me a sum with which to send my daughter to her Maker, I would be forever and with all my heart indebted to her. God will look upon such an act of kindness and mercy as a mark of a truly pious soul working in his holy name.

If the gracious lady will extend her generosity to a desperate mother, please give the money to my simple but trustworthy neighbour who delivers this note.

I am your humble and ever grateful servant
Henrietta Norris

Susan finished with a flourish and read the letter to Bezer, who beamed with pleasure.

'Now hurry up and make yourself ready. These letters must be disposed of. I think at last good fortune may be turning our way. And we're learning all the time,' she said.

Bezer dirtied his face with a little ash from the fireplace, put on an old coat, which was threadbare and too tight for his present girth. Susan ripped some of the hem down and fashioned a ragged cap from an old felt hat of her own.

'There, you look the part now,' she said, turning him round to inspect the full effect of his disguise. 'And remember to keep off the main thoroughfares for fear of seeing any from the Society who might recognise you.'

Bezer nodded, stuffed the note into his pocket and with more than a shred of hopefulness, set off to Belgravia, a new estate of houses for the very rich, beyond Buckingham Palace. It was a long walk, particularly by the alleys and side streets of his obscure route. He panted with the effort and also with growing excitement and anticipation of success, of money and of a fine supper. As he approached Belgrave Square, he found his way barred. Access, it appeared, was not available to the general public. He peered in through the gated entrance at the magnificent white terraces in the Italian style with columned doorways, tall windows, five storeys high. Gazing in envious admiration, Bezer stood for some moments until a porter or gatekeeper in livery came striding up.

'Away with you,' he said. 'No loitering here.'

'If you please,' said Bezer with a cringing bow. 'I have a very important letter for Lady Dartmouth's secretary and for the eyes of Her Ladyship herself.'

'Give it to me,' said the man rudely.

Bezer hesitated but knew that there was little point in arguing.

'I'm obliged to wait for a reply,' Bezer said.

The gatekeeper looked at him, now clearly in doubt about whether he should leave his post and this disreputable person unsupervised to deliver the letter, or let Bezer make his own way to the house.

'Her Ladyship is bounty itself, an angel to those of us unfortunate souls who have fallen on hard times,' Bezer said dolefully.

'Come, then,' said the man, beckoning Bezer

to follow him.

Bezer trotted obediently behind, admiring the circular park in the centre of the square, with newly dug flower beds and small trees just planted out. Some men were at work laying paving further along a wide walkway in front of the first magnificent terrace. Bezer's imagination leapt, as in his mind, he saw himself mounting the steps to one of the pillared porticoes, Susan on his arm, dressed in silk and fur.

'This way,' snapped the man hurrying down a small side lane to the rear of the grand houses into the mews street with stables, houses and service buildings. The man took the first staircase down at the back of the main house to a basement below and clanged the bell. A kitchen maid appeared at the door and the gatekeeper explained that the letter should be taken straight away to Mr Taylor.

'But for her Ladyship's eyes,' Bezer butted in, drawing looks of disapproval from the maid and the gatekeeper. The maid took the letter and then disappeared.

'Come back and wait at the gate' said the man to Bezer. 'If there's any reply, someone will bring it.'

He instructed Bezer to stay out of sight and placed him behind one of the great gateposts to the square. Bezer amused himself for the first half hour by conjuring more visions of himself riding into the square in a carriage. The gatekeeper opened the barriers to let in one such carriage, bearing its occupants to the far end of the square, where Bezer could just see a servant coming out of one of the houses to help two ladies down from the vehicle. As the time ticked on, Bezer felt a mood of despondency begin to creep over him, like dampness on a cold day rising through the soles of the feet. This effort might lead to nothing; he might wait and wait, and in the end receive nothing.

Two gentlemen on horseback rode into the square, turning in the direction of the stables. Then, from around the same corner, a boy came running, bearing something in his hand, a letter. Bezer's heart jolted with joy. A reply at last. He stepped out from behind the pillar and came to meet the boy while the gatekeeper looked on.

'Message for Mrs Norris,' said the boy.

'I'll take that,' said Bezer holding out his hand.

The boy recoiled a little, looked for approval to the man who nodded, then handed the letter over to Bezer. He tried not to snatch it in his eagerness but scurried away as quickly as he could, without a glance back at the man and the boy. His step was light, his heart too as he had felt a weight in the package a coin, a sovereign. All his weariness of body and mind had fled. With the coin in his pocket, he moved with ease first to the butchers where he bought a good lamb shank, thence to the greengrocer for a bag of potatoes, and finally to the tavern for a restorative brandy and water or two and a small bottle to take home. With ample change in his pocket, he returned to his wife.

Susan greeted him with a chuckle of glee at the sight of him with his spoils, though when he handed her the few shillings he had kept by for her, her face changed.

'So, her ladyship couldn't stretch to a guinea then?' she said. 'Skinflint. What did she give you?'

'Fifteen shillings,' he lied, 'but my dearest we shall dine well tonight and tomorrow, and who knows? There may be more.'

'What did she say in her letter?' she said.

Bezer had stuffed it into his pocket without reading it, after having extracted the guinea from the envelope. Now he pulled out the paper and handed it to Susan.

2 Belgrave Square

Dear Mrs Norris,

I was greatly distressed to hear your sad news and regret that my physician was unable to call upon your unfortunate daughter before it was too late. It is doubtful, however, given the severity of her illness, that he would have been able to save her. Please accept my sincere condolences and this monetary contribution towards her funeral rites.

Yours truly
Lady Wilhelmina Dartmouth

Bezer could see Susan's face creasing into a grin as she read and he laughed out loud.

'Come, my dearest one, let us drink to the memory of our dear departed.'

Chapter 7

Though the room was cavernous, high-ceilinged like a barn, it seemed to Nathan hardly large enough able to contain the turbulent mass of bodies in the Ragged School. The noise of the children filled the place: the combined cries of starlings, the screams of seagulls and the rattle of hundreds of coach wheels. Fifty, sixty, maybe more, tattered boys and a few girls milled around, climbing over the wooden forms and some even standing upon the long trestle tables. Nathan scanned the tumult in search of an adult in charge, but could only make out one or two older girls and boys of around ten or eleven years amidst the crowd. The rest were younger, smaller or perhaps stunted by poverty.

None in the room appeared to notice his presence, as he stood by the door wondering what on earth he should do. He was supposed to meet Mr Nicholas Greaves, the schoolmaster here but there was no sign of him. Nathan was tempted to turn and leave, pick his way back along through the filth and smells of Field Lane where this Ragged School was located. Miss Coutts had not been mistaken when she had told him that these schools were set up in districts of the most dire poverty and need. Should he turn tail and forget this foolish notion of his that he might be able to teach these children, help them at all towards a better life? The task was too great, the problems too gross, as he could clearly see now in this congregation of the deprived. In fact, he was not sure what had possessed him to agree when Miss Coutts had made this suggestion to him. He had been taken aback that she had shown an interest in him. He found her quiet directness surprising as well as her commitment to improving the lot of the poor. She appeared completely honest and pure in her intent. He was sure that her munificence was not self-seeking. But could he rise to the challenge that she had set him? How could he, a miserable recluse, survive in this den of noise?

Before he could think further on this, a man and woman appeared beside him at the door. The man was short in stature but with a strong, square face, and a direct, commanding gaze. He took off a battered looking hat, revealing a head of long grey hair. The woman with him was in height almost equal to her companion. She was slim, with a neat figure and a pleasant, open expression, her cape and bonnet well-worn and plain. The man held out his hand to Nathan and, over the hubbub, greeted him with some inaudible words of welcome. The woman smiled at him, while from his pocket the man took out a small round tin and, stepping further into the room, shook it vigorously. The strident clattering of marbles or shot against metal pierced the wall of noise and within a few seconds the children's din had begun to subside.

Nathan watched these rowdy pupils, faces turning towards the couple, their scampering, fighting and chattering slowing until the motion of their bodies was reduced to an almost quiet seething, like waves on shingle.

'Good morning, children,' said the man in a voice not much raised above that of a suppertime conversation. The children chorused noisily back.

'Good morning, Mr Greaves, Good morning, Mrs Greaves.'

'Sit down everyone, please,' said Nicholas Greaves, advancing towards the main body of the room, while the woman took her husband's hat from him, removed her own and her cloak and hung the items up on a peg by the door.

The children complied in a manner most astonishing to Nathan. They crammed themselves onto the long wooden forms, those who could not fit, squatting on spaces on the floor. Sixty grimy faces and fidgeting bodies assembled before him.

'Today, children, we must welcome someone to our school,' said the schoolmaster and Nathan was aware how, in this near hush, the attention of those who had previously not noted his presence, had been drawn to him.

'Mr Hines is going to be teaching arithmetic to the boys of seven and upwards. You must show him how well you can count and calculate, for these are important in life.'

The schoolmaster was now looking pointedly at Nathan and he was not sure whether any remarks were required of him in response to this introduction. Mercifully, Nicholas Greaves issued orders for the children to divide into groups according to their ages, and the girls were to go separately with Mrs Greaves. There was much shuffling, pushing and the crack of an overturned form and in the midst a few children stood forlorn and dumbfounded by the proceedings. Mrs Greaves approached Nathan, holding out her hand, which he clasped briefly in his, immediately reassured by her calm and unhurried manner.

'Thank you so much for coming,' she said, raising her voice above the noise. 'We are so pleased to have another teacher, as we have our hands very full, as you can see. I hope you are used to wild children. I'm afraid they're inclined to be impudent and boisterous. Many just come for the soup and are not always the best of scholars.'

She was smiling as she spoke, with a shrug, perhaps in recognition of the limitations of their efforts.

'Well, I am not the best of teachers,' said Nathan, 'so perhaps the children and I can learn together.'

'Mr Hines if you can teach them some basic arithmetic, we shall be delighted. My husband, you see, is a more literary soul, if you get my meaning. But please do not expect too much of the children. They mostly live in a wretched state of poverty and ignorance. This place gives them respite and warmth if nothing else. Ask my husband which are your boys for today and good luck,' she said, leaving him and herding her group of about six girls of various sizes over to a far corner of the room.

Nathan headed to where Nicholas Greaves was assembling a group in two rows in front of him, while a clutch of others were squabbling and chatting nearby.

'Ah, Mr Hines,' said Greaves, looking round at him then pointing at a loose assemblage of unoccupied boys, around twenty of them. 'Would you take these boys over there for adding and subtracting.'

'But how... what shall I...? Are there any books, Mr Greaves?' said Nathan, which he realised too late was a pointless question as the room contained nothing but the bare furniture.

'We have no books, Mr Hines,' he said. 'We have nothing, no blackboard, no slates, but we have high hopes now you are here and with our new benefactress Miss Coutts. But for now, I'm afraid you'll just have to improvise.'

Nathan, dismayed and a little fearful, moved in the direction of an empty space in the opposite corner from where the schoolmaster had his class and Nathan's charges followed. Some moved slowly, others cavorted towards the benches, grabbing spaces before the tardier ones. Once they had more or less settled and most were looking towards him, Nathan hesitated, wondering how to start.

'Don't yer know what to do?' said one of the larger boys near the front.

'Just ask us our numbers,' offered another helpfully.

'When can we have our dinner?'

'Shut yer bloody cakehole.'

'I can add up.'

Nathan watched in alarm as a straw-haired boy pushed another off the end of the form and the victim retaliated, leaping up and punching the first one in the face. A number of the others nearby joined in the fight. Nathan, knowing he must take action quickly, shouted, 'Enough!' surprised at the sound of his voice in the room. He saw Mr Greaves look up and a few of the children in his group tittering and grinning.

Nathan's class however, paid little attention, only a couple of the smaller boys at his feet on the floor stayed silent. He knew that another outburst from him would be unlikely to lead to a change in the boys' behaviour, so he ignored the squabbling ones and addressed the few who were quiet at the front.

'What's your name?' he said to a small dark child with a squint in one eye.

'Tom,' he said solemnly.

The boy beside him was Albert.

'Right,' said Nathan feigning confidence via briskness. 'If Albert has two pence and Tom here has two, how much is there altogether?'

The two boys looked at each other with puzzled expressions.

'But he ain't got no money, sir,' said a larger boy behind them.

'"S'easy,' said another of the larger boys. 'Two add two makes four, you dimwit.'

'Good,' said Nathan, heartened by this minor display of attention. 'This is what we'll do. We'll go round one by one; you tell me your name and then add two to the number before. Tom says two and Albert says four, two add two makes four. Right, who are you?'

He pointed at the next child at the end of the row.

'Jem,' he said.

'Right, Jem, add two on to four.'

'Six,' someone shouted from the back row.

'Well done,' said Nathan, 'but wait till you're asked. If someone doesn't know the answer, then you can help.'

So, to Nathan's amazement they proceeded to go around the class, with a few pauses, a few panic-stricken faces and considerable shouting out of answers right and wrong until they had reached 40. Nathan surveyed the group and found that they were all by now at least sitting down and most were facing in his direction. In his head he tried to run through their names again. Some had stuck, the cheekiest, the most forlorn and the filthiest. Then they moved on to subtraction in which most seemed happy to participate, though Nathan sensed that the attention of many was flagging. A few moments later, however, a welcome distraction came in the shape of a large man, barging backwards through the doors into the hall.

'Blimey, dinner at last,' said one of the boys loudly, jumping up, pointing at the huge round basket of bread that the man was wielding.

Nicholas Greaves's group had broken into a ragged, noisy hubbub too, until he once again rattled his tin loudly above his head and started issuing instructions for the children to set up the trestle tables in the middle of the room and the forms around them. Amidst the bustle, a wooden trolley was pushed through the doors, bringing with it the smell of some kind of broth and a couple of stray dogs. The trolley on four wheels, which bore two large pans of the brew, was being pushed by two nuns. Two others followed with large bags, which they emptied on to the table top. Out rolled a clatter of small wooden bowls and tin cups.

'Take your seats, everyone. No pushing. There's room for everyone, and a bowl for everyone,' called Mr Greaves, as the children rushed forward with snatching hands.

Miraculously, there seemed to be enough to go around, and some moments later, two of the nuns and Mrs Greaves had started spooning the broth into each bowl. Nathan saw the look of disapproval flit across the face of one of the nuns, as some of the children already had their mouths on the bowls.

'We must give thanks to God,' said Mr Greaves, standing behind the boys who had begun to slurp hungrily.

He quickly said a short grace while the stuff was being dispensed, Nathan suspected, to placate the sisters of this holy order. Nathan, aware that the bread was still to be handed out, moved around to where Mrs Greaves was standing and offered to help. She nodded and smiled and soon he was quickly distributing a chunk of the rough brown stuff to each child.

Some snatched it from his hand and others nodded, others tried to take two pieces, but in the end, all were supplied. As he finished, Mrs Greaves had appeared beside him.

'We do not get food every day,' she said. 'Today it was the Sisters of Mercy who supplied us. But we hope with Miss Coutts's support we may be able to have some bread and cheese every day.'

'It's good,' Nathan said, impressed by the efficiency of the operation and touched by the relish of the children for their fare. 'The children have a safe place to come, to take them from the streets.'

'Yes,' she said, 'but we're struggling against the odds, Mr Hines.'

There was a note of resignation in her voice, but she turned to him and smiled.

'You seem to have occupied your boys well this morning,' she said. 'How did you find them?'

In the presence of this woman, Nathan felt no embarrassment. He felt no sense that she would judge him. Her manner was frank and open and in this place, exposed to the eyes of others and to the impossible demands and needs of these children, there was no room for pretence.

'I confess I was badly at a loss at first about what to do,' he said. 'But we managed well for the most part. I will give some thought to devising calculations for the different levels of understanding,' he said.

She was studying him closely as he spoke.

Her eyes were grey, her expression open and attentive.

'Mr Hines, I'm sorry that we didn't have time to offer you any guidance and I'm so glad you're thinking of coming back,' she said. 'But you can never be sure which children will attend each day. Some of them come only once. It makes progress slow to say the least. I hope you will not find it too frustrating.'

He watched her as she turned and consoled a small weeping child, whose bread had been snatched by a bigger boy. Amidst the hum of noise and activity, he stood, wondering at himself and how he had arrived at this point, but with no doubt in his mind that he would return. Already he was thinking about the books on the shelf in his shop that people had brought in to pawn. There could be some that would be of good use in the school, should they not be redeemed. There were also the books he had read to his children, though these were too precious for him to part with.

That night, Nathan slept and dreamed of Kate. He did not wake in a sweat after a fitful hour, however, remembering the manner of her death, as he often did. In this dream, he had told her that he had become a schoolmaster and she had smiled then embraced him. When he awoke, he recalled the scene vividly and wondered if this change was fated to shake him from his torpor and depression. Already he felt that maybe this was the beginning.

The next morning early, Nathan called upon

his friend Silas, whose help he would need in his new venture into schoolmastering. Silas was always obliging and glad of the money that Nathan paid him for minding the shop, surviving as he did on casual labour in markets in the East End. He was not a physically prepossessing man, though Nathan saw beyond his superficial appearance and manner. He was inclined to be gruff, the result Nathan surmised, of a childhood in the workhouse and lifetime of sour looks and abuse from others because of his gargoyle-like appearance. He had worked on the docks as a ballast heaver, in coal yards and as a soap boiler. Born into another class, however, Silas could have excelled at many things. He had a quick mind, was adept at figures, literate and a book lover. Nathan valued his fidelity and friendship.

Silas expressed his agreement and even pleasure at Nathan's request.

'It may be that I am not suited to the work,' Nathan said, 'but I must try it for a while at least.'

'And maybe I'll not suit this business neither,' Silas said, his grizzled cheeks bunching into something like a smile.

In fact, Nathan and Silas both embraced their new responsibilities and after some weeks, the arrangement seemed mutually agreeable. As the school day finished at around three o'clock in the afternoon, Nathan was able to return to the shop to oversee the business of the day.

One afternoon, when Nathan returned, Silas seemed particularly satisfied with the transactions he had managed and the money collected.

'A good day today?' Nathan said.

'It was indeed.'

'Redemptions, I hope,' said Nathan, taking off his hat and coat.

'Yes,' said Silas eagerly, 'a ring, two greatcoats, a tidy sum. Sold some things too. But look here.'

He pointed to a small pile of books on the counter.

'Now you've turned schoolmaster,' Silas said with a grin.

Nathan smiled slightly. 'I've not yet earned that title.'

Silas handed him the first book, *Principles of Mathematics for Schoolboys* then another *The Paths of Virtue* and *Bible Stories for Children.*

'Thank you, Silas. I think Miss Coutts our benefactress would certainly approve. These will be useful.'

The schoolmaster and his wife had told Nathan of Miss Coutts's piety and her concern for the spiritual as well as the material welfare of the pauper children. Promoting Christian virtues was likely to present a particular challenge as many of the boys had little idea about who Jesus was, nor any notion of religious faith and belief. As for Nathan's faith, witnessing the suffering of the innocent had finally obliterated any shaky belief he had ever had in the existence of a loving God. Any texts, however, would prove useful additions to the sparse resources of the school, Nathan concluded.

Nathan looked around the shop. Since he had taken over, Silas had enjoyed tidying the storeroom where the pledges were kept on shelves, checking the cataloguing of the items and those unredeemed for sale. Nathan's only concern was that Silas might think it his duty solely to maximise income and profits, with smaller payouts and higher interest charged on pawned goods. It seemed, however, from Silas's immaculate bookkeeping that Nathan's fears were not justified. His friend shared his own values of what was fair.

'Sold a gown too,' Silas said, 'for twelve shillings and sixpence.'

'A gown? Which gown?' Nathan said.

'The silk one that was hanging in the cupboard in the storeroom.'

'No!'

Silas's face reddened at Nathan's outburst.

'I thought – It wasn't in the book, no label –. It wasn't – your Kate's?' he said.

'No, damn you, it wasn't,' said Nathan. 'I have her things in a chest upstairs.'

Nathan immediately regretted his show of anger and apologised.

Silas shook his head, his face a tragic mask.

'I didn't know –Thought it was for sale. I'll pay you.'

Feeling guilty at the abject look on Silas's

face, Nathan explained the story of Selina Harding's gown, how he had come by it and her letter in the pocket. Silas, shaking his head disconsolately, told him he had sold the dress to a woman who wished it to attend her niece's wedding and she went off with it, mightily pleased. Nathan reflected, as his dismay subsided, that perhaps it was better for the garment to be worn and appreciated rather than decaying in a forgotten cupboard. He would like to have given it to the daughter, if she were ever to be found alive, but he realised that this was never likely to happen now. His enquiries had led to nothing, even though he had extended his search to Sundays when the shop was shut. Nathan saw now that his peculiar interest in the gown and its owner was a foolish obsession, born of his grief. It set him thinking of Kate's clothes too and his children's, which lay upstairs. He knew he must some day soon look at them again, not leave them closeted and turning to dust.

Silas was still apologising as he took his leave after helping Nathan with the shutters of the shop, but Nathan told him to think no more about it. He still had the woman's handkerchief after all, which he could carry with him on his searches. After Silas had gone home, Nathan had supper but found himself in a restless state, thinking about the woman and her daughter. Though dusk was falling, he determined to go out again for a final search. There was a place nearby, a network of small alleys near Cow Cross, where he had seen a number of young pauper girls congregating. He thought them likely to be beggars, thieves or worse, child prostitutes. There was a chance that Selina Harding's daughter, if orphaned and alone, had been forced as so many others were, to beg on the streets. He took a few coins in his pocket.

He set off in a northerly direction, walking swiftly, passing a couple of lamplighters, ladders on their shoulders, going about their nightly business on the main thoroughfares. The sky glowed red behind the taller buildings and the ubiquitous smell of coal smoke, mixed with sour hops from a brewery and rotting vegetables, hung in the air. People were hurrying home, and stall holders packing up their wares and wheeling barrows away, late shopkeepers closing the doors of their shops. He soon arrived at the place where he remembered seeing the girls. Here again, between some tenement buildings, outside a shuttered shop, he saw a group of them standing talking and laughing together. Nathan moved closer and when he was within twenty yards of them, he recognised one, the very girl who had been masquerading as Mrs Harding's servant. He had carried a clear picture of her in his head and there was no doubt in his mind that this was the same one. The pinched white face, skinny body, slightly hunched posture and the deformed foot. He wanted to call to her, feared surprising her, but she looked up first, saw him and in that moment of recognition, turned quickly and bolted off down one of the alleys. Her companions stared after her, then turned back to him, seeming unsure about whether he was offering any kind of threat to them.

'It's alright,' he said to them as he approached. 'I mean you no harm. But your friend. I need to speak to her.'

The girls glanced at him recoiling a little, though one, a bolder creature of around ten years old, he reckoned spoke up.

'It'll cost you, mister,' she said.

He put his hand in his pocket and put a sixpence into her palm, which she held ready.

'Will you ask your friend to meet me here tomorrow. Tell her I only want to talk to her. I will not harm her in any way. I only want information, nothing more.'

'Friend?' said the bold girl. 'She ain't no friend of ours. Never seen her before.'

At this the three took off quickly down another of the dark tunnels that the unlit alleys had become. Nathan saw their small figures disappearing almost immediately into the obscurity. He shook his head, feeling foolish but knowing it would have been useless to attempt a pursuit. As he turned to go back the way he had come, he found a man standing only yards from him, clearly a witness to this scene. He was of middle years and too well-dressed to be a resident of these streets. It was likely that he was taking a shortcut to a more salubrious destination.

'Excuse me,' he said. 'I observed only now that you gave money to those beggar children.'

Nathan, taken aback, searched the face of the man for some clue as to the purpose of this unsolicited comment.

'Yes, sir I did.'

The man smiled briefly. 'Sir, I can see you are of a benevolent nature, and I wonder that you have not heard of the work of the Society for the Suppression of Mendicity.'

'No, I have not,' said Nathan, suspicious of the man's motives for addressing him.

He was obviously disapproving of Nathan's apparent act of charity, though this stranger was mild-mannered and gentlemanly. Nathan knew that clearing beggars off the street was the wish of many, though mainly for reasons of decorum rather than concern for the welfare of those who were forced into such a life.

'The Society is a worthy body of men that offers unfortunates who live by the occupation of beggary. They create a nuisance and eyesore and their degradation is abominable to society.'

The man plunged his hand into his coat pocket and brought out a packet of papers in the form of a small notebook or similar.

'Here are some tickets you can give to street beggars that you encounter. With a ticket they can report to the Society's office in Holborn. There they will be fed, clothed if possible and their case and circumstances explained to the charitable committee. If they are of good character, not thieves, rogues or other miscreants, they will be helped to employment or to emigrate. Or if they are from the country, they are sent back to their parishes.'

'And what of those who are not judged to be of good character?' Nathan asked, genuinely curious, reserving his judgement of such work.

The man looked at him, with a hint of disapproval.

'Well, those who would cheat the Society will be turned out on the street. Sturdy beggars and irredeemable ones, if they persist in their practices, will no doubt find themselves in front of the magistrate,' he replied. 'But we are merciful and benevolent in our dealing with paupers and unfortunates who have through no fault of their own ended up in need. Take some of these tickets and hand them out to persons you find in this condition, if you please.'

The man handed Nathan two tickets and then bade him farewell. Though Nathan's search had failed to bear fruit, it had not been a completely unrewarding venture. He had discovered the girl who had pawned the gown and had hopes that he might find her again if she lived in this area of the town. Also, he had now learned of another possible charitable body to whom Selina Harding may have appealed. He would go to the Holborn office of the Society as soon as he had the opportunity.

The next day at the school, in the third week of Nathan's taking up his post, Mr Greaves announced that they were to expect a visit from Miss Coutts. Nathan found himself in a state of some anxiety at the prospect of meeting his benefactress again. This stemmed, he knew, from his desire to demonstrate to her that he was worthy of the trust she had placed in him. Nicholas Greaves announced to the assembled children that the kind and bountiful lady, Miss Coutts, who gave money to the school was coming to inspect how well the children were learning and how politely they could behave.

Nathan took his group to the appointed corner. He saw how the numbers had swelled to nearly forty, with many new children who had little knowledge of arithmetic. He resorted to making the children chant multiplication tables, hoping that any new ones would be able to join in, parroting at least, though he wondered all the while about how he could keep them all occupied until the food or Miss Coutts arrived. Soup and bread had been promised, courtesy of Miss Philpott's Paupers' Aid Association.

In a pause after the second round of the chorus of tables which Nathan observed Nicholas Greaves's group had joined from the other side of the room, Ned one of the older boys shouted out.

'When's the lady coming, Sir?'

'Is she pretty?' called another, emboldened by Ned's remark.

'She going to give us any money?' squeaked another.

Nathan quelled the cacophony of questions, a skill which he had developed more effectively over the weeks, by staring in silence, raising his hand and waiting.

'Miss Coutts will expect you to show her what you've learned about arithmetic and Bible stories. So, I'll read to you again one of the miracles of Jesus,' he said.

'Loaves and fishes,' Ned pronounced. 'Then maybe Jesus'll come here and do his trick. We could do with some grub.'

Nathan suppressed a smile. Ned was an intelligent boy, quick with numbers and with the confidence of the impudent. Nathan had decided he would try and find a place for the boy in work where he might be able to prosper. With some new clothes and a bit of a scrub, he could be made to look presentable. Mrs Greaves had managed to find work for one or two of her girls in laundries or in service in kitchens. Perhaps she could help find a place for Ned.

The soup arrived before Miss Coutts, and the children were all well occupied with supping when she appeared. She came on foot, accompanied by a young manservant, as Field Lane was too narrow and cluttered with stalls and barrows to permit the passage of a carriage or hansom cab. Nicholas Greaves and his wife greeted her at the door and presented her to the volunteer women and Mrs Philpot, who had come to serve out the food. Nathan watched from the other side of the room. Miss Coutts was not a beautiful nor imposing figure, but she was quietly elegant, serious, shy almost. He found himself admiring these qualities in a woman whose vast fortune could have had her basking in some exotic foreign location - Paris, Rome, Vienna - in the palaces, concert halls and opera houses that the rich frequented, not this sordid den of child paupers.

She nodded to Nathan from the other side of the room, as the children, heads bent over their bowls, devoured their food. Mrs Greaves guided Miss Coutts around the room and she greeted him, he bowing his head to her.

'Mr Hines,' she said, 'I'm pleased to see you here. And how does it suit you?'

'Very well Ma'am, thank you,' he said, 'though I have much to learn about schoolmastering.'

'Mr Hines is acquitting himself very well indeed,' said Mrs Greaves, looking at him with a smile, which caused him a moment's embarrassment, though he hoped this had not manifested itself in his expression.

Though he was gratified at the praise of these two women, he was not at ease as the centre of their attention. Fortunately, Miss Coutts was soon discussing other ways in which she could help the school. She took an interest in the practical aspects of her project, such as the design of a new bath house in the vacant building next door. Her concerns were clearly for the material as well as the moral welfare of the children.

'We would be grateful for some slates and chalk pencils,' said Mrs Greaves, which Nathan was pleased to hear, even more so when Miss Coutts asked Mr Greaves to put his requests in writing and submit them to her.

When Miss Coutts made a request to meet some of the children, Nathan immediately thought of Ned, though as the boy was ushered before her, his confident expression was replaced by a look of terror. Mrs Greaves had chosen two of her small girls to meet the lady and they too were dumbstruck, fidgeting with their ragged clothes and glancing about as if for an escape route.

Nathan whispered to Ned that he should not worry, but just speak up and answer the lady's questions clearly and politely. The charity women and Mrs Greaves, meanwhile, were helping to clear up the bowls and quell the noise of the other children. Miss Coutts looked at the children with a serious expression.

'Now who can tell me what they've learned in school?'

The children were silent and Nathan looked hopefully at Ned.

'Miracles of Jesus,' he blurted. 'Want to hear the one about the loaves and fishes, do yer, mi lady?'

Nathan caught Miss Coutts's eye and read there her approval, tinged with a gentle amusement. Ned spoke with remarkable fluency, growing in confidence, which seemed to encourage the two small girls to utter brief responses to Miss Coutts's questioning. Then Mrs Greaves returned and led Miss Coutts to the back room, where her group of girls worked on their sewing.

'I done all right, didn't I?' Ned said to Nathan with a grin.

'You did,' said Nathan, looking at him with a sudden inspiration about how he might tame the rest of the boys, who had been energised by their food. 'Come and help these little ones with their work.'

Order was restored and in this, Ned proved a useful helper.

An hour later, Miss Coutts was ready to leave and awaited the return of the manservant who had been instructed to meet her at the school to escort her to a cab. However, after some time, there was still no sign of the man and Nicholas Greaves, a little agitated and embarrassed at the situation, asked Nathan if he would accompany Miss Coutts to the main road and find her a hansom cab. Nathan was pleased to oblige and speedily took his hat and led their benefactress out on to Field Lane. He offered her his arm to guide her past the dirtiest patches and obstacles on the road, which was thronged by shoppers at the small stalls in front of the shops. A child was driving a pig that was trotting quickly straight into their path and a clutch of men were arguing loudly outside a doorway. Miss Coutts seemed untroubled however by the squalid environment, though as they neared the end of the lane, she gasped and stopped suddenly.

'Miss Coutts?' Nathan said, turning to her, fearing that she might be unwell.

Her face was taut and her eyes fixed on something or someone on the corner of the street.

'Mr Hines,' she said in an urgent undertone.

'Will you please get me a cab as soon as you can. There's a person, a man, I do not want to see.'

Nathan looked in the direction of her gaze and saw a dark figure standing by a shop door, a gentleman judging by his clothes and his bearing. He was gazing around him, though it appeared that he had not noticed Miss Coutts. As he turned his face in their direction, however, Nathan was struck by something familiar in his appearance. It took him only a few seconds to identify him as the arrogant Irishman who had pawned his cloak about a month previously.

'We'll go this way,' said Nathan quickly, offering his arm then leading Miss Coutts to the left, thus shielding her from the man's gaze. He was unsure if this strategy had come too late and the man had spotted them.

They walked briskly along Clerkenwell Road. Nathan hailed a hansom cab that was passing by on the opposite side of the road and the driver whipped his horse in a tight but skilful manoeuvre to reach them.

'Mr Hines, could I prevail upon you for another favour?' Miss Coutts said in a tense whisper.

'Of course,' he said.

'Would you be so kind as to accompany me back to my house? I don't want to encounter that man. He is a very troublesome person and I would not have him speak to me.'

'By all means,' said Nathan, as he helped her into the cab, giving the address to the driver, telling him to make haste.

Nathan climbed in after her and the driver, taking the instruction seriously, whipped his horse up to a sudden and speedy departure. Miss Coutts sat back, visibly relieved, while Nathan thought it indelicate to question her about the undesirable individual whom she seemed to fear. He was tempted to tell her of his previous encounter with the man, of his visit to the shop, but was wary of being too familiar and indulging in gossip, particularly with a woman of her station. Miss Coutts recovered her composure quite quickly and enquired after Nathan's search for Selina Harding and her daughter. He told her about his sighting of the young girl who had brought him the gown and of his discovery of the Society for the Suppression of Mendicity.

'Yes, I know of the work of the Society,' said Miss Coutts. 'You could certainly make enquiries at their office. I'm afraid my own investigations with other charitable bodies have not been fruitful. I fear that the woman and her child may be lost to us for ever.'

Her distress was genuine and Nathan felt a sinking of his spirits too. It was wrong-headed, however, that he should feel responsibility to a woman and child he had never met. All around him was poverty and people in need. The Ragged School was a nest of want and deprivation. He would do better to expend his energies on these children rather than pursuing a hopeless cause.

The cab drew up outside Miss Coutts's

house on Stratton Street and Nathan jumped out. He glanced quickly along the street and was glad to note that there was no sign of the troublesome man. He helped Miss Coutts down. She took a gold sovereign from a small velvet purse at her waist and handed it to Nathan, bidding him to pay the driver and keep the rest. It was an excessive amount for two journeys by cab and Nathan felt a momentary insult that she was paying him like a servant. But then he reflected, that was what he was to her. He was not her social equal and had rendered a service. She thanked him for his help and went into the house by the front entrance. It was a puzzle to Nathan as to why Miss Coutts's manservant had not appeared as instructed. He paid the driver and decided to walk back home, as the day was fine and dry. It was also too late to return to the school as the lessons would have finished for the day.

He was only a hundred yards from Miss Coutts's house, however, when another hansom cab careered to a halt at the side of the road and the Irishman leapt out, planting himself on the pavement, squarely in front of Nathan. The driver shouted for his fare and the man turned and tossed a coin to him angrily, as though he felt entitled to a free ride.

'You there,' said the Irishman to Nathan, charging towards him. 'What do you mean by wheedling your way into Miss Coutts's company, you impudent fellow?'

Nathan was so taken aback, it was a few seconds before he could construct a coherent reply.

'I don't know that it's your business, sir,' Nathan said, 'but Miss Coutts requested that I accompany her home. Her servant was expected, but he did not arrive.'

The man's face reddened and he raised a fist taking a step to within a foot of Nathan's face. He was a well-made individual, not as tall as Nathan, but strong looking and he rooted himself in Nathan's path in a theatrical pugilistic stance. Nathan had no wish to fight with the man but was not prepared to wait to be struck. It seemed, however that the Irishman preferred to throw insults rather than punches.

'You. I know you. You're a bloody shopkeeper, a pawnbroker, the lowest of the low. What do you think you're doing consorting with Miss Coutts, the woman I love?' he said.

'Good day to you, sir,' Nathan said quickly. 'I have given neither you nor Miss Coutts any injury or insult. I'll ask you to let me pass.'

Chapter 8

From his room, Richard Dunn could see quite clearly into a good part of Angela Coutts's house. Not all, of course, but if he stood on a chair, he could glimpse a section of what seemed to be her drawing room. Also, from the coffee shop on the street below, he had another useful vantage point: he could watch the comings and goings of servants and others who used the access passageway that led to the rear of the buildings. The only drawback of his situation now was his lack of funds, seeing as he'd had to shell out to pay the servant George for his services. That young devil certainly knew which side his bread was buttered. Dunn knew he'd have to offer him more too, if he were to see through his more ambitious plans.

In his head, he ran through his list of friends and associates, concluding sadly that he had already touched most of them for cash. Others were in Dublin and some of those had given him the brush off the last time he'd tried to borrow from them. He'd have to pawn something else - his watch maybe - though he was reluctant to do so as it was a vital possession for a professional man like himself. He had a spare pair of boots and a couple of older linen shirts, but they'd not bring in much. Also, he'd have to steer clear of that bastard in Fleet Street, that one he'd seen in a cab with Angela. The cheek of the man, ingratiating himself like that. He might well have the face and figure of a man of a superior sort, but he was common as dirt and had no right to be around a lady.

It had all been going so well until that shopkeeper poked his nose in and took her home in a cab. Young George had tipped Dunn off about Angela's visit to the slums, the school for pauper brats. Dear God, the woman must need her head examined to go into a place like that full of squealing urchins crawling with vermin. But then she was of a soft turn of mind as some rich ladies of a religious disposition were inclined to be, all serious and godly. Well, he'd show her that there was a lighter side to life beyond fretting about beggars. He'd fixed it with George for another guinea, not to turn up, so that he, Dunn could wait near the school and come upon Angela, by accident so to speak, without her manservant and thus offer his services to escort her home. She could hardly refuse in a lane like that full of thieves and cutpurses ready to steal the nose off your face given half a chance. But the pawnbroker had appeared, God damn his soul, though Dunn had scared him off, that was for certain.

However, what were obstacles but a test of his constancy and his resilience in the quest for the idol of his heart? Had he not endured the humiliation of prison for her sake? Thinking about the next stage of his plan heartened him greatly and he took pen and paper to write.

First, he would write a letter as he felt his prose style was at times almost as elegant as his verse for conveying the profundity of his feelings. He would write a poem too, for good measure, as these two documents would reinforce each other, impress her with the intensity and sincerity of his feeling. But he found himself singularly bereft of inspiration, dogged as he was by the awareness of his wretched financial circumstances, tempted also by thoughts of a drink or two. There was nothing for it but to take a risk with the cards. He'd not had much success in gambling exploits in the past and he knew that he could lose the last of his meagre funds, but his position was pretty desperate. Money was essential for the success of the next part of his plan. So, gathering together his coins and pocketing his watch, just in case, he went out.

He headed to Soho, to the *St James Tavern*, dreaming fondly as he went of the day when he would be married to Angela and would be able to join *White's Club* to mix with men of standing and influence, the aristocracy, the gentry, top professionals and not play greasy card games in some back room of a squalid tavern with the unwashed. He pushed on grimly until he came to the place and on enquiring of the landlord, discovered that there was a poker game in progress in a private room.

The upstairs room was a poky space, thick with the fog of smoke, which hung like a cloud above a round table where five men sat, heads bent over a game. Their faces were in shadow as the dim light came from one solitary oil lamp affixed to the wall above them.

'May I join you, gentlemen?' said Dunn as they finished a hand.

There was no reply beyond a nod from the dealer, who turned a gaunt and expressionless face to him, then indicated an empty chair in the corner. Dunn scarce had time to sit down before the dealer's hands were at work on the next round.

To his delight, the first few hands went his way. God was on his side for a change and his winnings grew with each game.

'Bloody Irishman,' said one growling man withdrawing from the game, having lost a substantial sum. 'If you're cheating, I'll make mince of you.'

'Come, sir,' said Dunn convivially, 'I'm a gentleman. You offend my honour to suggest such a thing.'

The man spat on the floor and left. Dunn would have gone on, but when he lost a hand, a premonitory force seemed to hold him back and he withdrew from the game £10 the richer and with his watch still in his pocket. Scarcely able to conceal his delight at his good luck, Dunn returned to his rooms. Knowing he should be thrifty and circumspect in conserving his funds, such as paying the landlady for another month's rent, he nevertheless treated himself to a hearty meal at *Wilton's* and readied himself for the serious literary work ahead, for which he had much more appetite now. He had a deadline too, as he had to meet the servant George that evening at the back entrance to the house in order to gain access.

The prospect of his daring escapade excited him. Inspired now, he set to work with pen and paper.

My dearest, loveliest Angela,

Whatever pain and cruelty you choose to lay upon me, I will bear with patience and fidelity to you, for I love you more than my life. Indeed, the indignities I have borne for your sake, such as my imprisonment, have made me stronger, have fortified me against adversity. My adoration is as tough as armour, as stalwart as a fighting steed that will not be cut down in the heat of battle.

It was flowing nicely now. Perhaps he could throw in a bit of suffering, though. She might respond to that, she being so soft about lesser beings such as waifs and beggars. He could put that in the poem and he might as well lather it on thick.

All in the cold stone, iron-barrèd cell
I dreamed of you, my Angela, my love
Who had with cruel heart thrust me away
To sink in abject solitary days
Only to pray to God to give me strength
And thus the light of His pure mercy came
To grant me fortitude, enrich my love
For thee. Pierce me with arrows sharp and strong

Bludgeon my body, crush and break my bones.
Such agonies will I endure for thee
And more, until this very love of mine
Ceases to throb in fleshly life, although
It will continue for eternity.

That should do it. She was fond of suffering creatures, puppies and whatnot, so that kind of dog-like devotion was sure to count for something.

That evening at dusk, Dunn descended to the street from his rooms, the two folded papers tied with red ribbons and carefully placed in his coat pocket. Out on Stratton Street, men were making their way home from work, clerks and their superiors, while others passed on horseback and an omnibus crawled by, over-loaded with passengers. A few young girls were visible in doorways; prostitutes readying themselves for their nightly trade. Glad of the cover of a busy evening, Dunn felt less conspicuous as he waited for George to appear. Suddenly the servant was there, whispering in Dunn's ear that now was his chance. Miss Coutts and Miss Meredith were out and the other servants were all drinking tea in the kitchen. If Dunn was quick, he could come in and leave his messages where he pleased.

With a nod, Dunn followed the man down the narrow passage to the back door leading into the scullery. He heard voices chattering and laughing as they passed through the cool, stone-flagged room to a passageway leading to a staircase at the end. Upstairs, on the next floor, they entered through the butler's pantry into the corridor that opened into the main entrance hall. The place was empty and silent but rich with red turkey carpets and flock-papered walls, gilt mirrors, a brass-faced long-case clock and ornate balustrade of carved mahogany leading to the upper reception rooms. And this is just her town house, Dunn mused. She had others in the country too, most likely. If he played his cards right, all this and more could be his. He shivered with delight at the thought as he mounted the staircase after George.

The parlour that they entered was opulently furnished with velvet drapes at the windows, landscapes and portraits adorned the wall and a marble fireplace was the centrepiece of the room, which was comfortable rather than grand. A large, tall object, covered with a paisley shawl stood on a stand in the window and as Dunn stood surveying the room, he started at the sound of a strange and sudden squawk.

'It's only the parrot,' said George. 'Come on. Be quick, before it starts up.'

Dunn, hearing no further sound from the cloaked creature, grinned at the servant, sat down in an easy chair by the fireplace and looked around. George's face changed.

'I've told you. You can't tarry long. You'll be discovered and I'll be out of a job.'

The young man was twitching like a hare but Dunn was enjoying his moment luxuriating in what one day would be his. He pulled out the first folded paper, the letter from inside his coat, kissed it, stood up and looked around for a suitable place to position it. Seeing a small occasional table, he propped the letter against a bronze figurine and satisfied with the arrangement, followed George out of the room.

'The bedroom,' Dunn said. 'I must see her bedroom.'

The servant's face contorted into a look of disbelief and he shook his head.

'You're mad,' he said. 'You've got to get out. It'll be another guinea if you want to stay longer or I'll call the butler and say I found you intruding.'

'Och come on with you, man,' said Dunn shocked that the little snake was prepared to betray him. 'Just two minutes, that's all it will take.'

George gestured with his hand. 'This way, and then you must get out of here.'

They climbed the next flight of carpeted stairs two at a time and George flung open the second door on the right on the landing. It was a flowery affair, with light oak furniture, a dressing table, draped four poster bed and extravagantly fringed curtains at the windows. He ran quickly to the dressing table and propped up the poem against the mirror, smiling for a second or two at his reflection in the mirror, catching his profile in one of the angled ones. At the back of the dressing table top he noticed a small book with an embroidered cloth cover, a diary perhaps. Shifting his body to hide his hand from the eyes of the waiting servant, he slid the book quickly into his pocket and turned around.

'Right you are, then,' he said to George, whose face was white, his eyes black with panic.

They ran back down both flights of stairs, down the passageway past the kitchen and through the scullery again. Dunn felt the man push him out the door and heard the bolt being shot behind him. Exhilarated, Dunn strode out of the alley on to Stratton Street and headed off to *The Bull*. He owed himself a drink.

It had been more than a week and still there had been no reply to his declaration, no response of any sort from Angela. He had watched for several hours every day to observe servants and visitors going in and out of the place but had not once seen Angela nor her companion leave the house. The notebook that he had taken from Angela's bedroom was a considerable disappointment too. It wasn't a diary with her private thoughts recorded; it was simply a memo book with lists of people to contact, the names of organisations, notes of sums of money and scribbles that made no sense to him. However, he had something of hers, which could be handy for the future, though he could not think exactly how at that moment.

As for visitors to her house, there was one particularly flamboyant dandy of a gentleman who fetched up there in a cab one morning, so Dunn had gone to the coffee shop opposite the house to see if he could find out who the man was.

'Probably that writer, that Charles Dickens. He's a very famous man,' said the proprietor, who had obligingly appeared from the kitchen and now stood in his huge apron, hands on hips, peering out of the window. 'Have you never heard of him? There's all sorts visit Miss Coutts. Lots of folk after her money, I shouldn't wonder. A good catch for some gentleman.'

'Is this Mr Dickens married?' Dunn asked the man, thinking that he might vaguely have heard of this rival.

'As far as I know, but these famous folks, they're always up to some hanky-panky, if you get what I mean. But I can't stand here talking all day, sir. Are you ordering a drink or what?'

It was clear that Angela had many important friends, but it irked Richard Dunn that so many of them were men. However, thankfully, quite a large number of them seemed to be old: white-haired vicars and other ancient-looking banking types, from what he had seen of her visitors. Even the old Duke of Wellington was a regular. Dunn ordered a coffee and stared out of the window, seeing a carriage drawing up at the door of the house. He moved closer to the window, brazening out the stony looks of a couple at the next table. He watched the door of the house opening, a servant emerging and then Angela and her companion. As they climbed into the carriage, Dunn cursed himself for being taken by surprise and rushed out of the café, past the waiter who was carrying his coffee, out across the street, just in time to see the driver whipping up the horses and the carriage moving away. He stood gazing for a moment or two. They had taken no heavy luggage, so they could not be going very far, he reflected. He strode rapidly to the front door of the house and rang the bell, feeling a dampness about his brow, a manifestation of his annoyance and bad luck. If he had only known she was going out in a carriage, he could have hired a horse.

The door was opened by a man servant, the butler by the look of him. In one glance Dunn knew he'd get no information from the man.

'You are not welcome here, sir,' said the butler, with a look so haughty that Dunn would have needed no invitation to punch him in the face. 'I must ask you to leave.'

Dunn tried to assume an expression of indifference.

'I have a gift for Miss Coutts,' he said. 'She is expecting it.'

'Good day to you, sir,' said the butler and slammed the door shut.

Dunn knew that the sneaky devil would have servants staring out of the windows to see if he had moved away, so he strolled off down the street until he was out of sight of all of the windows. He stood for a moment or two, wondering what kind of reception he would receive if he returned to the coffee shop and resumed his surveillance. It was worth a try, as it was the best vantage from which to observe any members of the household coming and going. If he could catch George, he could find out where Angela had gone.

The proprietor asked him to pay first before he was prepared to serve him with another drink. Dunn told him a story about his sudden sighting of a long-lost acquaintance on the other side of the street, which had necessitated his swift departure. He ordered a glass of wine this time, to steady himself and watch. He had only to wait for a quarter of an hour before he saw a housemaid coming out from the passage at the rear of the house. She was wearing a hat and cloak and carrying a basket. Dunn leapt up and bade a hasty farewell to the proprietor.

'Just seen another long-lost acquaintance, have you?' he said, sourly.

An hour later on a slow old grey horse, Dunn was plodding his way to Norwood and the hotel where Angela had gone to dine with a group of friends. The maid had been quite obliging, after a bit of flirting and flattery, though he'd had to pay her two shillings for the information and had made him promise that he wouldn't be a nuisance to Miss Coutts.

The hotel, when he eventually reached it, was an imposing older style mansion, converted, he assumed, from a private house. He urged the sluggish animal up the driveway and was met by an ostler's boy who took the reins and offered to stable the creature. Dunn dismounted and made his way to the front doors. A doorman stood waiting.

'I've an invitation to join Miss Burdett-Coutts's party,' Dunn said with authority.

The man stared back at him. 'Really sir? No one else is expected. I'm told to admit no others.'

Dunn swore silently.

'Look here my man, I have been invited. Miss Coutts will be displeased if she hears that any of her guests have been refused admittance.'

Dunn felt his armpits dampen. The man was standing in his way, legs astride and in the next instant he called over his shoulder. Two other men appeared behind him. They were young, smartly dressed hotel employees by the look of them.

'Escort this gentleman off the premises,' said the doorman as the two young men slipped past their colleague, advanced on Dunn and rudely grabbed him by both arms, so that his body was gripped tightly between.

'This is an outrage!' Dunn shouted, anger boiling.

She had everyone working against him, damn her eyes. Couldn't she see that he was devoted to her? Couldn't she pity him for what he had endured at her hand, she who had smiled so demurely, so fetchingly that day for only one reason? She was a coquette. How long did she expect him to endure this rejection? He writhed in the men's hold, but there were two of them, the brutes, and they were marching him briskly, dragging him back down the drive.

'My horse,' he said.

'Shut your mouth,' said one of the men.

Dunn struggled. He'd not allow himself to be handled by oafs such as this. He kicked with his heel and caught one in the shin. The man yelled and Dunn felt a thud on the side of his head, then a blow to the stomach, which brought the ground hurtling towards his face, then a horrible crunching of his hand and an arrow of pain in his spine before his sight went black.

Chapter 9

Bezer's euphoria at their early success with Lady Dartmouth and the funeral expenses was rudely dispelled, only a few days later. The landlord's agent came knocking on their door at an early hour. Bezer, shivering in his nightgown, was forced to hand over all but a shilling of his money to pay their rent arrears. Their breakfast was therefore taken in a gloomy silence, though Susan's face bore a thoughtful look as she chewed slowly on a crust of bread.

'We need to find other means to get people to loosen their purse strings,' she said suddenly.

'My dearest one,' said Bezer miserably. 'I pray that the fruitfulness of your mind can devise such means, for I fear I am doomed without you.'

'Stop your pitiful moaning and listen,' she said. 'This is what I propose, but you will need to play your part well for it to work.'

Bezer was glad of his wife's ingenuity but knew that any plan would undoubtedly involve him in some tedious or risky pursuit, more bowing and scraping and more insults from uppity servants. In his day, such folk would have licked his boots. Still, he and Susan were sorely in need of funds and thus desperate measures were inevitable.

'Are you not obliged to visit the Society offices to pay back what you owe them?' she said.

'Yes, but I don't have the wherewithal to pay

them a penny at the moment, as you well know,' he said.

'Of course, but listen. You know where the correspondence from benefactors and supporters of the Society is kept, don't you?'

'Yes,' he said, puzzled but disinclined to interrupt her.

'You could lay hands on some letters, couldn't you?'

'But why? For what purpose?'

'For samples of their writing, to copy,' she said, 'just the richest ones of course.'

Bezer wondered if his wife had lost her wits, as he had no notion of what her plan could be. Stealing documents from the Society's offices would be exceedingly difficult to accomplish as it was staffed by at least one clerk all day and locked up securely at night. He nodded patiently, not at all taken by the thought of returning to the place of his humiliation, to bear the scorn of his former colleagues. Susan was fired up, however, carried away with her idea, which had obviously been fermenting in her mind.

'Don't you see, once we have letters written in the hand of Lord Such and Such or Lady So and So, we can write promissory notes, letters and contracts,' she said, getting up from her chair and coming to him, clutching his arm.

'You mean copying, forgery?' said Bezer with wary fascination. 'But my sweet one, it is not an easy thing to do.'

'Pah!' said Susan. 'I have a good eye and a steady hand. It just takes practice.'

Bezer kept his remaining doubts to himself.

'So, let's say that some rich lord has sired a bastard child by a girl up from the country or some whore,' Susan went on, 'for isn't that a common sort of thing? The girl has letters from this lord promising payment of a goodly sum to support the child. She demands the lord pays her or she'll tell all to the wife and family. Wouldn't most fine gentlemen wish to keep their little dalliances secret? And there's even some would pay as a matter of honour.'

Bezer stared, letting the notion sink a little further into his mind. It was true that he had heard gossip about several of the vice presidents of the Society and their liaisons or affairs, their weaknesses, whether for pretty young girls or boys. Lord Burton, it was said, was unaware of how many children he had fathered. Bezer could probably remember which others among the great and good were in the habit of straying.

Susan's colour had risen in excitement at the blossoming of her idea.

'There are other possibilities too, once we can provide evidence of the obligation to pay out,' she said.

'But my treasure,' Bezer said, 'how can I gain access to papers in the Society without being seen?'

She pursed her lips in exasperation.

'Have you no brain? You can get into the office, can't you? You need to get rid of the clerk from the room, feign a sudden illness, collapse, say you saw an intruder in the hall.

Use your wits.'

Bezer did not like her tone of voice, nor the fear that was building inside him. He was more than a little glad, therefore, to have hit on another obstacle.

'It's a grand plan, my angel, but what shall I do for money? I cannot present myself at the Society without a sum to pay.'

'We'll have to pawn something,' she said looking round. 'We have things in the house that would raise five pounds. That would be sufficient to satisfy them.'

Bezer nodded. It was a hazardous ploy, but the fruits could be worth the risk. Susan started on their dresser, finding two china plates that had belonged to her mother, the others having been sold long ago, a string of glass beads that from a distance might be taken for pearls, one of their pewter inkpots, a glass decanter, Susan's spare petticoat and Bezer's silk handkerchief. He gave it up to her reluctantly.

'That will suffice, surely,' he said.

Susan said nothing but placed the items in a canvas bag.

'Go and put on your beggar's clothing,' she ordered.

They debated a while about whether this was the best approach. She argued that a beggar might provoke pity in the heart of the pawnbroker and he replied that from what he knew pawnbrokers had no hearts; they were only intent on paying out paltry sums and squeezing extortionate interest from folk. Bezer suggested that if he appeared in a more respectable guise, he might command a degree of respect as a well-informed individual temporarily down on his luck. That way he might be able to negotiate a higher price for the items.

'Such fellows as pawnbrokers need a firm hand, my love,' Bezer said, feeling a little of his confidence return at the thought of not having to play the beggar again.

'Very well,' she said. 'Go to that one in Fleet Street, Hines. They say he doesn't charge as much interest.'

After another briefing from Susan, Bezer set off with a sense of purpose to the pawn shop. The streets seemed more crowded than usual, even though it was not yet time for shops and offices to close. He strode past St Paul's Cathedral, feeling a little more like his old self, a man out to do business. No one seeing him would have guessed the sort of business in which he was about to engage. He dodged through pedestrians, hopped around horse droppings on the road and soon found himself on Fleet Street outside the shop, *Licensed Pawnbroker.* The window displayed an assortment of the usual items for sale, walking sticks, ladies' bodices, boots, crucifixes, clocks, candle sticks. He pushed the door and went in.

Behind the counter was a small, hump-backed man with a grey beard and a face pitted with the scars of the pox.

'Good afternoon,' said Bezer. 'Am I addressing Mr Hines?'

The man shook his head. 'Not here,' he said.
'Not here?'

'He's put me in charge. I'm doing his business,' he said. 'Buying or pledging?'

Bezer put his bag on the counter and slid it towards the man.

'I hope you'll give me a good price for these,' he said. 'I have only a transitory embarrassment when it comes to ready cash.'

Bezer sniffed in an effort to dissociate himself from the type who would perpetually frequent such a place as this. The man gave no response, simply reaching into the bag and taking the items out one by one. He laid them out before him on the counter, examining each one carefully and recording the description in a large ledger.

'Want a price for each one?' he asked.

Bezer gave a dismissive sweep of the hand.

'One price for the whole, my man,' he said. 'I shall want to redeem them all of course.'

The pawnbroker added up the figures, scribbling quickly in the ledger.

'Four pounds and twopence,' he announced.

'What?' said Bezer, unable to conceal his affront. 'Is that all?'

'It's fair,' said the man with a shrug, 'take it or leave it. Mr Hines left me a list of the usual prices. And there's a half penny to pay on each item per week, so that will be twopence halfpenny. You have fifteen months in which to redeem these. Name please?'

Bezer could see no other option but to take the money. He would have to hope that the

Society would agree to accept four pounds as his first payment of the debt. The paltriness of the sum as a proportion of what he owed struck him painfully. Drastic action was needed. He would have to proceed with the plan.

He took the pawn ticket from the man and the money, which he tipped into a small purse Susan had given him. As he made his way to Holborn, to the Society's office, he rehearsed in his head the strategy he would employ and a fall back method, should this fail. With luck, Larkin the clerk would be there on his own in the office that contained the cupboard. This was not normally locked as it contained no valuables as such. But he would have to get Larkin out of the office for enough time so that he could lay hands on some of the letters. Bezer was hopeful, however, as Larkin was a humble man, a quiet, biddable sort who had never questioned Bezer's actions in the past.

Bezer climbed the steps to the place of his former employment, number 13 Red Lion Square. The entrance hall was silent and deserted. His heart leapt with joy at the realisation that there were no meetings scheduled today and therefore only a few staff would be present and no one of importance. The porter who usually manned the door on meeting days was also not in evidence.

Bezer, emboldened, strode up to the second door on the right hand side of the hall, the office where Larkin and the assistant clerk worked. The door was shut and he rapped lightly upon it. A faint voice from within replied. Bezer, assuming the posture and expression of a man deeply sunk in a state of depression, opened the door slowly and found Larkin at his desk.

'Mr Blundell?' he said, rising suddenly from his seat.

'Good day to you, Larkin,' said Bezer in a lugubrious tone, 'though by good I do not refer to my view of it.'

The clerk stood awkwardly behind his desk for a moment.

'Can I help you, Mr Blundell?' he said.

'My dear man, if only you could,' said Bezer tragically. 'I fear I am much cast down by my situation. I have lost everything, my employment, my status and my self-respect. In fact, I wonder daily why I go on with this painful existence. It is only the thought of leaving my poor dear wife on her own which stops me from throwing myself into the Thames. You cannot know how I suffer.'

At this, Bezer, overcome with emotion, swayed on his feet and managed, very convincingly he thought, to squeeze a few tears from his eyes.

'Forgive me, Larkin,' he spluttered, 'for this unmanly show, but I am weak through lack of bodily nourishment. May I?'

He gestured at a chair at the side of the room, close to the cupboard, which he eyed quickly, noting that it was not padlocked.

'Er... yes, I suppose you may,' said Larkin, coming out from behind his desk as Bezer stumbled towards the chair.

Larkin hovered, ill-at-ease, glancing at the door as though he expected someone to come to his aid. Bezer plunged his hand into his pocket in search of his handkerchief and then, remembering that he had hocked it, felt the purse of money. He decided against revealing it at that moment and wiped his brow with his sleeve.

'Larkin, I'm not well, a fever I suspect. Would you by any chance be able to fetch me a drink, a restorative, tea or even a cup of water?'

The clerk hesitated.

'Well, sir, I don't know that you're meant to be here. I mean...'

Bezer broke into noisy sobs.

'Have pity, man, as you are a Christian. I have done wrong, I confess that. I am a weak sinner, but I am repentant. Please help restore me so that I can at least walk out of here with a shred of dignity.'

'Very well,' said Larkin nervously. 'I'll be back in a moment.'

He scuttled out of the room and Bezer leapt up and dived for the cupboard doors. Inside, the shelves were stacked with books and papers. Bezer dug his hands into a bundle that looked like correspondence but discovered that they were bills of sale for stationery items. His fingers trembled as he grabbed the next stack of papers, his senses sharpened so that his beating heart threatened to burst from his chest and his ears pulsed with listening for the sound of Larkin returning. This bundle, he saw, contained about half a dozen letters in various different hands, so he stuffed it inside his coat, hearing footsteps. Bezer slammed the cupboard door shut and clutching his chest fell against it, collapsing on to the floor, as a man taken by a seizure.

'Mr Blundell!' said Larkin, his face taut with shock.

He put the glass containing a brown liquid on his desk and crouched down beside Bezer's groaning body.

'Can you breathe?' Larkin said. 'shall I loosen your clothing?'

'No!' said Bezer too sharply for a man in this state of collapse, groaning loudly to cover this faux pas. 'I shall be recovered presently. Don't worry yourself on my account. I shall be on my feet in a minute.'

Larkin stood up and brought the glass of drink to Bezer, who had pulled himself up to a sitting position and was looking with interest and anticipation of the burning power of a brandy. He clutched his chest with one hand to ensure that the bundle of letters was not visible, then reached with his other to accept the drink, which he downed in one. It was not the hoped for brandy, but a sickly sweet cordial which clung to his throat.

'It's Mr Carter's favoured tonic for the nerves,' said Larkin.

Bezer breathing heavily and with the assistance of the clerk, raised himself to the chair.

'Thank you, Larkin,' Bezer said, his chest heaving. 'You are so kind. Now I must be on my way and trouble you no further.'

'But, sir –,' said the clerk.

Bezer was unsure whether Larkin's concern was for his state of health or that he might leave without explaining the purpose of his visit, but Bezer had no wish to tarry in order to find out which. He had to get out of the building as quickly as possible and what's more, he wanted to keep the money that clinked in the purse in his pocket. Ignoring Larkin, who was following behind, he went out into the hall and headed for the front door. There, however, to Bezer's shock and dismay, stood Mr William Carter, the Honorary Secretary of the Society.

The man's face changed swiftly from surprise to anger and Bezer felt a quiver of nausea in his stomach.

'What do you think you're doing here, Blundell?' said William Carter.

With a mighty effort to conceal the effects of his fractured nerves, Bezer reached into his pocket and withdrew the purse. He returned Mr Carter's stare with an expression that he hoped conveyed stony disdain.

'Sir, I have come to pay the first part of my debt. You see, I am a man of my word.'

A moment later, Bezer was out on the street, with a quick flurry of speed to put distance between him and Red Lion Square. Then, sufficiently clear of the place, he fell back into a sluggish pace for the rest of his homeward journey, thinking that he might simply expire through lack of food. There was a measure of comfort however, in his accomplishment. He had a bundle of letters safely pressed to his breast. Susan could start that very evening perfecting her calligraphic skills. He wished that he had her confidence in the likely success of their new stratagem.

It was only a matter of a week before they received their first reply, which Bezer opened with a thundering heart and started to read aloud to Susan, who hung impatiently at his elbow.

Christchurch, Mayfair

Dear Miss Roper,

Your letter has caused much distress at this doleful time for my family. The memory of my dear uncle should not have been so tainted by such spectres from an erring past. No man is without sin, though we pray daily to the Almighty to help us strengthen ourselves against the power of the Devil –

'Stop!' shouted Susan. 'I'll not listen to any more of this windy nonsense. Will they pay us anything or won't they? I've no wish for a sermon about it. Come on, get on with it.'

She made to grab the letter from Bezer, but he raised his hand and turned away from her, sensing the familiar sting of her anger directed so unjustifiably at him. He felt that his rendition of the sentiments expressed had been deeply moving. True, it was probably yet another refusal, but it was a reply at least, which always raised his spirits a little. He proceeded to read the rest of the letter, while Susan flounced to the sofa and dropped down upon it.

This was the over-lengthy reply to Susan's plea in the person of Betty Roper, debauched and impregnated at sixteen by the late Lord Hazeldean, the recently deceased uncle of the writer. Susan's, or rather Betty Roper's, letter had included a statement in the hand of the sinful old goat. It was not until Bezer had read nearly to the end of the verbose reply that he found anything which might offer a glimmer of hope for them.

My uncle's weakness, I am forced to acknowledge, led to some unfortunate short lived and imprudent encounters. However, we are comforted that as a man of honour, he acknowledged his responsibilities and obligations in the form of monies sent to you. I would be willing, therefore, to make a monetary contribution towards the base-born child's Christian education in a suitable training school for pauper girls. Send me word, in strictest confidence of where we may meet, for I must examine the said child with my own eyes, to ensure that she is sound in body and mind. Furthermore, I will need your solemn promise that after the payment has been made, you will never contact me or any of my family or my uncle's under any circumstances. His note to you has been burned.

Bezer sighed. Why were obstacles always to be thrown in the way of their plans? He prepared himself for an outpouring of rage from Susan and when this was not forthcoming, he dared to glance up from the letter.

'It's working, Bezer, don't you see,' said Susan getting up from her chair and pacing back and forth on a tight square of floor as she often did when thinking. 'I can copy anyone's hand and make it convincing. All we need is a child. It's as simple as that.'

Bezer was taken aback, shocked in fact that she expected such a thing, since for the first ten years of their marriage they had energetically worked at producing offspring, all to no avail. After that, between the sheets they had grown more sluggish and Susan seemed to accept without too much protest the fact of their childlessness. Was she really suggesting now that they should re-double their efforts to produce what God had not seen fit to bless them with?

'But...,' Bezer began.

'There's beggars aplenty on the streets, brats that would do anything for a square meal,' she said.

This reassured Bezer in one sense but troubled him in another. He wondered from where such square meals for a child might originate, as they themselves had not had anything that he could define as such for some time.

'A child would come in handy,' said Susan, unaware of Bezer's lack of enthusiasm. 'There's always sympathy for the young and if the worst comes to the worst, we could send it out on the streets.'

'But,' Bezer began again, 'what shall we do for money in the meantime, dearest? Children are inclined to be hungry, I fear.'

'Nonsense,' said Susan. 'If we get a small one, a girl would be better, she wouldn't need much. In any case I have a necklace we can hock if need be, to get some ready cash, but let's get to work on the last of these papers. There must be someone else in here we haven't tried.'

They both turned their attention back to the small pile of letters on the table, the last of those purloined from the Society. Bezer, trying not to indulge in his private feelings of despair, took up a paper with a list of past benefactors. A name, a familiar one, jolted his memory and he soon remembered why.

'Ah ha!' he cried out, holding up the paper. 'Here we have something promising, my sweet one.'

Susan looked up at him from the other side of the table.

'What is it then?'

'Sir Francis Burdett. He was a donor to the Society for many years. And he was quite a fine gentleman in his day. Very sad to read of his passing only last week. But here's a thing or rather several things.'

He had her attention now, and he felt his pride swell. This was exceedingly hopeful.

'Well, he said,' leaning forward, hoping that she would not prick the bubble of his idea with some spiteful comment. 'I know for certain that Sir Francis had his dalliances, along with a wife and a full-time mistress, Lady Oxford. Everyone knew about it and the child too. It was commonly talked of. Then his youngest daughter, the legitimate one of course, inherited a huge fortune. The richest woman in all England, they all said at the time. Don't you remember hearing about it, my dear, the young lady Miss Burdett-Coutts, or Miss Coutts as she is now called, on account of her rich banker grandfather?'

Susan's eyes narrowed as though she doubted Bezer's account, but when he detailed the good works of the generous Miss Coutts, her donations to the causes of the poor, her financing of the building of a church and a hostel for homeless girls, a Ragged School for paupers, Susan's expression slowly became more accepting and open.

'She gives generously to many causes,' said Bezer, 'so her heart I'm sure will be softened if we approach her with the fact of another of her father's little strangers. Miss Coutts must know of Lady Oxford and of her bastard, so she will surely be unable to deny the possibility of another child, or even more than one.'

Susan smiled and Bezer saw the flame of

inspiration in her eyes.

'So, we most definitely need a child as proof. This Miss Coutts will probably want the evidence of her eyes too, so we must be prepared. Come Bezer, we must go a-hunting. And bring your cane, as we may have to venture into some noisome places.'

Susan retreated quickly to the bedroom to get her bonnet and cloak and Bezer understood the aim of their expedition that afternoon.

They headed for the alleys of Queen Victoria Street near the river. The docks always had gaggles of drifters, paupers and beggars and Susan reasoned it was far enough away from their district to get a child well clear of its stamping ground. However, there were only boys, mudlarking and begging in the streets where they ventured and so they turned north towards Spitalfields and the alleys and yards around the market where the crowds would provide the hubbub necessary to locate a suitable child. It would have to be one that professed to being an orphan of course, though there were plenty of them about, with disease regularly taking off a lot of poorer folk. They couldn't risk the possibility of interfering parents seeking to reclaim their children. They needed a destitute one, a hungry, compliant, quiet one, Bezer thought, dreading that Susan might light upon some terrible little rogue.

On Commercial Street, arm in arm, they joined the streams of shoppers, costermongers with their barrows and portable trays selling any sort of small goods and trinkets. There were children here too, some attached to the vendors holding out samples of the wares to passersby, others begging in pairs or on their own. Susan was alert, constantly glancing as they passed along the street, like a bird on the lookout for crumbs. Bezer was unsure of the wisdom of kidnapping as a way out of their dilemma, but as he could think of nothing better, he submitted himself to his wife's better judgement, as he always did. Suddenly, he felt a tug on his sleeves and followed Susan's gaze.

She was gesturing towards the entrance to an alley between an ancient dilapidated building of three storeys and another tall tenement with blackened windows. At street level was an apology for a shop, with a grey window concealing a clutter of indeterminate items. At the opening of the alley, by the side of the shop was the crouched figure of a small child, hunched over with its head drawn down to its knees.

Susan pulled Bezer across the street nearer to the spot and they stood for a few moments looking.

'Is it a girl?' he whispered.

'Yes,' said Susan, 'and a filthy one, a little ragamuffin, but she'll do. Come on.'

The child remained motionless as Bezer and Susan approached, oblivious of their presence.

'Hello, my dear,' Susan said, in a voice Bezer had never heard before. It was velvet-throated, as though she was sucking a smooth sweet lozenge. However, this effort on Susan's part seemed fruitless, as the child gave no response, appearing deaf to any kind of sound. Bezer wondered for a moment whether the child might in fact have expired, hunched in the alley like this. It was certainly a common enough occurrence in such streets. Sometimes, even in the fashionable West End thoroughfares, the bodies of paupers and beggars were found cluttering doorways and pavements. He had no wish to investigate, to poke the child's body with his cane, to see if it were stiff and cold, make it topple over at their feet.

'Would you care for a bite to eat?' Susan tried, moving a step closer to the child.

Bezer watched, wishing that his wife would more often address him in such caring tones. This time, the small body moved. It shuddered.

'Come and have supper with us,' Susan said.

Maybe, Bezer mused, there was another side to his wife that he had yet to discover, so sweet and welcoming was her approach to this child. The girl shifted now and at last looked up, revealing a dusty, pale face with watery blue eyes. She was clothed in rags, her arms protruding from a tunic which had at one time been blue in colour.

'Come along, my little darling,' Susan said, 'we can give you a nice home.'

She held her hand out to the beggar child who pushed herself up to a standing position. Bezer could see a smirk of satisfaction flit across Susan's face. It was clear that this was exactly the sort of child they needed, small with a miserable look about her. Bezer was ignorant of how to gauge the age of a child; she could have been anything from seven to twelve years old. He could see how filthy she was however, and thought with some disgust of the lice and vermin she was likely to bring into their house. Susan, he hoped would take care of all that, sluice her down and launder the filthy rags.

Susan took the child's hand in hers in what Bezer thought was a very tender gesture, then she walked between them as they made their way slowly along the street back to their lodgings. It was dark by now and they would likely be able to evade the notice of their neighbours.

The next morning, Bezer felt that something had changed. He had had a bad night's sleep, imagining the urchin child to have transformed herself into a demon, which had come to devour them in the night. But he was reassured on waking early to find only Susan snoring beside him. He prodded her in the ribs to lessen the noise, but succeeded in waking her instead.

'It's an idiot child we've taken,' he said. 'She cannot speak nor hear, it would seem.'

'What? Susan mumbled, half awake.

They had given the girl a blanket and a rug to lie down upon in their parlour in front of the fire. Susan had tried to clean her up a little, wiping her face and taking off some of her dirty garments.

'Well, what of it, if she is a mute, all the more pity and sympathy she will arouse when it comes to getting people to pay up.'

'But what if she's only pretending and means to make off with our belongings, or stab us in the night?' said Bezer.

Susan pulled herself up in bed with a grunt of contempt.

'You're not afraid of a poor pathetic scrap like that, are you?'

'Well, I don't like children. They're dirty, dishonest and light-fingered.'

Susan clouted Bezer on the side of his head.

'What a ninny you are Bezer,' she said.

On rising a little later, however, they discovered that the girl was sitting by the door, her hand was clutching the handle, tugging, attempting to open it. Susan had locked the door, and taken away the key, suspecting that the child might attempt an escape once her belly was full.

'No, you don't,' said Susan, taking the hand that was attached to the door handle.

The child submitted to Susan's command and was led back to the kitchen and ordered to sit down on the rug. Susan questioned her again about her name, but the girl simply hung her head and remained silent. As Bezer watched Susan's ministrations, he felt irritation bubbling inside him.

'Ought to be grateful, little tyke,' he muttered. 'Maybe a good beating would get a sound out of her.'

Susan threw him a disapproving look.

'Well maybe it's best that she doesn't utter a word. A simpleton needs food and clothing like anybody and your finest lords and ladies spawn idiots as readily as street drabs do. So, read me the letter to Miss Rich-Pickings-Coutts then, while I drink my tea. That one can watch us breakfasting and maybe she'll learn to speak up when she wants something bad enough.'

Bezer joined Susan at the table. He picked up the letter that he had written out the previous day, in a manner and style he felt very suitable to the writer, a simple tart of a girl he imagined.

Side Alley, Percy Street

Dear Miss Coutts,

I have heerd of the sad news about Sir Francis your pa, that most noblest of gentlemen and I know he will be singing with the angles in heaven most like. God will forgive him his transgreshuns. I am only a common sort but Sir Francis was always kind to me and when I came to bed with his childe he was generous to me and the babe. It greeves my hart that so kinde a gentleman as Sir Francis has left this earth and I worry for the sake of my poor child, a fatherless girl who without your mersiful helpe will be left to beg upon the streets or die and join her pa. I am desperate ill you see and close to deaf myself. Oh Miss

Coutts for pity's and your deere pa's sake and his good name, for I will not say nuffing, send some relief to us. Ten guineas should see us rite.

                    Your humble sarvent
                    Fanny Mercer

Chapter 10

Angela's mind was swamped, weighted with sorrow, just as the heavy black crepe of her mourning dress burdened her body. The loss of her mother, who had for years been sickly, she had borne with sad resignation and acceptance, but the sudden death of her father had knocked her down, reduced her to a state of woe that she had never before experienced. Prayer helped to strengthen her to continue from day to day, as she knew she must, but for some time she had not felt equal to receiving visitors, nor of pursuing any work on her various projects.

Other worries assailed her too, rousing her to anger as well as hurt. The first arose from a letter she had received purporting to be from a woman with whom her father had had a liaison. The ill-educated writer claimed that she given birth to the child of Sir Francis and that he had supported her and the child financially in recognition of his obligation. Angela knew of other slanderous claims: her father's supposed affair with Lady Oxford, though she had never accepted this as truth. These were wicked falsehoods, spread by mischievous individuals and political enemies. Her father had been a highly principled, morally upright gentleman and would never have consorted with any woman or lady in an illicit liaison. All the world might claim such things to be true, but Angela would never believe them.

'It is a fabrication, a lie,' Angela had said to Hannah when she had received the letter. My father would never have strayed. I will never treat with people who would slander his good name and his reputation, especially as he is no longer here to defend himself.'

Hannah had to calm Angela with soothing words and a herbal infusion to help her to regain her equilibrium.

'Let me burn the letter,' Hannah offered.

'No, give it to me again,' Angela said, snatching it from her friend. I will send this to the Society for the Suppression of Mendicity. It is not genuine. The Society seeks out dishonest people who masquerade as needy individuals. The Society employs constables who can track down criminal fraudsters of this type. You must send the letter to them with my complaint.'

'Yes, of course, my dear,' said Hannah. 'I will do it straight away.'

Angela immediately regretted her sharpness to her loyal and constant friend. Hannah had been at her side with comforting and encouraging words and prayers through this difficult time. She had set aside her own affairs to minister to Angela's needs. She had even delayed her marriage to her ever patient betrothed Dr Brown. And it had been he who had waited on Angela and treated her during her periods of debility.

'I'm so sorry, Hannah,' Angela said, as they sat together in the drawing room, after they had dealt with the unpleasant letter.

The little dog Fan snoozed comfortably at Angela's feet and even the grey parrot was silent.

'I have been very remiss. I have been so taken up with my own concerns that I have forgotten about yours. Have you set a new date for your wedding?'

Hannah smiled and reached for Angela's hand.

'Don't worry, my dear. Dr Brown has agreed to a delay of six months. He really doesn't mind. He is the most patient sort. I need to make sure that all is well with you before we go ahead.'

Another source of anxiety, which had returned to trouble Angela when they had all thought the matter closed, was the persistent and increasingly threatening actions of the madman Richard Dunn. The discovery that he had actually gained entry to the house unnoticed and had left some offensive letters and notes in the parlour and in Angela's bedroom was deeply shocking. The matter had been reported to the police and the servants had been questioned closely. All denied any knowledge of the intruder. Strict security measures were put in place; doors and windows were to be locked whenever anyone went in or out. No entry point to the house was to be left unsecured.

His latest outrage had occurred when he had pursued Angela on an outing to lunch with friends at a hotel in Norwood. This had resulted in his sustaining injuries at the hands of two young hotel employees. They had been acting on Angela's orders that on no account should any gentleman not of her party be admitted to join it. She, having become nervous of Dunn's persistence, had asked for the assurance of the hotel staff that any such person should be removed from the premises. Now, it seemed he was going to press charges of assault against the two men and bring Angela's name into the case as the instigator of the attack. She shrank at the prospect of Dunn's continuing assault on her person and her peace of mind.

Some weeks later, however, and in spite of these events and her state of mourning, Angela had agreed to receive visitors. Hannah had recommended this as a distraction and restorative to her spirits. In this there was hope for a little cheer and entertainment, as their first visitor was to be Mr Charles Dickens. He would most likely have some business to discuss, as he and Angela were keen collaborators in a number of social welfare initiatives. Mr Dickens, like Angela, always had some new project in mind to improve the lot of the poor.

At three o'clock, a maid brought the visitor to the library and Angela felt her mood lift the moment he entered.

'Good afternoon, ladies,' said Mr Dickens, with his usual ebullience, though tempered a little out of respect for Angela's situation.

Angela observed his bright, dandyish appearance, a mustard-coloured coat and checked trousers, a claret silk stock. He wore his outfits with such panache, set off by his slightly wild dark hair and sharp eyes.

'Miss Coutts,' he said approaching quickly, taking her hand and bending to kiss it. 'You look well, in spite of the sad times you have endured. And Miss Meredith, what a pleasure to see you again.'

He quickly moved the conversation to matters of his own and Angela found herself keenly attending to his latest report on the hostel for homeless women and girls.

'The place is ready and we have found suitable staff, a very capable superintendent and two matrons. It just remains for us to find the girls and women to fill it.'

'Such places are so badly needed,' said Angela. 'Each evening, when I look out upon the street, I see such women below my very window. I hope that this one will be the first of many.'

'And how should these women and girls be chosen?' Hannah said.

'Ah yes,' said the writer, 'it must be by their own volition. For you know that little can be achieved by people through coercion and punition.'

'Yes, I suppose you are right,' Angela said, thinking of the imprisonment of Richard Dunn and how his containment had not appeared to dent his malicious and foolhardy actions in any way. However, she thought it wise not to allude to this particular example of the failure of correction for malefactors.

'I will keep you informed of my plans, Miss Coutts,' said Dickens, 'by letter as I am due to visit Paris and shall be out of the country for some time. Now tell me about the progress of the Ragged School, if you will. Have you visited?'

Angela was clearly gratified to report positive news of this establishment.

'It is attracting more children each day, and the teachers are doing their best against the odds,' said Angela. 'Mr and Mrs Greaves now have the assistance of a new master, Mr Hines, who is proving to be quite an asset. He is by trade a pawnbroker, but a most surprisingly charitable and thoughtful individual.'

'A pawnbroker?' said Dickens, looking shocked if not disapproving. 'Really my dear Miss Coutts, is this the sort of person who should be guiding the young?'

Angela felt herself blushing, surprised by the strength of her friend's objection, but roused to defend the admirable Mr Hines, who had risen even further in her estimation.

'Come, Mr Dickens,' Angela said. 'Didn't our Lord Jesus Christ consort with thieves and usurers? And Mr Hines seems to be a man not suited nor with much liking for his profession, which he has followed out of necessity, rather than choice.'

Charles Dickens smiled. 'But a man who makes money from the misfortunes of others is hardly one to admire, Miss Coutts.'

'But you haven't met him, Mr Dickens,' Hannah said, returning his smile. 'I did not imagine that you were a person given to criticise others because of their station in life, and the necessity that drives them to follow a particular course.'

'Miss Meredith, you have the better of me,' he said, laughing. 'If you and Miss Coutts hold this fellow in high esteem, then I am sure that he is a worthy individual.'

This visit from Dickens and the resumption of her work put Angela more firmly back into her positive and productive frame of mind. She hoped that this would strengthen her mind and spirit to deal with the ongoing trouble caused by Richard Dunn. Hannah confessed that Dunn had accosted her while she was out on an errand only a few days previously. Her friend assured her, however, that she had refused to listen to the man's mad ramblings and had called on a passing gentleman to protect her against his attentions.

'More blooming letters! More blooming letters!' squawked the grey parrot as the maid brought the correspondence to Angela and Hannah in the drawing room the next morning. The maid, blushing, deposited the letters quickly on a side table and scuttled out.

Hannah gathered them up and started opening them.

'A letter of thanks from Miss Macpherson for your donation to *The Home of Industry*,' Hannah read out, as she dealt with them one by one. 'And here's an invitation for you to attend the inauguration of the *Young Women's*

Christian Association and the offer to you to become president of the *Women's Mission.*'

Angela stroked Fan as she listened to these welcome pieces of information. Then at the last one, Hannah's tone changed quickly.

'This one is from your solicitor, my dear,' Hannah said. 'I'm afraid it relates to the unfortunate incident of the forced removal of Richard Dunn by the hotel staff in Norwood. The dreadful man has brought charges and it will come to court. He has demanded that you appear too, as having incited these two to an act of violence against him.'

Angela was aware of a sudden fluttering in her chest, which tightened and seemed to stop her breath. She gasped and clutched the arm of the chair, while the room swirled around her. Then she was conscious that Hannah was at her side, holding her hand, murmuring to her and her maid was there also. She was being guided to her bedroom, then stripped of her gown and laid in bed. She felt the palpitations in her chest subside and, aware of her faint, whispered embarrassed apologies to Hannah, who shushed her and ordered the maid to bring a glass of warm fruit cordial.

'I shall send a message for Dr Brown to come immediately,' Hannah said. 'Rest, my dear. The shock will soon pass.'

Angela nodded and squeezed her companion's hand. The shock would certainly pass, but the prospect of a court appearance would remain. She fell into a troubled doze.

On awakening, she found Dr Brown at her

side with Hannah and was pleased to discover herself in a state of drowsy calm.

'Miss Coutts, I hope you feel a little rested now,' said Dr Brown. 'But on my orders, you should remain in bed for the rest of the day.'

Dr Brown's warm and reassuring presence, his patient but competent manner made Angela realise why Hannah had chosen to be his wife.

'As for this unpleasant matter, Hannah and I have contacted the Duke and the Bishop to exert their influence with the judge. You have many friends, my dear Miss Coutts. You are not unprotected.'

Chapter 11

He'd have the bastards, those two lackeys, in court, Dunn thought as he lay in bed. They thought they could wriggle out of criminal charges, but no, the police had seen his injuries. They knew he was not faking and the two idiots had no more sense than a clod of earth between them, admitting that they'd been instructed by the hotel manager and others in Angela's party, to set about him. He'd have them in the dock all right, the lady herself to boot. They hadn't reckoned for his knowledge of the law. The two blackguards were bailed of course, not left to languish in jail as he had previously been forced to do.

Though Dunn was pained by his injuries, his mind was clear. He was seeing the truth now, with perspicacity. At last, he could see Angela for what she was, a heartless strumpet, a cold, unfeeling woman who revelled in teasing men, provoking desire in them with coquettish looks and simpering modesty. Those eyes of hers had been so full of unspoken promises of a fortune and a future life of luxury. He had been fooled by her, dazzled by her attention to him, enticed by her apparent evasions when he came near her or sent her his letters and poems.

It was just his bad luck too that there were these others on the scene, who were intent on gaining her favour, that puffed up writer Charles Dickens and the wretched pawnbroker fellow. But they were a distraction - that and her do-gooding nature. Maybe she was not in her right mind and there was madness in the family. Would he risk becoming attached to a madwoman who might have him murdered in his bed?

Dunn stretched out his painful leg where he lay on the bed and rested his injured right hand on a pillow. They'd broken two of his fingers, the ruffians. He had them splinted and wore a sling on his arm. There was no doubt in his mind now. Something had changed within him. Though he'd been buffeted by ill fortune, not only by the blows of those louts, but also by the cruelty of Miss Angela Coutts, there still remained that stalwart determination to get something from all his trouble. He was damned if he would withdraw empty-handed. In fact, he deserved compensation for the injuries he had suffered. His hand would never be the same again, he feared, which could cost him dear in his profession. That wretched woman had ruined him and he was within his rights to seek for justice.

He lay for some time pondering on what he now saw was a clever strategy with a good chance of bearing fruit. This plan, unlike his previous one he'd tried a few days ago with the Meredith woman, did not involve direct contact with either of those two harpies. The last time he had been in a weaker position to negotiate. He had approached previously with a very reasonable proposal, which would have suited them all very well in his opinion, but he had again been rebuffed. That poisonous witch

Miss Meredith, Angela's companion or servant of whatever the woman was, was permanently at her side, so it seemed. She protected Angela as ferociously as a dragon its young. So it was when he had approached her, when she was out on an errand of some sort along with a maidservant. He had simply begged a moment of her time. Then she'd had the gall to be rude to his face when he offered a very decent sort of proposal and he a man obviously still in the pain of his injuries. She'd called to her maid and said she'd create a hullabaloo if he didn't go away.

'Hear me out, I beg of you madam,' he'd said, though the words nearly choked him in his throat as he was forced to cringe and crawl like a dog to a woman who was only fit to clean his boots. 'If you will just pause a moment, this may be the last time you ever have to set eyes upon me again.'

That stopped her in her tracks, though it was hardly flattering to himself.

'Take pity on a man who is beaten down, thoroughly defeated. I have been disabled by the power of my passion and my terrible wounds, but am now fully able to see reason,' he said in the same humble tone, that seemed to be having some effect in making her less belligerent.

In spite of the situation, he was proud to see that his powers of persuasion had not completely deserted him.

'Say what you need to say,' said the Meredith woman, like she was someone of importance, 'and then be gone, sir.'

There was something unnatural to his mind about these two women that had not occurred to him before now when he looked at her. He knew about she-devils like her who preferred those of their sex to men, pawing and fawning on each other like cats. It gave him the shivers to think of it and of the practices in which they most likely indulged. He was well out of this but could maybe turn such suspicions to his advantage. He had wasted enough of his time on Miss Coutts and she would pay for the suffering she had caused.

'It's a fair proposal,' he said to the woman. 'Miss Coutts has wealth enough to pay me by way of compensation for the injuries and indignities I have suffered, which have all arisen from her actions in encouraging my attentions.'

Miss Meredith's face turned a darker colour, or maybe that was just the dulling of the daylight.

'You have brought these injuries on yourself by your unseemly behaviour,' she snapped, all haughty, like some kind of duchess instead of a jumped up governess.

The maid was standing gawping at her side and it irked him that a servant should be listening to their conversation.

'Does this girl need to be here?' he said. 'I'd not have servants tittle-tattling about my private business.'

The woman's face took on what she most likely imagined was a fearsome look, but he would not be put off by her acting.

'My maid will act as witness to your proposal, whatever it is, so make it quickly. If what you suggest is honest and harmless, then you need fear no tittle-tattle.'

What a bisom the woman was, he thought. She needed a damn good belting to keep her in order. He drew himself up, putting his good hand in his lapel.

'For a consideration,' he announced to her, 'I'll be more than happy to leave Miss Coutts to a life of spinsterhood.'

'A consideration?' said the Meredith woman. 'You expect money?'

'Aye well, madam,' he said, thinking that she was not exactly quick on the uptake. 'I think that money's no object to Miss Coutts.'

'How dare you,' said the woman. 'You expect Miss Coutts to pay you to stay away from her? Is this what you mean?'

Maybe she wasn't so slow after all, and he could see that she was starting to edge away from him. He was in danger of not even being able to name his price.

'Get out of my way,' she said sharply, 'or I shall call for help.'

He took one step alongside her, seeing that two gentlemen had paused on the corner of the street, obviously having witnessed something of their encounter.

'Five thousand guineas would do it,' he said, 'and she'll never see me again.'

She grabbed the arm of the servant girl and with the other waved to the two gentlemen who started moving towards her. Game up. The bitch had won, so Dunn had turned immediately on his heels and started walking off in the opposite direction, then crossed the road, assuming a nonchalant stroll, but seething inside. His failure smarted but it was this surge of anger that had first suggested the next course of action to him. He had Angela Coutts's notebook, albeit that it was not a scintillating or incriminating thing in itself, but what he had was her handwriting.

Now, as he lay on his bed, the idea turned into a plan. He sat up, picked up the newspaper that he had taken on a previous occasion from the coffee shop on Oxford Street, while no one was looking. He folded up the page with the item he needed and studied it again.

Professional Scribing and Compositional Services
of the Highest Order
Scholarly, companionable, litigious, whatever your needs
Our writers will copy any style and hand at your convenience
for a modest fee
Enquire for Mr E Fortescue c/o The Bear Inn, Commercial
Street

Dunn wondered at the level of the quoted 'modest' price and whether Mr Fortescue might be a man to work on the strength of a promise. There was only one way to find out. Would he also do as he was instructed and ask no questions? These were essential matters if the plan were to work. With some difficulty, because of the bandage around his broken fingers, he scrawled a quick note to Mr

Fortescue requesting an appointment, which he decided to deliver in person to the landlord of *The Bear Inn*. Feeling a terrible thirst come upon him for a glass of good Irish whiskey, he found sufficient in his pockets for a small glass or two.

As he sat in the tavern, the first few sips were all it took for a maudlin, nostalgic wave to envelop him. That he should have left the Emerald Isle for this benighted hornets' nest of greed and injustice, where those born to riches spurned all whose talents might unsettle them from their position of power and influence, where passion and love given freely were thrown back in his face. He drained his glass sadly, wondering if the landlord would let him have another on tick, to save his diminishing funds. He raised his empty glass to the man, though it was he who spoke first.

'You're in luck, sir,' the landlord said, nodding in the direction of a portly man of middle years who had just entered the tavern.

Dunn watched the new arrival approach the bar.

'Here's your man, Mr Fortescue,' the landlord said.

After introductions by the landlord, who would clearly have enjoyed the role of host at a soirée, Dunn's note was handed back to him and he shook hands with this Mr Fortescue, who might just be the answer to his problems. Dunn was unsure whether the man expected him to offer to buy a drink and he decided that his last shilling might be well spent in standing him one. It might provide the right impression of his promised wealth. The whole business was risky, Dunn knew, but he had exhausted all other routes to access the mean-spirited Miss Coutts.

Fortescue seemed delighted at Dunn's offer of a brandy and Dunn, seeing the man's frayed cuffs concluded that here was someone who would be sorely tempted by what he proposed.

'It's a delicate matter,' said Dunn, as they settled themselves in the quietest corner of the tavern, 'requiring the most professional approach and the utmost secrecy, but the rewards will be great.'

'Sir, I am your man,' said Fortescue, with gusto. 'In my previous career I was entrusted with matters of great confidential import.'

'And could you copy a lady's hand from a sample which I can provide?' Dunn said.

Fortescue leaned forward in his seat with a confident smile.

'Of course, sir. Anything you ask can be arranged. Would you care to call at my place of work to discuss matters further, and the remuneration, of course?'

Dunn smiled back. He would meet the man, hand over the notebook and dictate the letter he required. The exact fee could be discussed when they met, Dunn said. And there would be a bonus of course, for Mr Fortescue's promise of silence.

Chapter 16

At school that day it was clear to Nathan that Nicholas Greaves was ailing. His face was waxy pale and sweat lent his skin an ugly silken appearance. His wife was solicitous, but the children were particularly rowdy, causing Nathan to resort to threats to calm them down and set them to work. Nicholas Greaves sat on a chair in the corner of the school room and managed to read to a group of the smaller children gathered around him.

'Let the girls come and join me for arithmetic,' Nathan said to Mrs Greaves.

The tension relaxed from her face a little and she touched his arm.

'Thank you so much Mr Hines. I must get my husband a restorative drink.'

Nathan herded the children onto forms in front of him, the small girls at the front. He asked them to call out numbers for the boys to multiply, which Nathan wrote upon their newly acquired blackboard. Grouping the children in threes and fours, he made them copy the sums upon the slates that had also been supplied from the money gifted by Miss Coutts. He then wrote a short Bible text upon the blackboard and had each child copy a sentence each. He finished with reading from one of the books that Silas had found in the shop. Thus, the morning was spent in quite an orderly and productive fashion, the girls proving themselves the equal of the boys in mental arithmetic. Bread and cheese were delivered that morning too, thanks to Miss Coutts's new dinner fund, so, from an unpromising beginning, the day was proceeding quite smoothly.

The schoolmaster was worse by the afternoon, however, and Nathan found himself growing anxious, with a renewal of those memories of the times when he had tried and failed to help the sick. The anguish of watching helplessly, while someone dear is suffering, he remembered as the worst form of punishment. The man at least did not have cholera; he had not vomited nor had he diarrhoea. His breathing was rasping and thin and he had a fever, certainly. Nathan saw the wife's powerlessness, re-lived his own but knew he had to do something.

'Mrs Greaves,' he said as she knelt at the sick man's side. 'Your husband must go home to bed. Let me get a doctor. We can dismiss the children early.'

The woman looked at him with a grateful sigh.

'You are kind,' she said. 'Would you do that?'

'Thank you,' murmured Nicholas Greaves, who was struggling to breathe.

He grasped his wife's hand and Nathan heard his breathless apology to her. 'Marianne, my dear, what a burden I am.'

Nathan picked up the tin of beads and rattled it fiercely, calling the children to near silence.

'Boys and girls, you must go home now. Mr

Greaves is not well and must be taken home. We will see you tomorrow,' he said, wondering if it was a promise he would be able to keep. He would most likely be here in sole charge with above fifty pupils.

Most went willingly, though some, including Ned, hung back.

'Ain't we going to get more 'rithmetic, sir?' he said.

Nathan looked at the boy, surprised at this request.

'Not today. I'm sorry.'

'Is he going to croak then?' said Ned

Nathan shook his head. 'He needs rest and a doctor,' he said hopelessly, unsure how else to respond.

He would never speculate about who was destined to die and who to recover. Life and death were matters of blind chance or luck, no more. There was little comfort to be had in imagining that any being, human or immortal, had sufficient power to influence events that were already rolling towards their conclusion. Maybe a doctor or nurse could ease a person's pain in their sickness, but he knew that the acts of medical men could instead induce for the sufferer an agonising passage to death.

The last of the children were leaving as Mrs Greaves was helping her husband into his coat. It was clear, however, that the man was not capable of standing, nor of movement.

'Let me help you,' said Nathan, slipping his arm around the sick man's body to ease him to his feet. His wife supported his other side, but he was a heavy, dead weight and they struggled to get him to the door.

'If we can get him to Clerkenwell Road, I'll find a cab,' Nathan said, as they struggled to get him out of the door on to the street.

A few passersby stared and one man, a stallholder or market trader pushing an empty barrow paused.

'What's up with him?' he said. 'Need a hand, do you?'

Nathan exchanged a look with Mrs Greaves and she nodded.

'Yes, if you could get him on your cart, please,' said Nathan to the man, knowing that they would otherwise have trouble getting the near senseless man to the road.

The barrow man obliged by wheeling his vehicle nearer and lifting the sick man's legs up as Nathan laid him on top.

'Where to?' said the man, as though this were all part of his usual day's work. 'You live far, eh?'

Nathan realised that the helpful man might be a quicker means of returning the sick man to his house.

'Not far, St John Street,' said Mrs Greaves. 'Could you carry him there?'

'Yeh, I reckon I could,' said the man.

'Thank you,' she said. 'I will pay, of course.'

The man nodded in acknowledgement.

'And do you know of a doctor nearby?' Nathan asked the barrow man.

The man shook his head.

'Never could pay for no doctor,' he said.

Nathan knew of several doctors, though he would not, even if fearing for his life or anyone near him, ever consult them again. There was one, however, who had been recommended, too late as it happened, a Dr Simpson in Aldwych. He left Mrs Greaves and her husband in the hands of the barrow man, whom they had no reason to mistrust, as he had offered his help freely for the sake of another. Nathan promised the anxious wife that he would bring a doctor as soon as possible and, not knowing whether she would be able to pay, determined to meet the fee himself.

He set off, weaving his way through the busy streets, knowing he could probably go faster than an omnibus, until he arrived at the home of Dr Andrew Simpson, as the plate outside on the wall proclaimed. Nathan rang the bell, wondering what his next course of action would be if the doctor were not at home, or if he would not agree to attend the sick man. Fortunately, not only was the doctor in, but he very obligingly left his supper to come with Nathan to the Greaves's house. Nathan proposed that they take a cab and he hoped that his money would stretch to this as well as the doctor's fee. On the way, the doctor asked about Nicholas Greaves's symptoms and listened attentively.

Half an hour later, in the small parlour of the Greaves's house, the doctor explained his diagnosis. He had little doubt about the seriousness of the man's condition.

'It is pneumonia. His lungs are congested.

We can only wait and pray that he is strong enough to come through it. Give him this draught when he is restless and bathe his face and chest to keep him cool. I will call back tomorrow.'

'Thank you, doctor,' Mrs Greaves said, going to the desk in the corner, but Nathan stopped her, catching her arm lightly.

'There is no fee. I have made the arrangement with Dr Simpson,' he said quietly to her.

'But Mr Hines –,' she said, her eyes filling.

She looked away, murmuring her thanks. The Greaves's threadbare carpet and meagre furnishings indicated to Nathan that he had been right to pay. The place was clean and neat, however, with a bookcase full of books their only extravagance, it seemed. She showed the doctor out and turned to Nathan.

'Mr Hines, thank you for your kindness and generosity,' she said.

'We will repay you, of course. Nicholas would not wish to take your money.'

Nathan shook his head. 'In good time,' he said. 'But have you anyone else to come and sit with him?'

'No, it's all right,' she said. 'I shall doze as I sit beside him.'

She reached for his arm touching it briefly. Her face was strained, pale with fatigue, though with no sign of fragility. There was a core of strength in the woman; Nathan had witnessed this in her calm and quiet firmness with the pupils at school.

'You should close the school until Nicholas and I can return,' she said.

He smiled.

'You do not think me capable of managing on my own?'

She blushed slightly.

'No, I didn't mean –'

'It may not be so orderly as when you are there,' Nathan said, 'but I will do my best. I will come by tomorrow, when I hope to find Mr Greaves improved.'

As Nathan made his way home, he was struck by the nature of his undertaking over the next days. He had not betrayed his doubts about the recovery of the schoolmaster. The doctor's manner and the state of the patient had indicated to him that death was the more likely outcome. But good fortune, he knew, sometimes lighted on people in the most unexpected ways. Nicholas Greaves had not appeared to be an ill man, though he was, Nathan realised, many years older than his wife, Marianne, as he had now discovered her Christian name to be.

His strategy the next day was to appoint some of the older children as monitors to supervise the younger ones. An appeal to the children's sympathies also seemed to have a sobering effect on them, at least initially. Some of the children were silent and solemn at the news of Mr Greaves's sickness and the absence of his wife. Nathan assumed that this was because, even in their short lives they had almost certainly witnessed death, of parents, siblings, even strangers in the street. Ned proved an apt and stern substitute schoolmaster, though his recourse to threats of physical violence against anyone who was found wanting or inattentive was a source of mild concern to Nathan. The small group of girls were set to copying excerpts from the Psalms, Miss Coutts having paid for a set of twenty new Bibles. Nathan himself wrote a board full of calculations for another group. He paced between the groups, helping, intervening, reprimanding and praising as necessary.

The arrival of food brought cheers as the Sisters of Mercy entered with baskets of bread and sausage and apples. Nathan just managed to control the lines of hungry bodies to ensure that all received something.

'You are on your own today,' said one of the nuns to Nathan.

When he explained the circumstances, the nun crossed herself.

'We will pray for him,' she said.

He wished that he could believe in the power of prayer, but acknowledged that to some its worth lay not in the outcome but in the process, the comfort that eased away despair. With some trepidation, he went again to the Greaves's house after he had closed the school. Marianne Greaves came to the door and welcomed him in, reporting that her husband was no worse and in fact had rallied a little that afternoon, taking a little broth. She was hopeful, she said, of seeing an improvement the next day. Nathan left her, glad that his suspicions had been false.

Returning home, he found Silas at work in the storeroom.

'Sorted the stuff for auction,' he said.

'Thank you, Silas,' Nathan said, having to admit that the shop and the storeroom were much tidier and better organised than when he had been in charge. Listless, worried and uncommitted to the work, he had done what was required, no more no less, to keep the business running.

'We are obliged to put up notices about the auction of unredeemed items for two weeks,' Nathan told him, 'then we must make space in the shop and a little in the storeroom to accommodate the buyers. There are not usually many, however.'

Silas nodded. 'I'll write the notices tomorrow. Want them printed, do you? Which printer?'

Nathan told him, noting that Silas looked smarter, more presentable today. He was wearing a respectable looking coat and a white linen shirt. His hair had been cut, too. Putting him in charge of the business had clearly benefitted them both.

'Done well this week,' said Silas, pointing to the cash box, which lay below the counter.

Nathan opened the box and counted out over ten pounds. He handed Silas coins to the value of five pounds.

'You've worked beyond what I expected,' he said.

Silas squirmed slightly.

'No need. Glad to do it. My pay's enough.'

'Take it,' said Nathan. 'Keep it safe. There is always something unexpected round the corner. You need a bit set by, don't you think?'

Silas nodded sheepishly grateful and put the money in his pocket.

'Probably be set upon on my way home,' he said with a twisted smile.

'Well, that's a risk, Silas, since you're looking like a prosperous man these days,' Nathan said.

'And you're getting more like a schoolmaster every day,' snorted Silas with a laugh.

Nathan smiled and bade Silas good night.

Later that evening, Nathan opened the chest where he had stored Kate's and the children's best clothes. The others that had been worn in their sickness, he had burned. Kate's Sunday gown and shawl, his daughter's too and his son's new breeches, jacket, shirt and cap. The smell from the trunk was musty and the garments bore the folds and creases of his hasty miserable packing a year ago. He picked each item up one at a time and folding them again, put them into a large canvas bag which he had got out for the purpose. He kept his daughter's handkerchief embroidered with her initials, the sampler, too, that she had stitched, his son's toy soldiers, carved and crudely painted from sticks and his wife's cream silk fringed shawl, embroidered with beads and small plush designs at the edges. This he had given her on the day of their marriage. He held it to his face, felt its cool softness, folded it again and placed it on the bed alongside the other precious things that he would keep for ever. He recalled the children's heads, bent over their handicrafts that night by the fire, only weeks before the sickness came.

He lifted the canvas bag downstairs, putting it beside the door ready to take tomorrow. Those that were living could make good use of the belongings of the dead.

Chapter 12

'Ned, I have some clothes here that might fit you,' said Nathan to the boy, whom he had drawn aside from the hubbub at the beginning of the day. 'You must find yourself a place of work and for that you need to be better turned out.'

The boy stared at Nathan suspiciously and at the bag of garments at his feet.

'You want to get rid of me?' said the boy.

'No Ned, not at all. But you want a job of work, to earn money, don't you?'

'Yes, but I want schooling too,' he said with a sulky expression.

Nathan sighed. 'You're an intelligent boy, but we can't teach you much here, not in the Ragged School. So, what I say is that you should get a place, in a shop for example as an errand boy, or a hotel or a place in a grand house. Then, when you're older and have a bit of money, you can take up your learning again.'

The boy looked at him dubiously. 'How do I get a place then?' he said.

'I will enquire on your behalf, as will Mrs Greaves. Miss Coutts our benefactress may also be able to help.'

'If I take them things, Ma'll just pawn them. No point taking them.'

Nathan realised that he should have foreseen this possibility.

'Leave them here, then, until you need them to go for a place. When you get work, you can tell your mother you need to look smart.'

The boy grinned at him and Nathan took the bag of clothes and locked them in the corner cupboard. He then picked up the rattling tin and brought the room to a state of near silence. Mildly gratified at his accomplishment, he surveyed the heads of the fifty or so children assembled there, awaiting their instructions.

That afternoon, he was late to close the school as there was mess and dirt to be cleared from the place in readiness for the next day. The children had run off without completing their assigned jobs, such as cleaning the blackboard and slates and sweeping the floor. Nathan did these jobs, straightening the furniture as well, rebuking himself for not having kept the children under a tighter rein. Though he was tired with the day's work, he knew he must go again to see how the schoolmaster was faring and to offer what help he could to Marianne Greaves. He admired the woman for her devotion to her husband, her uncomplaining nature and commitment to the children in the Ragged School. She and her husband had not been able to have children, he assumed, perhaps because Nicholas Greaves was advanced in years. and thus, these boys and girls were their substitute. He knew little about the couple beyond the fact that they were people of better education than financial means. He suspected that they were non-conformists too, a fact that would probably not have pleased Miss Coutts, a devout Anglican.

His lateness made him decide to take a short cut through Verulam Street, which joined Leather Lane leading to Cross Street, where the Greaves lived. It was close to the junction where he had espied the girl who had brought him Selina Harding's gown and as he picked his way through the filthy puddles of the alley, he glanced at the few people he encountered as he passed A woman and two children sat on a doorstep, the children holding out their hands as he passed. He gave them a halfpenny each and continued on his way, hearing 'God bless you, mister,' a woman's voice calling after him. Ahead, coming towards him, was another small limping woman or girl carrying a bundle under her arm. His recognition of her gait and her skinny shape made him advance at greater speed towards her. Was it her, the same girl who had visited his shop with the gown that day? He could not be sure unless he could get close enough to see her features. Only twenty paces from her, he called out, 'Miss, a word, please. Just a moment. I mean you no harm.'

But the girl had seen his rapid progress towards her, had stopped and looked around and then, as before, she turned quickly and ran. He saw her dodge past a man with a blackened face, lurching along with a full sack of coal balanced on his back, then she bolted off away from Nathan. She was still visible ahead of him and he was gaining on her as he ran. Then she dived into an opening to her right, a cart entrance between two warehouse buildings. Nathan ran after her, plunging into the entrance, which led to a large courtyard surrounded on all sides by two storey dilapidated brick buildings. At the far side of the yard, he saw the girl approach a hole in the wall, a black opening where bricks had crumbled or had been broken down.

'Wait, come back,' he shouted, knowing it was futile.

She disappeared through the black hole that gaped like an open black mouth. He ran to it, poked his head through into a dark and rancid smelling passageway, devoid of nearly all daylight because of the high walls of buildings on both sides. He could just make out the girl's figure about fifty paces along near the end of this stinking tunnel. He ran, splashing in puddles, seeing the small bobbing figure ahead. Then another shape appeared, that of a large man who exchanged a few inaudible words with her. He let her pass and then charged down the passage towards Nathan, his bulk blocking out the only patch of grey light. Before Nathan had a chance to utter a word or retreat even a step, a heavy fist crashed into his face and he hit the ground with a crunch as a splintering pain struck his back.

Though Nathan thought he had opened his eyes, he could see nothing, nor was he aware of anything about his body except for pain, a jabbing knife in his back and a pulsing of his nose. He put his hand up to his face and felt sticky moisture that he knew was blood. He discovered that he could move his legs, then his arms and groped with one hand to feel the hard surface of a wall. With an effort, gaining more control and awareness of his body, he eased himself up to lean against the wall. His clothes were soaking from the noxious puddle in which he had fallen and he shivered. His coat had been stripped from him, his shirt torn and his boots gone. Turning back, he saw a faint light patch at the end of the alley and felt his way slowly along towards it. He was back in the yard again and remembered clearly now what had brought him this way, his pursuit of the girl. Standing shivering there in the dark, he realised now that the thief had taken not only his clothes but his watch and the last token of Selina Harding that was in his possession, the lace handkerchief embroidered with her initials. This was the second and greater failure of his efforts to speak to the girl.

It was a painful and slow walk back home, and as he staggered along, his head throbbing, he would have been mistaken for a drunken dissolute, one of many desperate creatures on the streets at night. He had no idea how long he had lain senseless in the alley, but he guessed that it must now be late in the evening. As he stumbled the last yards toward home, he noticed that a faint light was glowing through the cracks in the shutters on the shop window. The only explanation for such an apparition was that Silas was still there. Only then did he realise that he would have been condemned to sleep on the streets or break and enter the shop as his keys had been taken along with everything else. His feet were sore, lacerated and bruised with walking and he knocked on the door feebly. In a brief moment Silas was there, extending his hand to Nathan, steadying him over the threshold into the place.

'God in Heaven,' Silas said. 'What happened?'

While Silas washed the blood from Nathan's face, Nathan explained how he had sighted the girl and followed her to the place where he had been attacked.

'Bloody thieving gang, that's what,' Silas said as he wrung out the bloodied cloth into a basin of water. 'She's part of it too. She knows you're after her, little thief.'

'But I only wanted to talk to her,' Nathan said. 'I know that she must have stolen the gown, but I only needed to know–'

'Give it up,' said Silas. 'You'll not find the woman.'

'But the child,' Nathan said, glad that Silas's dabbing at his stinging wounds had brought other tears to his eyes. 'I know that the woman Selina Harding is certainly dead, but her daughter might still be alive.'

'There's beggars and homeless children aplenty out there. You going to save them all, are you? Hundreds, thousands maybe. And those little paupers in your Ragged School... see to them, why don't you?... and not drive yourself mad.'

Nathan knew that Silas was right, the

chances of finding Selina Harding's child were by now non-existent.

'What is it o'clock?' he said suddenly remembering where he had been going before he had been beaten.

'After eleven,' said Silas. 'Do you think anything's broke?'

Silas was inspecting Nathan's ribs, which ached dully.

'I need to go and see Mr Greaves. He's sick and his wife –'

'You need to see to yourself not others,' Silas said, in the manner of an irate parent. 'Tell me where. I'll go and bring you word, if you'll let me stop here for the night.'

Nathan was suddenly swamped by a wave of helpless gratitude to this man. He reached out to his friend, grasped his arm, at which Silas simply nodded and told Nathan to get to bed at once.

The sound of the clatter of dishes downstairs in the kitchen woke Nathan. It took some moments for him to realise where he was and what had happened. He was stiff with a dull pain in his back and his face felt tight, but he got up and splashed his face with water, dressed, resorting to all that was left to him in his wardrobe, his best shirt and coat, his spare boots and went downstairs. Silas was slicing a fresh loaf and Nathan saw a pat of butter on a saucer, some jam and a pan of water on the stove.

'Need a servant, you do,' said Silas.

Nathan tried to smile but it stretched his face uncomfortably.

'Are you offering your services?' he said, then asked about Silas's visit to the Greaves.

'The man is bearing up,' Silas said. 'He's taken water and is sitting, so his good wife told me. Nice woman, that one.'

Nathan was relieved to hear this and set himself to the task of shaving, a painful process with his bruised face.

'Looks like you've done a round with the Beast of Stepney,' said Silas.

'That bad?' said Nathan.

When he opened the door to the schoolroom, he found a dozen or so boys around him.

'You been fighting, sir?'

'What's up with your face, eh?'

'Tell us who done it and we'll get him.'

'Bloody Nora!'

Nathan was surprised and a little perturbed that the evidence of his involvement in violence should have created so much interest in the boys. He offered them only a vague explanation of his mishap and called them rather hastily to order. They obeyed a little more promptly on this occasion and he instructed his monitors to do their work as before. As he moved around among them, he realised that Silas was right. Here were children that needed his attention. He would think no more the lost girl. She, however, would join with his other painful losses, not to be forgotten but with the yearning dulled and smoothed by time. The constant activity of the day took his whole attention until the close of the school and, exhausted, he saw the children out and on their way.

He was locking the door with the intention of going once more to the Greaves' house, when he heard a voice calling his name.

'You Mr Hines?' said a boy, not one of their own.

He was breathless, clearly having run at full speed on his errand. He gulped and wheezed for a few seconds before he could speak clearly. When he did so, he said he had a message from Mrs Greaves that her husband had gone, passed away in the night and could Mr Hines come to her.

Chapter 13

'A fortune!' This one'll make us a fortune,' Bezer said. 'Five per cent of £100,000. Just think.'

Susan stirred the pot of soup vigorously then turned to her husband.

'But this gentleman, this Mr Dunn, has he given you an advance or some surety?' she said, with her familiar sharp tone.

Bezer had hoped that she wasn't going to ask this.

'Well not in actuality, at this time,' he said, not looking at her and taking a seat at the table, adding quickly before she had time to continue her criticism, 'but he's a gentleman. Irish, I give you that, but a gentleman all the same. He's given his word.'

Susan said nothing, turning back to the pot of soup and hoisting it off the range. She splattered some into the bowl in front of Bezer. He looked down at the small lumps of grey meat and knew that he ought to be grateful. He stuffed the end of a piece of cotton cloth into his collar, to serve as a napkin, as they'd long ago pawned all their linen ones, then scooped up the first spoonful hungrily.

'You'd best give some to the child,' he said, pointing with his spoon to the silent girl who was crouched on the floor by the fire. 'We don't want her dying on us.'

Susan sighed. 'She's as stubborn as they come. She'd starve rather than speak.'

She poured some of the soup into a bowl

and took it to the child who did not look up. Susan sat the bowl beside her on the floor. Bezer took another mouthful and chewed on the rubbery piece of flesh, uncertain of its animal origins.

'So, this gentleman,' said Susan, 'when is he coming?'

'Tomorrow and I may tell you my dear, the person from whom he will gain his riches is none other than Miss Angela Coutts herself.'

Susan snorted.

'It never is! But she hasn't paid up for her father's little bastard, has she? Does this Irishman think he'll get anything out of her?'

'He is confident, my love and he has good reason to count on it. In any case, Miss Coutts may still intend to honour her father's memory by doing the right thing. We can always hope.'

'Hope won't put bread on the table, Bezer. You'll have to get something out of this so called gentleman. We're down to our last shilling and we've precious little left to pawn. I reckon it's time to make that one earn her keep.'

Susan nodded towards the girl, who, Bezer saw, had finished her bowl of soup. She was the most miserable and forlorn-looking creature he'd ever seen, not the dirtiest by any means, just sunk deeply in her muteness. He could not help a moment's sympathy for her and he realised, as Susan did, that she might become an essential asset to them in their endeavours, whatever strategies they were to adopt.

Bezer had decided not to tell Susan the exact details of the story the Irishman had told him. The advertisement for their writing services had produced only his request and one other, from an unemployed dockworker who had approached him in the inn, requesting a letter to be written to his brother in Essex. Bezer had dashed off a missive quickly on a page torn from the back of an almanac on a shelf in the inn, while the landlord wasn't looking. He'd charged the man a shilling, which Bezer reckoned was cheap at the price for an accomplished piece of composition designed to wring the heart of the brother in Essex. The man had gone off with it satisfied.

Mr Richard Dunn's proposition was an altogether different undertaking; daring but potentially extremely lucrative. It was risky too. It was forgery. He had never really considered their other letters as actual criminal acts. The people to whom they appealed had generally more money than they knew what to do with, and they were the high-minded sort who wished to do good works and benefit the needy. He and Susan were certainly needy. He supposed that even when Miss Coutts paid out that vast sum to Richard Dunn, she would hardly notice its absence. She was the richest woman in England, after all. Still, it was a dangerous plan and would demand the highest level of Susan's skills to accomplish.

The next evening, Richard Dunn turned up at their rooms. Susan had tidied the parlour, stoked up the fire with coals she had bought from two mudlarks. She put the girl in the bedchamber out of the way.

'It will create a more scholarly, professional impression,' she said to Bezer as she laid out paper and pens on the table in readiness and lit their last wax candle.

At his knock, Bezer sprang to the door.

'Good evening, Mr Dunn. This is such a pleasure,' said Bezer with a respectful bow. 'Do come into our humble dwelling.'

The man did not smile, nor return this overture, his dark features set in a scowl. Bezer tried to ignore this inauspicious start by introducing Susan, who smiled sweetly, curtsied and took his hat. He had no cloak nor topcoat, though the night was chilly and his right hand, as before, was heavily bandaged.

'May I trouble you for a drop of something?' Dunn said as he took a seat at the table.

Bezer glanced in inward panic at Susan, who gave an almost imperceptible shake of the head.

'I'll make you a refreshing infusion, sir,' she said in her most oily tones.

Richard Dunn snorted with displeasure. 'Have you nothing stronger, for God's sake?'

'Ah but sir, don't we all need clear heads for this undertaking?' Bezer said, rather pleased that he had hit on a rational argument.

Their visitor did not try to hide his disgust. Bezer could see Susan's anger in her quivering lip.

'Well sir,' she said in a brisk manner, 'if you

would be kind enough to provide a down payment for our work, I shall be happy to go to the tavern and purchase a bottle of something to your liking.'

Bezer cringed inwardly for a second or two, wondering if Dunn would take off, insulted by Susan's directness. He saw for a nasty moment their best chance of making a fortune disappearing. However, Dunn hesitated, appearing almost flustered.

'No matter then, no matter,' he muttered. 'Let's to business.'

He took out of his pocket a small notebook with an embroidered cloth cover and opened it to reveal the pages of notes in a lady's neat hand.

'Here is the sample that you must use to create a statement from this writer,' he said, pushing the book towards Bezer. 'I would have done it myself, except that I am incommoded as you see by this injury. And it is a lady's hand, which I do not think I could replicate, my education and training being of an entirely manly style.'

Bezer examined a page of the book closely, noting its regular, even slant and the style of letter formation. He handed it to Susan who in turn held it close to her face to scrutinise it.

'My wife is a specialist in ladies' writing styles,' Bezer said proudly.

Dunn glanced at her.

'Of course, I will need to inspect the letter once it's written,' he said.

Susan looked up at him with a bold

expression.

'And you will give us part payment at that stage?' she said.

Dunn nodded, though his black eyes darted away from Susan's persistent stare.

'If I am satisfied with the work, I will of course remunerate you. But you must understand that the bulk of the payment will be made after I am in receipt of the monies. Now, let me dictate the exact wording I require.'

Bezer dipped the pen and slid a piece of paper in front of him.

'I will take down the letter as I have a speedier hand, then my wife will convert it to the form you desire.'

Dunn leaned closer to Bezer and then glanced at Susan.

'This is highly confidential,' he said. 'No word of this meeting must ever be breathed to a soul, nor any mention of our arrangements. Do you understand?'

'Of course, sir,' said Bezer. 'Please be assured of our silence on the matter.'

'Very good,' said Dunn with a sudden glimmer of a more affable self.

He leaned back in the chair and dictated slowly and in a lugubrious tone while Bezer wrote. In ten minutes, the text of the letter was written.

1 Stratton Street,
Piccadilly

My Darling Richard,

How I repent of my cruelty to you! I implore you to forgive me and look with favour on one who loves you truly. I will do everything in my power to ensure that you are never subjected to insults or injuries for my sake. Take also, my dear one, a gift to compensate for the wrongs and ills you have suffered for your devotion to me. I beg you to present yourself to the Chief Clerk of Coutts Bank and claim for yourself the sum of £100,000 from my account.

My heart's joy, only to see you will give me the peace and happiness I crave.

With my tenderest love,
Angela Burdett-Coutts

Bezer suppressed his desire to question Dunn as to whether this whole business was a fabrication. He could see that Susan was curious about the matter too. Dunn, appearing to sense their need for some explanation or justification took the letter from Bezer and stared at him, in a disconcerting gaze, with a tilt of the head, like the look of a Bedlam lunatic.

'She made up to me, the minx,' Dunn said, after some moments, 'with her smiles and her come-ons and now she has the gall to deny it all. I've been arrested, beaten, insulted, humiliated, all because of my desire to return her love. Well, I tell you, I shall have my due.

She owes me this and she will pay.'

Bezer's stomach clenched as he watched Dunn utter these words; the man's eyes threatened, his brow glistened with sweat and Bezer heartily wished him gone.

'We will have the letter ready for you tomorrow,' Bezer said, shifting in his chair then rising awkwardly from it.

'Good,' said Dunn, getting up. 'Until tomorrow.'

Without further words, Susan brought his hat, opened the door for him and a moment later he was gone. Bezer and Susan exchanged looks in silence for a few moments after the man's departure, as though they feared that he might be lurking outside, eavesdropping.

'Come,' said Bezer, with a secret heavy feeling inside. 'You'd best make a start.'

Susan nodded and picked up a scrap of paper, on which, with Miss Coutts's notebook open before her, she started practising forming the letters and words.

The next morning Bezer was aware that Susan had left the bed very early. Bezer drowsily recalled the previous evening of toil, a laborious business, not helped by the whimpering of the child who slept fitfully on the rug in the kitchen. The only sound she seemed capable of uttering was a thin, dog-like whine. Bezer blearily roused himself to leave the bed and found Susan, head bowed over her meticulous copying of the lady's hand, which expressed this outrageous confession.

'Have you nearly finished, my love?' he said.

'Yes, I have just to complete the signature. See here.'

Bezer approached and examined the finished text, comparing it with the script in the notebook. To him, Susan's version appeared to be a veritable work of art.

'You are truly a marvel, my darling,' he said, kissing her plump cheek. 'With such skill we could go far. This is simply the beginning.'

Susan sat back in her seat and sighed. Bezer took up the letter carefully.

'It should be addressed on the outside to 'Mr Richard Dunn'.

Later, once the letter had been completed to their satisfaction, Susan announced that she intended to go out and take the girl with her. She would go to one of the better streets in the West End, maybe Regent Street, in the hope of attracting the attention of a better class of person, do-gooding ladies for example, whose hearts might be moved at the sight of a poor sickly-looking child. Susan planned to set the girl to beg and she herself would watch from nearby. She was not prepared to demean herself by dressing like a beggar, but the child looked the part. The child's state of muteness would not be amiss. She would be viewed as a poor, half-witted creature, the more to be pitied. Her ragged appearance and her thin, mournful face would give a vivid enough picture of her need.

Bezer bade Susan farewell and good hunting and went back to bed. Moving about always made him hungry and there was nothing to eat. He lay in bed, imagining the glorious supper he and Susan would have once they had the first instalment of Richard Dunn's fee. It was a delicious imagining. Some time later, he awoke to the sound of the door banging shut then the key turning in the lock. He was unsure about how long he must have been sleeping and the next he knew was a slap in the face and Susan standing over him.

'Wake up, you lazy fool,' she said.

He sat up quickly, his cheek smarting.

'What is it? I was only –.'

'She's gone,' Susan spat out at him, 'that little wretch – run off.'

'What?' said Bezer. 'The girl?'

'Yes, damn her and she only raised a sixpence for us.'

Bezer thought fondly of what a sixpence might buy, but he could see that Susan was enraged.

'How? When did she run off?'

Susan held out the few coins in her hand and told him how she had taken the girl to a very good spot not far from *Dickens and Smith* on Regent Street, where the well-to-do shopped and there were quite a few folk on the street. There were a couple of other beggars at the same game further along the street, but Susan had thought it was worth a try. She had placed the girl on the pavement and ordered her to put her hand out, told her to step forward and look up at folk as they walked by. She hadn't much of a clue, but after some time, she'd collected a few pennies in her hand from people who passed swiftly by. A lady's maid following her mistress stopped briefly, dropped a coin into the child's hand and said a word or two to her. Then all of a sudden, the girl lifted her head and was staring at two folk who had just come out of the door of the shop, a gentleman in a bowler hat and a woman on his arm, wearing a green outfit, a cape and a striped gown. They crossed the road and the girl was gaping like she'd seen the Queen and Prince Albert right there on the street. Then she threw down the coins and bolted off across the road after the couple.

Susan had rushed to the spot, picked up the pennies where the girl had dropped them and tried to get back across the road, but an omnibus was in her way and then she was nearly knocked down by a hansom cab as she tried to go round it.

'I lost her, the little wretch,' Susan said bitterly. 'The little devil. What was she doing, taking off like that?'

The next day, with scant hope and a little desperation, Bezer went to *The Bear Inn* to see if any mail had arrived for him. There was the possibility of a couple of responses to letters they had sent recently, with the address of this public house for replies. Others, quoting their own address and also from two other hostelries had yielded nothing. It was dispiriting work, this business of begging letters, though he did not like to think of them in these terms. 'Speculative requests' was a more respectable expression, he thought to himself. There was a chance, too, that someone else might require their writing services. After all, their advertisement had attracted the attention of Richard Dunn. The Irishman had come back and taken away the letter to Miss Coutts and her notebook, but had offered them no money. Susan had looked ready to explode with anger at this and told the man in no uncertain terms that should he not pay, she might be tempted to drop a hint to the authorities about the forgery. This was a risky threat, Bezer reflected, but it drew from Dunn a solemn promise of part payment the next week.

Bezer could not help the heavy feeling of gloom weighing upon him, his optimism all spent. They would starve. Now the child had gone, there was even less chance of a small but regular income to be gained from her begging. The spectre of his need to get work was haunting him too. He could do clerking, he supposed, though the pay would be pitiful and so far beneath him, a man of his education and talents. Also, he was not made for manual labour. He was a brain worker. Maybe, he thought, they should emigrate to the colonies where literate people like them might be more valued, but the idea of a long sea voyage to a place full of savages was deeply terrifying to Bezer. Maybe he and Susan could start a school and charge a modest fee, to attract the less affluent sort of person who had aspirations for their offspring. However, he disliked children with their noise, their mess and impudence.

The warm fug of the public house cheered him a little, the bartender pouring a jug of ale in front of the shining mirrors, the clink of pewter and glass, the low rumble of talk and laughter. The landlord saw him enter and signalled that there was indeed some mail for him. He had to part with sixpence to the landlord for his services in keeping Bezer's mail and he thus had only enough left to order a small gin and water.

'Here we are, Mr Fortescue,' said the landlord, handing him two letters.

The landlord, as with the others, had seemed happy enough with Bezer's explanation about his itinerant lifestyle on business and his need for a city address amidst many house moves. Bezer's main challenge was remembering which name he had used in which public house. He went to the corner of one of the small back rooms and opened the first letter.

His heart leapt with painful joy when he discovered a cheque for £5 made payable to 'Mrs Teresa Allen', from a Lady Montmorency of Oxford. This was in response to one of Susan's pleas in the guise of a poor woman, Oxford born and bred, widowed when her husband was drowned in a well and she with a withered arm and seven children, forced to quit their tied cottage and now destitute in London. Susan might need to prove her identity as Mrs Teresa Allen, but could easily provide some suitable document, a reference from a vicar or landlord or similar belonging to her fictitious beneficiary.

The other letter, however, struck Bezer with considerable alarm from its first words and his hand trembled as he read its content.

15 Albemarle Crescent, Bath

Sir,

Your offensive and libellous letter with its untruthful claims will be dealt with in a manner as befits such fraudulent and criminal action. I and my family absolutely refute your wicked allegations made against my late father. He was crippled and confined to a wheelchair these last ten years before his sad death three months ago. He has fathered no child since myself thirty years ago. The child you claim is his, cannot be. No person outside his lawful blood relations has any claim upon him nor upon us.

I have therefore reported the matter to the Society for the Suppression of Mendicity and to the Justice of the Peace in the borough from which you have sent your evil missive.

I hope you will, after due punishment, repent of your sins and resolve to live by honest means.

Yours
Arthur Blackstock

Bezer gulped the last drop of his drink and glanced furtively around, then, getting up quickly, he quitted the place. He could never return. The authorities would be investigating and would come to the inn and speak to the landlord. As he hurried along the road, he thanked God and Susan that they had had the foresight to use multiple addresses. He hoped that the letters written from their own address would not provoke any similar actions from recipients. Bezer's stomach churned uncomfortably as he wondered if he should propose an immediate relocation.

He reached the steps leading up to their rooms and galloped up them, causing his rising gorge to burn his throat. He burst into the kitchen. Susan was chopping an onion.

'My dearest, the worst has happened,' he spluttered.

Susan tutted as though he had simply brought in a little mud on his boots.

'Sit down, you fool, will you and catch your breath. Is it a murderer or rabid dog that's after you?'

Bezer glanced behind him and ran to turn the key in the door. Then he fell into a chair and pulled the letters from his pocket. Susan slumped down beside him and took them from him.

'But here's good news indeed,' Susan said holding up the cheque for £5.

'Yes, but the other, read the other,' said Bezer, his heart thudding.

Susan read it quickly and he saw her face change. Her mouth twitched and she tossed the letter down.

'Just our luck to write to a cripple,' she said. 'Who'd have thought it?'

'But what will we do?' said Bezer, sniffling.

'Be quiet and let me think.'

Susan got up and was about to start her pacing to and fro when they heard a sharp knock on the door. Bezer jerked out of his chair, grateful for his foresight in locking the door. Was it a constable already, or an inspector from the Society come to arrest them? Susan held her finger to her lips and they stood in the kitchen in a fearful silence.

'Blundell! I know you're there!' called the voice of the landlord's agent. 'Don't think you can fool me. Three weeks' rent, that's what you owe. Pay it by Friday or I'll get someone to press you a trifle harder.'

Bezer shrank down, his head almost level with the tabletop. Susan sat motionless, staring at the door with eyes as sharp as arrows. If only they could be fired straight into the heart of the landlord, Bezer thought, to make him leave them in peace, just until they were back on their feet again. After another knock and another threat or two, they heard the footsteps retreating down the steps.

'Shall we make ourselves scarce, my dear, tonight?'

'No, you idiot. Richard Dunn would not find us if we fled, and he would not put himself out if we weren't here to be paid, would he?'

Bezer sat back in his chair.

'Is there anything to eat, my love?' he said in a plaintive tone.

'Onion gruel,' she said. 'But we have the cheque for £5, haven't we? Don't give me that look. We'll eat better tomorrow.'

An hour later as they scraped the bowl for the last drops of the watery stuff, Susan suddenly thumped a hand on the table.

'The cheque, show it to me again,' she said, rising from the table and grabbing the paper.

She was peering at it closely and Bezer had no mental energy to speculate on what she might be thinking. He licked the bottom of the bowl again like a dog.

'Look,' said Susan sharply, laying the cheque before him.

She was pointing to the figure 5 and the space which lay behind it.

'Get the ink pot,' she said, clicking her fingers at him and pushing the empty bowls aside.

Bezer did as he was commanded and watched his wife dipping the quill a few times into the pot, testing the colour on a scrap of paper. She ordered him to bring a little water to dilute the colour, trying again and again, until she had matched the colour of the script on the cheque. Bezer watched, fascinated. Carefully, with fingers so delicate in movement that she could have stolen meat from a sleeping lion, Susan stroked the pen to create two noughts after the five. Next, she inserted the word 'hundred' after 'five'. The former word looked to Bezer just a jot smaller than the latter, but when Susan held it up for his inspection and as the ink dried, he was profoundly moved.

There were several other people in the bank, well-dressed gentlemen being attended by solicitous bank clerks behind the counter. Bezer and Susan had done their best to look like respectable and regular customers to such an establishment. In reality, Bezer was twitching with anxiety. Susan, on the other hand, appeared unperturbed by what she was about to do. Bezer watched nervously as the customer in front of them completed his business and left the clerk. He busied himself for some moments scribbling on papers, then looked up and saw Bezer and Susan waiting.

'May I help you, sir?'

Bezer was aware of the man's scrutiny of them as he and Susan moved to the counter.

'Actually, we are here on my wife's business,' Bezer said as casually as he could and turning to Susan. 'Come my dear, present your cheque to the clerk.'

Susan plunged her hand into her small velvet bag, an item she had saved so far from sacrifice at the pawnbroker's, and brought out the cheque with a flourish. The clerk took and examined it closely, adjusting his glasses.

'And you are Mrs Teresa Allen?' he said.

'Of course I am. Who do you think I am, Her Majesty the Queen and Empress of India?'

Bezer felt that this was perhaps not the appropriate tone to take with the man, but the clerk remained blank-faced.

'This is a very large sum of money,' he said.

Bezer's stomach churned, partly with nerves but also with indignation that he could no longer suppress.

'My wife, I will have you know, my man, has earned every penny of this,' he said with a disdainful glance at this little upstart.

'And how has she done that?' he asked, with an undisguised smirk.

'Gowns,' said Susan sharply, adopting the story they had agreed on the night before. 'I am a costumier to many of the most fashionable ladies in town. This cheque is drawn from the account of Lady Montmorency of Oxford. She ordered a large number of gowns for herself and her daughters.'

The clerk looked at the cheque again, then stood up.

'I will have to consult the Chief Clerk. Wait here a moment, please.'

Bezer wondered if this might be the moment to make a hasty escape, but Susan's determined expression and the prospect of their imminent penury, kept him standing there beside her. He looked around the banking hall, pretending casual observation of the architectural features, which he had to admit were splendid: marble pillars supported an ornate plasterwork ceiling, with intricate frieze. His admiring survey was interrupted, however, by the arrival of a grey-haired, serious looking individual, the Chief Clerk, followed by the clerk.

'Good day sir, madam,' he said, nodding politely at each in turn, a courtesy which Bezer found immediately reassuring.

'Mr and Mrs Allen, the cheques are to be cleared tomorrow in the clearing house at Lubbocks Bank. Monies can be paid out after that. If you would be good enough to return in two days' time, we will be able to complete the transaction.'

Chapter 14

'Mrs Brown,' said the Duke to Hannah, 'I believe that I should give you my best wishes and congratulate Dr Brown on your recent nuptials.'

Angela saw Hannah bow her head, acknowledging this courtesy. The wedding had been a quiet affair and Angela still had to remind herself that this woman, who had been closer to her than any other person through her youth and into adulthood, now had a separate life. But she also knew that Hannah's loyalty and their friendship were too profound to be disrupted even by her marriage.

'And I believe that you are still to be regular visitor to Miss Coutts,' he said, glancing at Angela, who was sitting beside Hannah, stroking the silky coat of Fan, who was sitting in her lap.

Angela smiled. 'Yes, wasn't it fortuitous that the house next door became available just at the right moment? Now I need never be parted from Hannah.'

The Duke's expression remained one of benign acceptance of a fact that he could do nothing to alter. He turned pointedly to Angela, the angle of his head excluding Hannah from their conversation. It troubled Angela that the Duke, though always courteous to Hannah, seemed to consider her to be of the servant class. Angela was determined, however, that the bonds of love between herself and Hannah would never be severed, in spite of Angela's growing regard for the Duke.

Recently, he had become very tender towards her, so affectionate and attentive, that Angela sometimes thought that what she was feeling might be in the realms of romantic love. True, he was old enough to be her father and perhaps this affection filled a void left by that parent's death. But the stirrings in her breast, the thrill in expectation of his visits, were sensations she had never experienced in relation to any other man. The Duke's dignity and power showed in his face and figure, and were those of a much younger man, the kind of qualities that if he had been younger, would have been commended to her by those who would have her married. The Duke also had no other motive for his attentions, other than his regard for her, which was far from the case of the younger men who had attempted to woo her. She valued his support, advice and revelled in his fascinating accounts of his military and political life. He had even intervened and smoothed the disagreements she had had with Mr Marjoribanks about her pressure to improve the pay and conditions of the clerks at Coutts Bank. He was a powerful ally and a dear friend and these stronger urges that she felt caused a certain confusion and embarrassment that she would never admit.

He was taking tea with Angela and Hannah in the drawing room, where the old parrot had greeted his arrival with its favourite squawk, 'More blooming letters.' They laughed and the dog Fan frolicked around the Duke in the hope of receiving some sweet offering.

'Actually, I have had a letter today with some very sad news,' Angela told the Duke. 'It's about a very worthy and learned man, a master at the Ragged School in Field Lane. He has passed away, very suddenly, of a malady of the lungs.'

'Not that pawnbroker fellow you took on?' said the Duke.

'No, it was Mr Greaves, the first schoolmaster. His wife informed me. She is mistress to the girls that attend the school. She and her late husband were responsible for establishing the place with Mr Dickens's support. It appears that the poor woman has returned to the school already, although she is in mourning.'

'Is that seemly?' said the Duke.

'Maybe not, but the woman has a strong sense of duty to the children, she and Mr Hines. They wish to keep the school open, though it is hard with only two.'

'Well, I hope another master can be found,' said the Duke. 'It is a worthy mission, to teach the illiterate scum of the earth to read and count. More able ones among them can be set to rudimentary work in support of industry. Such dedication to the welfare of the lower orders is highly commendable, my dear Miss Coutts.'

He smiled, indicating that he wished to change the subject.

'I have a present for you, my dear,' he said. 'Mrs Brown, would you ring for Coleman and have him bring it to us?'

Angela felt a surge of excitement. They had exchanged small gifts in the past, but this was evidently something of significance. She kissed her dog's head as a child might do in anticipation of a birthday gift. A short time later, the butler appeared.

'Coleman, be so good as to bring up the present for Miss Coutts,' the Duke said to him.

'My dear,' said the Duke, looking intently at Angela, leaning closer, 'you look very well today. I believe that we have known each other long enough now for you to call me Arthur, that is if I may call you Angela, when we are in private of course.'

Angela feeling a flush on her face, smiled. 'Of course,' she said, like some silly girl at her first ball.

When Coleman returned, he was carrying a small creature enfolded in a blanket. The thing was wriggling in his arms and he was struggling to control the look of distaste on his face. He edged towards Angela and bent down, with the bundle held towards her, lifting the flap of the blanket to reveal a small terrier pup that poked out its curious pointed little nose at Angela.

'Oh, my goodness,' Angela said, her face glowing at the sight of the small creature. 'Hannah, would you take Fan for me, please?'

The dog Fan responded to the intrusion with a yelp, then leapt from Angela's lap, shaking himself with hurt at his displacement by this interloper.

'My groom's bitch had a litter with some to spare,' said the Duke, as Angela took the puppy from its wrapping and held it to her cheek.

'Oh... oh... oh,' she squealed a moment later, laughing, holding the little dog at arm's length as it trickled on to the carpet and on to the edge of Angela's gown. 'Take it, take it, Coleman... and get a maid to clean this up.'

Coleman's lip curled as he took the puppy, holding it as if it had the plague, while the Duke roared with laughter. The parrot, aroused by the outburst, squawked, hopping from foot to foot.

'What a shocking bad hat! What a shocking bad hat!' it shrieked.

Angela and Hannah wept with laughter at this scene of a mad menagerie in the drawing room.

When all was calmer and they had taken tea, the Duke left and Angela sat contentedly with her new pet on her lap. Fan sulked in the corner with his muzzle on his paws, his eyes fixed on his cruel mistress. Hannah rose to take her leave, excusing herself on the grounds of having to instruct the cook about dinner.

'Shall I call a maid to take the dogs?' Hannah said.

'Yes, thank you, my dear,' Angela said.

At that moment, however, there was a knock at the door and one of the housemaids entered with a tray on which was a letter for Miss Coutts. Hannah relieved Angela of the sleeping pup so that she might open the letter.

'Thank you, Betty,' she said to the maid. 'You may take the dogs for supper.'

At that word Fan leapt up and Hannah handed the new arrival over to the maid, who left with Fan trotting at her heels. Hannah stayed, however, curious about Angela's correspondence, as it frequently involved work for her.

Angela picked up the envelope and examined the handwriting, recognising it as Mr Marjoribanks'.

'It's probably his latest thoughts on the matter of the bank clerks' pay,' Angela said. 'I really thought I had won that battle. Those poor men are trying to bring up families on ten shillings a week. I shall not give up.'

However, on opening the letter, Angela discovered instead a cryptic message.

'It is indeed from Mr Marjoribanks,' she said, looking at Hannah. 'He requests that I come and see him as a matter of urgency. Perhaps he hopes to wear me down with his objections.'

Hannah smiled.

'He should know better than to do that,' she said, 'particularly now that you have the Duke on your side.'

Angela and Hannah took a cab to the bank for the appointment with Mr Majoribanks the next day. Coutts and Co conducted business from an elegant premises on the Strand, designed by the famous architect of the previous century, Mr Nash. A black-coated doorman greeted them and led them across the spacious central hall, illuminated by light flooding in from the stained glass upper windows. Angela was always impressed by the grandeur of the place on her occasional visits, with its intricately patterned plasterwork ceiling and Italianate floor tiles and marble pillars, more suited to a palace than a bank. Coutts and Co, as the bank of royalty, the aristocracy and gentry, reflected the wealth and power of its customers.

Mr Marjoribanks was reservedly polite, and Angela was ready to continue her arguments for an improvement in the working conditions of the poorly paid bank clerks. This was not a mission that she would relinquish easily and Mr Marjoribanks knew to his cost about Angela's quiet determination in such matters. In the banker's spacious office, Angela offered her hand and he invited them to sit. Angela sensed from Mr Marjoribanks's demeanour that today's meeting was of a different character. He hesitated before speaking.

'Miss Coutts, I am sorry to have to impart some surprising and distressing information to you. I have received a letter from a certain person. a Mr Richard Dunn, making some statements –.'

Angela gasped, unnerved by the mention of that name. The violence of her reaction shocked her, as though her mind and body had suddenly fallen out of her control. She found herself struggling to breathe.

'Miss Coutts, are you unwell?' Mr Marjoribanks said, rising from his seat.

Angela felt Hannah take her hand and heard her ask Mr Marjoribanks if he could order some tea or cordial.

'Of course,' said Mr Marjoribanks picking up a bell from his desk and ringing it sharply.

'Be calm, my dear,' said Hannah. 'The man cannot harm you. Believe me.'

Angela let out her breath and dabbed her mouth with Hannah's proffered handkerchief.

'I'm sorry,' Angela said, with an effort. 'It was the shock of hearing of this man again. He means to make me appear in court, I assume.'

A moment later a clerk came into the office and was instructed to bring tea and a glass of brandy forthwith. Hannah, still holding Angela's hand, resumed her seat. She told Mr Marjoribanks about Richard Dunn's pestering and intrusive activities and his recent demand that Angela appear in court. Two men had been arrested on a charge of assault against Dunn.

'He has harassed Miss Coutts on countless occasions, in spite of the involvement of the law in punishing his crimes.'

'Dear God, Miss Coutts,' said the banker. 'What a dreadful ordeal for you. We must take action against him, for he is now making further claims about you.'

Angela, who had recovered herself sufficiently to respond, told Mr Marjoribanks that she had already engaged the services of her solicitor to deal with the troublesome fellow. The clerk brought in a tray of refreshments and after Angela had drunk a little of the tea, she had regained her composure.

'I'm so sorry, Mr Marjoribanks, for that show of weakness. I am myself again and I need to know the nature of this latest communication.'

The banker glanced at Hannah, as though seeking some sign from her about whether it was safe to comply with Angela's request.

'Please, I promise that there will be no more outbursts or fainting fits,' Angela said. 'I wish to be informed of the whole story, no matter what.'

The banker opened the drawer in his desk and drew out a folded paper and read it out to them in a slow and deliberate voice.

6 Stratton Street

Sir,

I write to you on a matter relating to Miss Angela Coutts, a lady who gave me reason to believe that she held me in an affectionate regard. Acting on these signals and my own powerful feelings, I respectfully pressed my suit as a gentleman. Such overtures as I made were rudely and viciously rebuffed by various people in the lady's company or service.

However, my passion was so unflinching that I was compelled to seek an audience with Miss Coutts, who I knew without doubt was ready to succumb to my requests. I knew this when I received a letter from her expressing her regret for my rough treatment, declaring her devotion to me and offering me a sum of money as compensation for the wrongs I had suffered for her sake.

Sir, if you have reason to doubt the veracity of my claim, I will be only too pleased to bring Miss Coutts's letter for you to examine, when I present myself at the bank to collect the monies owed to me. It is with profound regret that, should Miss Coutts deny these truths, then I shall be obliged to take out a court summons for her to be charged with breach of contract.

I am yours respectfully
Richard Dunn, Barrister at law

'This is an outrage,' Hannah burst out.

Angela shook her head, now feeling oddly detached, almost numb, in spite of the enormity of the claim in the letter.

'These are absolute lies, Mr Marjoribanks, in every detail,' she said calmly.

'I take it you have never made such a statement of intent to this man, Miss Coutts,' said Mr Marjoribanks.

'Never,' said Angela. 'I have never offered him anything, given him any promises, or assurances spoken or written. It is a fantasy on his part.'

'And how much is the sum of money that this rogue is claiming Miss Coutts promised him?' Hannah said.

The banker raised his eyebrows. '£100,000,' he said.

'The man is clearly mad,' said Angela, reassured that this monstrous and ridiculous claim was proof enough of the fact.

'He must be stopped,' Hannah said.

Hannah's alarm and Mr Marjoribank's solemn expression, made Angela aware of the dangers presented by someone suffering from such delusions.

'I agree,' said the banker. 'If he brings himself here, I shall tell him that we have taken this matter to law ourselves. I shall demand to see the letter, which is certainly a forgery. My staff who know your hand will also examine it. This might be sufficient to make him turn tail. If he is a forger and discovered to be one, the penalty is very severe. He will not risk that. However, I think it would be wise to contact your solicitor too.'

Angela nodded, reassured by the banker's robust response. Hannah took her by the arm and together they re-entered the banking hall and awaited the cab that had been ordered for them. On arriving home, Angela was suddenly afflicted by the onset of a terrible faintness and palpitations which forced her to retire to bed. She gave herself into the hands of Hannah and her maids and soon succumbed to sleep, induced by a medicine administered by Dr Brown, who had been called as a matter of urgency to attend her.

Chapter 15

The woman, Marianne Greaves, was still sunk in the depths of her grieving. Nathan had known that state too well and sometimes, even now, would feel the sorrow dragging him down. He and she were managing to maintain the lessons at the Ragged School, although sometimes there was little productive learning and the children's attention could not be harnessed successfully to engage in their activities. Nathan, exasperated one day by the noise, burst out angrily at the boys.

'For the sake of heaven, sit and listen and learn! Do you wish to be ignorant for ever? Be quiet!'

Ned, who had been attempting to calm the more rowdy boys, grabbed two who were engaged in a scuffle by the hair and pulled them apart. The others, shocked by Nathan's outburst shrank down on the forms or on the floor at his feet.

Nathan, surprised by the effect of his anger, and shaken by it himself, breathed deeply and stared at the boys. He hoped that this quelling of their impudence would endure for at least part of the day.

'Now boys, we will start our lesson again, in an orderly way. You will sit and listen, answer when spoken to. If you don't, you will get nothing to eat.'

He hated himself for making this threat but he knew that such a measure would be the only sure way of establishing order. He put

Ned in charge of a small group of boys and appointed another monitor, James, a thin boy, taller than the rest, who seemed as quick as Ned in his learning. Marianne had gathered her girls in the corner for reading. Nathan regretted that she too would have witnessed his loss of composure, but he hoped that she might overlook this because of the circumstances.

The pace of learning was painfully slow, Nathan reflected, with only a small number of children showing any progress at all in reading and arithmetic. Some were too hungry or listless to concentrate and others too wayward and inattentive, like small scavenging dogs, trotting from one whiff of food to another. He wondered frequently about whether what they were doing was of any value whatsoever. Would the lives of these children be changed as a result of a year or so attending a Ragged School? He doubted it. As the boys were now quietly working on the sums that Nathan had given them, he looked over at Marianne Greaves standing by the blackboard and with her pointer taking the girls through a short piece of verse, written in her immaculate hand.

Tyger, tyger burning bright,
In the forests of the night,
What immortal hand or eye
Could frame thy fearful symmetry?

Though the woman was pale with fatigue, all colour drained from her face by her black mourning dress, she could, even in her state of bereavement, regard her pupils with care and concern, almost with love, it seemed. One girl read the verse in its entirety, haltingly. Nathan watched Marianne's face reflecting her pleasure at the girl's achievement. The child's expression was of pure joy. This was all there was, he realised, small triumphs insignificant beyond the narrow limits of this place, irrelevant in the outside world. He would expend no more energy in bewailing the weight of the disadvantage under which these children and so many others laboured. Instead, he would work for what was, in small ways, achievable.

He decided at that moment to propose to Ned that he should present himself for a position as a grocer's errand boy in a shop not far from Nathan's own. He had seen the notice in the shop window that morning. It was a neat and well-kept place, owned by a Mr Gladwell, with his shining bald head and immaculate white apron. Nathan knew the grocer slightly and his wife, who worked alongside him in the shop. So, at the end of the school day, Nathan called to Ned, who was stacking the Bibles back upon the shelves.

'I have seen an opportunity for you, Ned,' he said, telling the boy about the vacancy.

'Nah, I couldn't work for no grocer,' he said, squirming as he stood in front of Nathan, his eyes on the floor.

'Why not?'

'Wouldn't take the likes of me.'

'What do you mean?' Nathan said. 'You can count, read and calculate. You can run, you can carry things, can't you? You can do as you're told?'

Ned scratched his head, glanced at Nathan then away again. Nathan had to admit that the boy's appearance was against him. In the time he'd been working at the Ragged School he had become accustomed to the sight and smell of unwashed clothing and bodies. Marianne Greaves was putting on her hat and coat in readiness to leave and Nathan caught her eye.

'Mrs Greaves, we need your advice,' he said. 'Do you think Ned would make a good errand boy?'

She paused and considered them both for a moment, then approached.

'Yes, I do,' she said, looking at Nathan, knowing what was in his mind. 'But he would need to smarten up a bit, some new clothes maybe and a good scrub of his face and hands.'

Ned submitted himself to the wet cloth wielded by Marianne Greaves when Nathan brought it and a bowl of water and a little soap. Nathan then fetched his son's clothes from the bag he had brought previously. There were no shoes, but Ned had a filthy scuffed pair. Marianne looked doubtfully at them, picked them up and finding the butt end of a tallow candle, softened it and rubbed it over the shoes, then buffed them with a rag. Nathan exchanged a look with her, a shared approval of their action.

'So, Ned, do you think you could be an errand boy now?' Nathan said, looking at the child they had transformed.

As Nathan walked to Fleet Street with Ned at his side, he felt a flutter in his chest at the sight of this child in his son's clothes. The two, he realised, could have been father and son returning from their day's occupation.

'You must promise to be honest,' Nathan said to him as they made their way to the shop. 'Mr Gladwell will need to be able to trust you. And you will always be polite to customers.'

'Or I'll get a bashing?'

Nathan shook his head, though in truth he knew little about Mr Gladwell, beyond his apparently mild-mannered demeanour.

'Only if you did something bad. I'll tell him your character, Ned and you must live up to it, remember.'

Ned fell silent and Nathan was struck with doubt about whether he had been wise to persuade this boy to go along with his scheme. The boy knew nothing about service to others; his only work had been begging, scrounging and scavenging in the streets. His family, Nathan suspected, lived on the edge of criminality. Yet, how else could this child climb his way out of poverty? Nathan suppressed his doubts about his motives and pressed on.

The opening of the shop door, *Gladwell's Quality Foods*, set a bell tinkling and caused Mr Gladwell, who was standing behind the counter, to look up. The tidy shelves were well-packed with stone pots and glass jars showing their contents, and packets with numerous labels. On a small separate counter, at right angles to the main one, was a marble slab with half a haunch of cured ham.

'Good afternoon, Mr Gladwell,' Nathan said, ushering Ned closer to the counter. 'I believe that you are in need of an errand boy.'

Gladwell narrowed his eyes and peered at Ned then back at Nathan.

'Yes, Mr Hines,' he said, 'that is the case. I take it you have brought me a likely lad.'

Nathan nodded. 'This is Ned Burrows. He is a pupil of mine and I can vouch for his diligence and reliability.'

Ned's leg had started twitching, Nathan noticed and he was gazing at the shelves in a mixture of longing and terror. Mr Gladwell pursed his lips as he examined Ned.

'Well, you're smart enough to look at, from the outside, but what are you like inside, my lad? That's the principal question,' said Mr Gladwell. 'Are you a good, Christian boy? Where do you live? Who are your parents?'

Nathan's hope shrank away at the man's questions. Ned stood mutely as he had when Miss Coutts had first addressed him at the school that day. His answers, if he gave them at all, were likely to condemn him. Nathan was unsure whether to prompt the boy or stay silent. Fortunately, both he and Ned were relieved of the need to say anything, as Mrs Gladwell suddenly appeared through a doorway behind the marble counter. She was a solid-looking woman with a pleasant, plump face, maybe the result of too much indulgence in some of their own merchandise.

'What have we got here? Good day to you, Mr Hines,' she said, looking from Nathan to Ned and then to her husband. 'Is this a boy looking for a place then?'

'Yes,' said Gladwell, 'but he hasn't got a lot to say for himself.'

His wife let out a chuckle, looking Ned up and down. 'That's good. I don't like backchat in a boy, nor impudence. So, will you speak to me then?'

If only they had asked him to multiply six by nine or to spell his name, the boy would have answered swiftly and correctly.

'Ned can read and count,' said Nathan quickly, touching the boy on the shoulder and pointing to the shelves behind the counter. 'Read the names on those labels, Ned.'

'Borax Dry Soap, Brown and Polson's Paisley Flour, Cod Liver Oil, Hot Mustard, Borwick's Five Gold Medal Baking Powder, Oxo,' Ned said, without a second's hesitation.

Mrs Gladwell let out her breath. 'Well, he's a clever one, a bright spark, and he comes on your recommendation Mr Hines?'

Nathan nodded.

'Ned is an able pupil, helpful around the schoolroom too, supervising the smaller boys, clearing up at the end of the day.'

'That's good enough for me,' said Mrs Gladwell. 'What do you think, George?'

Gladwell, apparently unmoved by his wife's appeal, looked at Ned again.

'Well, boy. It seems, I need to give you a try, but we'll see if you can step up to the mark. Only a week to start with, you understand.'

Nathan glanced at Ned, who looked stunned for a moment, though his hand fidgeted with the edge of the unfamiliar jacket as though he had something to say. Nathan, guessing what this pressing matter was, spoke up.

'And you'll pay him for his work, for the week and beyond, if he acquits himself well?' Nathan said.

Gladwell sucked in his lips.

'We can pay three shillings a week and his dinner each day,' he said.

Ned's eyes widened and Nathan saw his mouth twitch. He nodded at the couple and agreed to start at six o'clock the next day.

Mr Gladwell wagged a finger at Ned, as they made ready to depart.

'Make sure you're on time and your hands are clean. You'll be helping me stack the shelves and pack the deliveries. The carter comes at half past seven.'

Nathan thanked the couple and exhorted Ned to express his gratitude, which he managed to mumble sheepishly.

Outside on the street, they walked along for a moment or two in silence.

'Have I got it then?' Ned said. 'A place in a shop?'

Nathan nodded, praying that the boy would be able to maintain the position with satisfaction and that circumstances wouldn't conspire to destroy his chances.

'You have, Ned, but you must work hard and show what you can do, so that they keep you on. I'll come by and see how you're getting on. And tell your mother. She'll be proud.'

Ned grinned at him, then turned and ran back in the direction of the maze of streets, where he lived. Nathan, as he proceeded along the road, allowed himself to indulge in Ned's imagined future: some years as an errand boy and general dogsbody, then as counter assistant, learning the trade under the Mr and Mrs Gladwell's instruction, then to a partnership in a flourishing and lucrative business. Nathan arrived back in a more buoyant mood than he could remember for a long time. He greeted Silas, who was closing up the shop and invited him to accompany him to supper at *The Old Bell* which was serving its speciality that evening of eel pie. Silas hurried to close the shutters, looking inordinately pleased with the invitation.

The next day, Nathan walked past Gladwell's and was gratified to see, as he glanced through the window, Ned in his shirtsleeves lifting a wooden crate of groceries from the counter. Nathan silently wished the boy well, though he knew that he would also miss him from the schoolroom.

Although it was before the hour when school began, Nathan wanted to prepare for the day, finding a text for reading and writing up sums on the blackboard. He found the entrance door already unlocked and at first thought that there must be an intruder who had picked the lock and gained entry, as only he and Marianne Greaves had keys to the place. It was only after he had glanced around that he saw the woman in the far corner. She had not heard the sound of his arrival and gave no indication that she had noticed his presence. She was sitting on a stool, head bent over something she was holding in her lap. Nathan, reluctant to invade her solitude, moved quietly to the other end of the room, hearing a muffled sob. She was, he assumed, overcome by some reminder of her dead husband. He knew that sensation well himself, realising now that he thought about it, that the tender, raw pain was now a dull ache. Sometimes, however, the protective cloak that smothered the sharpness of his memory was pulled aside, revealing those terrible last scenes again.

He turned and heard her weeping, small, plaintive cries escaping from her. He knew that slackening, those weak moments which could not be forestalled, when grief returned as intensely as at first. He went to her, and she, seeing him, rose, flustered, pulling a handkerchief from her pocket, dabbing her face, though her pain drew him closer to her. He wanted only to take a share of her woe, join it to his, which was healing now, and soothe her thus. He took her in his arms and she leaned her cheek against his chest, while with one hand he stroked her hair.

Silas was agitated by something when Nathan came home from the Ragged School and for a while, he seemed reluctant to reply to questioning.

'A woman came in, with a –. Well, I gave her three shillings for it. Desperate, she was. A child's but–'

'What's wrong with you Silas?' Nathan said puzzled and disturbed by his friend's incoherence.

But by now, Silas had disappeared into the storeroom and returned a moment later holding a jacket, the one that had belonged to his son, the one that he had given to Ned.

'I recognised it,' said Silas, 'but the woman, she said she had children to feed.'

Nathan breathed deeply to steady himself from the shock of seeing this garment again and of what its reappearance signified.

'Said she'd redeem it next week,' said Silas.

'Let me see the ledger,' Nathan said.

Silas opened the book on the counter and Nathan looked at the entry for the pawned jacket. It was under the name Sarah Burrows, Ned's mother. She had pawned it already and the boy had hardly been more than a day at work. Nathan recalled his glimpse of Ned in his shirtsleeves at work in Gladwell's shop and had assumed that he had removed his jacket for the purposes of manhandling loads. He looked at the address that the woman had given to Silas and felt anger building in his chest.

'Did I do wrong?' Silas said.

'No, don't think that, but I must go and see the woman,' Nathan said, picking up the jacket from the counter and going quickly out of the shop.

As he walked, his frustration simmered. How could a parent thwart her child's fragile chance of employment, even when this offered an income to the family? For short term gain, Ned's mother had reduced his opportunity to be kept on. What would the Gladwells think of a boy without proper clothing? How would he manage in colder weather? The idea occurred to Nathan that he might go first to Gladwell's and give the jacket back to Ned. However, he did not wish to confront the boy in his place of work and thus reveal to his employer the unscrupulous nature of the mother. So, he proceeded to the place given by the woman.

It was indeed a poor, dark place, close to Field Lane, with tenements and shacks erected in gaps between the brick buildings, where previous dwellings or shops had collapsed or been demolished. He found what he thought was the door of the house on the street. A small window at the front was hung with sacking. He knocked hard on the door. There was no reply. He looked around and found the street deserted, as though the inmates were hiding like rabbits from a predator. He knocked again and standing close to the door called for Mrs Burrows. There was absolutely no sound from within and Nathan was about to give up his quest, wondering what sort of activity the woman and any other inhabitants were engaged in that would take them out at this hour.

Turning to go, he was startled to find a small girl, who had appeared suddenly to within a few yards of him. She was carrying a wooden tray held by a strap around her neck, of the type worn by street sellers. On it lay a few small bundles of shrivelled flowers. A glance at her face reflected back a likeness of Ned too defined to be denied.

'Good evening,' Nathan said. 'Are you Ned's sister?'

The girl eyed him and the jacket which he was holding in his hand, but said nothing.

'I'd like to speak with your mother,' Nathan said.

Still the child just stared and said nothing, though her eyes flitted around and she edged back a little from him. He remembered the other young girl who had successfully evaded his pursuit. This one was much younger and frailer than the other and looked hardly capable of such an escape.

'I mean you no harm. I am Ned's schoolmaster,' he said gently.

The girl's face changed. The eyes softened and her mouth twitched with excitement.

'Will you learn me to read like Ned?' she said.

Nathan, taken aback, couldn't help smiling.

'Maybe, if you'll take me to see your mother.'

'This way,' she said, with no hesitation and turned back, walking a few yards to a rotting wooden door, which she pushed open. Nathan followed the girl into a dark passageway, except that it brought them instead to another door and thence into a poky hole of a room that served as living quarters.

'Ma,' the child said. 'There's a man here wants you.'

In the corner, Nathan made out a woman sitting with a heap of dried foliage of some sort in front of her and some scraps of ribbon on the floor beside them. A small child of around two or three was sitting on the floor and stared at him with round dark eyes in a white face. The woman looked up, with the same sick white face as her child. Her hair was ragged, her body tied with a miscellany of faded garments. She peered at him and at the jacket he was holding, while the girl dumped her tray at her mother's feet then went to sit by the smaller child on the floor.

'What do you want?' said the woman sourly. 'What do you mean bringing that?'

Nathan introduced himself and the woman looked away, shifting where she sat.

'Yes, he's told me about you. He's told me about –.'

She was shaking her head, staring down at the pile of dried flowers in front of her.

'Ned needs this jacket for his job,' Nathan said more sternly that he had intended. 'He must be properly dressed if he's to keep his place. He must have it back.'

The woman looked up at him again, with a tight, angry face.

'Think I don't know? I had rent to pay else

we'd be out on the street, all of us. Is that what you want?'

Nathan swallowed, ashamed. 'With Ned's wage, you'll be better off, surely.'

'And it's you done it all, ain't it?' she said.

Nathan shifted awkwardly on his feet. He didn't want the woman's thanks, if that was what she meant by her question.

'Ned's a bright boy. He could make something of himself,' Nathan said, desperately, smelling the damp sourness of the room, seeing the black trails of water staining the walls.

The woman stretched out her hand to him. Nathan hesitated, though he knew that he had no choice but to give up the jacket to her and trust that she would return it to Ned.

'How did you get this anyway?' she said fingering the cloth.

'You pawned it in my shop,' he said, 'and my assistant recognised it.'

'Never,' said the woman. 'You're never one of these dolly shop men. You don't look the part.'

Her mouth twitched. Was it with amusement?

'Well, you'll have to wait for your money, Mr Pawnbroker or Mr Schoolmaster or whatever you are,' she said, 'just till Ned gets his first wages.'

Nathan shook his head. 'There is no need to pay.'

She peered at him again.

'I'll take it to a different shop next time,' she said with a twisted grin.

The shock and disapproval must have been visible on Nathan's face as the woman snorted.

'No, I'll not do it unless I've got to. But see, I've got no husband and just Connie here sells flowers and Ned does street sweeping and running errands sometimes, when he's not off book learning with you. I know he's got brains, the boy. His Pa would've been proud of him with his reading and counting. But me, I'm only good for sorting the flowers now, since my legs are no use to me.'

Nathan could say no more. He could throw more hollow words of advice or exhortation at this woman, about how toiling hard would raise herself and her family from this state. It would have been an affront, a futile and patronising suggestion. Ned, he realised was her only hope and she knew this too. He left, dispirited by this encounter and at his judgemental intention in visiting the woman. This thought strengthened in him a determination to look out for the boy. By doing this maybe he might save more than one.

Nathan returned to the shop too late to see Silas, who had locked up and gone home to his lodgings. He ate a meagre supper and went to bed, only to fall into a sleep that was disturbed frequently by a return of the spectres that had haunted him and those prompted by the encounters of the day.

Unrested and troubled by his dreams, he woke early the next day and set off for school before his usual hour. On his way, he thought about Marianne Greaves. He remembered how he had held her as she wept for the husband she had lost and how their shared sorrows had seemed to comfort them both. Another recollection which troubled him, however, was his awareness of the shape of her body in his arms, the pleasure of holding another human being close, a woman. Such feeling smarted with the pain of disloyalty to his dead wife; shame knotted itself inside him. It was also crude and unseemly to take into his arms a recent widow in mourning who was not a relative. He tried to deny to himself, as he walked, that he was looking forward to seeing Marianne Greaves again today.

On arriving at the school, he found the door already open again and, expecting that Marianne was already there, he went in. She looked up and smiled as he entered, breaking off from her busy action of straightening the tables and forms and re-positioning one of the blackboards. Her face was a little flushed with the exertion, but also with excitement.

'Good morning, Mr Hines,' she said. 'I have just received a message about a visitor to the school today.'

'Really?' Nathan said, wondering if she was referring to Miss Coutts.

Marianne looked at him, picked up a couple of books that were lying on one of the tables and clutched them to her chest.

'It is such a privilege. Mr Charles Dickens is coming here.'

Nathan knew that the writer had been a moving force behind the establishment of the

Ragged School and had persuaded Miss Coutts to support it with financial aid. It was to this that Nathan owed his new found career. He knew of Dickens's works however, only by reputation. However, clearly Marianne Greaves was one of his enthusiastic readers. So they discussed the best way of receiving their visitor while managing the children.

'Maybe he will bring us word of a new teacher too,' said Marianne. 'But have you read any of his works?'

Nathan strongly wished that he had, though he remembered an article written by Dickens that appeared in *The Morning Chronicle* in which he denounced the incompetence of the administration of parish relief. Here was a public figure, of considerable celebrity, who was speaking out for the impoverished underclasses, the needy, the ignorant and desperate in society. Nathan felt some of Marianne's admiration for the man too.

At ten o'clock, Charles Dickens arrived, alone, dressed very smartly, almost showily, with a coloured silk stock, patterned waistcoat, his hair quite long and a little unkempt, his features strong and confident. He walked with the air of one in his prime. The children stared, two boys giggled and pointed at his outfit.

'It's excellent to see such an orderly congregation of children,' said Dickens scanning the many heads of the children. He shook hands vigorously with Nathan and bowed to Marianne who curtsied, her cheeks reddening again, bringing a bloom to her appearance that Nathan had not seen in her before.

'Now, may I speak to some of the children?' Dickens said.

He proceeded to circulate amongst them, engaging some in conversation. Nathan heard one boy remark that Dickens couldn't be a barber as his hair needed a good cut. Another asked him what a 'toff' was doing here. He laughed loudly at their comments, then asked for a demonstration of what they had learned in school. Two boys recited some multiplication tables and another girl was able to spell all the words that Dickens called out to her. Other children, overawed, mutely stared at this strange, exuberant man moving among them. The children grew more restive, having discovered that their visitor was more of an entertainer than a threat.

At Marianne's suggestion, Mr Dickens agreed to read an extract from one of his books to the children. Nathan was unsure whether this was wise, but was soon reassured when Marianne handed him a book and he strode to a position in front of the waiting crowd of children. Nathan and Marianne ushered the few straying boys into the fold and there was a strangely full and expectant silence.

Then the writer started, in a sonorous voice signalling the beginning of his story, except that it was a preamble, explaining how the cruel miser Scrooge detested Christmas celebrations as he did the world and everyone in it. The storyteller revelled in his central role, his power to bind his audience as though by a spell, just as the miserable Scrooge is terrified by the first apparition that appears to him in his bedchamber. Nathan found himself entranced, as the children were. This man had the ability with his voice to re-create the very creaks and groans of the floorboards, the thick, dark terror of the bedchamber, the delicacy of the wavering candle flame. The children, though some had little idea of the message of the story, were rapt all the same by the magic of the teller and the atmosphere he created. Some were frightened, grabbing hold of the arm of the nearest boy and others watched open-mouthed and astonished. The reading came to an end, in a heavy cadence, with promise of the further visitations to the miser. The author, thankfully, explained to the children that Scrooge was changed by his experiences, utterly, to become a generous, gleeful soul devoted to the relief of the poor and hungry.

After Mr Dickens had left, there followed a hiatus of stunned silence, which remained for a time, albeit a short one. Then the Sisters of Mercy, in an apt enactment of their name, arrived with food to distribute, to satisfy the bodily hunger of those who had had their spirits filled.

'I must read Mr Dickens's works,' Nathan said to Marianne as she handed a basket of bread to one of the girls for distribution.

'Yes, you must. I have copies of everything that he has published. Books were our only extravagance. My husband would rather have gone without meat than books,' she said.

She handed Nathan the volumes that she had brought.

'Take these, Mr Hines.'

As he reached to receive them, he noticed as though for the first time the neat features of her face, the curve of her mouth, the small, feather-like lines around her eyes. He knew he was staring too long for comfort and looked away, thanking her for the books, taking them to the chair where his coat hung and placing them in his pockets. He glanced again at her from this safe distance and watched her breaking up a tussle between two boys over a piece of bread, then talking to one of her girls. Her manner was always gentle, even when delivering a rebuke. It was extraordinary how she managed to be stern without cruelty. He wondered at himself that he had not observed these qualities in her before now, but then he reflected that when he had first met her, she had been another man's wife.

Chapter 16

It was a busy day at the bank, for which Bezer was grateful. The presence of a goodly crowd always made him feel in a sense protected, offering as it did, a chance to disappear, should this prove necessary. Even Susan seemed tense, though as Bezer reminded himself, they stood on the brink of gaining a fortune. Was that not enough to throw anyone into a state of agitation and excitement? Bezer had spent many happy hours indulging his vision of their new life. They would take a house in Piccadilly or the Strand, somewhere fitting to their new station and they would travel abroad, to Paris, Rome, Vienna even. Such imaginings had lifted his spirits as they had sat over their bowls of gruel the previous evening.

Susan suddenly gripped his arm and pointed to one of the bank clerks who was beckoning them forward. It was not usual for his wife to hang on to him, as though in need of protection. She had never seemed to require it at all, in fact, though it offended his manly pride to admit, it was he who relied entirely upon her. Now here was she, clinging to him, as they moved forward to the desk clerk. Bezer suppressed his anxiety on this count by the thought that it could be part of her act.

'Good day,' said Bezer straining to adopt a cheerful tone. 'My wife, Mrs Allen has business with you.'

The clerk raised his eyebrows and looked

them up and down.

'And how may I assist you?'

'I have come for my money,' Susan said, firmly. 'I brought a cheque two days ago, from Lady Montmorency of Oxford for services rendered.'

'We were instructed to come here after clearing,' said Bezer attempting a tone of authority.

'Ah,' said the clerk. 'You are Mr and Mrs Allen, are you not? The cheque was to be drawn on the account of Lady Montmorency and for how much, may I ask?'

'£500,' Susan said, though Bezer noted a slight quiver as she pronounced the sum. 'A couturier, that's what I am, gowns for ladies and such like.'

'£500? And how many gowns would that buy?' said the clerk.

Bezer saw specks of pink appear on Susan's cheeks. 'It's not any of your affair how many gowns I've sold.'

The clerk showed no sign of contrition for his forward remark. In fact, with a furtive glance over his shoulder, he seemed exceedingly dilatory in his service to them.

'£500, you say?' he said, pursing his lips.

A terrified sense of anticipation seized Bezer. What was wrong with the fellow that he had to keep repeating things? Was he deaf or simply an imbecile?'

'Please wait here,' the clerk said, rising quickly from his seat.

Bezer, aware of something thrumming in his

chest, watched the clerk go over to a desk on the other side of the banking hall, to the desk of another employee. This second man looked up, as though he were expecting the interruption.

Bezer glanced at Susan and patted her arm, in a weak attempt at reassurance.

'Well,' he said, trying to smile, 'he would hardly have £500 sitting under his desk, would he? He most likely has to get a superior to open the vault or strong box or something of that nature.'

Susan said nothing, her face fixed in a grim expression. She too had been following the movements of the clerk. Now they saw him whispering to his colleague, who rose from his desk and looked across directly at them. Bezer heard Susan emit something like a growl.

'Damn him to hell,' said Susan in a sharp whisper. 'The game's up. Let's quit while we can.'

Bezer, appalled at the suddenness of her instruction, hesitated, resisting the tug of her hand.

'But the money – we –, £500.'

'You fool, can't you see. They're not going to pay up.'

Bezer glanced again at the two men, saw them advancing, realised that Susan had gone from his side and was weaving her way quickly back through the queue of people awaiting attention. Bezer turned and plunged after her. He skidded and almost fell on the steps leading down on to the street, drawing indignant looks from two gentlemen whom he brushed past. Susan was now about fifty yards ahead of him, on the street, mingling with the crowd. Hot with fear, Bezer followed his wife, not daring to look behind. Someone could well be in pursuit by now, that clerk or even a constable. Puffing hard, Bezer gained on Susan and caught up with her at the corner of a side street on their left leading from Lombard Street in the direction of the river.

'Down here,' said Susan. 'There's a market.'

Her face was a lurid red, shining with sweat but she lurched down the side street, which was long and straight. At the end were just visible the canopies of some small stalls and the movement of people around them. Bezer stumbled on after her, on legs that felt ready to give way. At the end of the street, Susan stopped, her chest heaving, leaning against the wall of a house in the small square containing the market. Bezer joined her, wheezing, noting that they were well shielded from the view of anyone looking down the street. They stood for some time, gathering their breath, Bezer wondering whether his heart was truly going to explode in his chest.

'My dear one,' he said at last. 'Maybe the bank manager was bringing the money after all.'

'You stupid dolt,' Susan replied. 'Didn't you see what they were doing? They were ready and waiting for us. They were going to get us arrested. Did you want to wait there till we were seized?'

'No, no, my dearest,' Bezer said shakily, with the pulse still pounding his brain.

He looked at the market stalls and the people milling around. He noted too, a tent on the far side of the square, which appeared to be selling refreshments. A small stall outside attended by a woman, contained pastries and pies by the look of it.

'Do you have any money at all, my dear one?' Bezer said.

Susan stuffed her hand into the pocket of her gown and produced two threepenny bits.

'A pot of ale each,' she wheezed as they tottered towards the tent.

Inside were a number of tables and chairs, most occupied by shoppers or clerks of the lower sort. Bezer and Susan squeezed behind a table at the rear.

'What you having, Squire?' called the man in charge from behind his makeshift counter of a plank balanced on two kegs.

'Two cups of your best ale, if you please,' Bezer said, sliding gratefully down into his seat and whispering to Susan. 'We'll be safe here, won't we dearest?'

Susan snorted. 'Unless they send out a search party. But they don't know where we live, nor our names even. What's more, we've taken nothing, not from the Lady Montmorency nor from the bank, so what purpose would it serve to chase us?'

Bezer sighed, partly in relief but also with a horrible new sense of disappointment.

'We've received nothing either. We've even

lost the £5.'

He drank the ale gratefully and too quickly, gulping air which formed a knot in his gullet. They were well and truly sunk now, with all avenues to money cut off, their scribing business was lost too, as they could no longer pick up enquiries from *The Bear Inn* and neither had their recent begging letters borne any fruit. Even the exceedingly wealthy Miss Coutts hadn't coughed up. Sometimes, rich people were the most parsimonious on earth, he reflected. Susan, whose normal colour had returned, was clearly engaged in the same sort of miserable thoughts as he was, judging by the ugly downward curve of her mouth.

'What in the world can we do now, my dearest one?' Bezer said, creeping his hand towards hers over the table, to indulge in a more companionable sort of gloom. But a solution to their predicament was probably beyond even her powers of invention. She smacked his hand sharply, though Bezer hoped rather to announce an idea than to reprimand him.

'That man Dunn. He owes us for his letter, doesn't he?' she said.

'Yes, but I dread to say it, sweet one, I think he will not pay, even though he is in our debt. He is, I regret to admit, not entirely honest. Besides, we don't know where he lives, so we cannot appeal to him again.'

'It wouldn't be hard to find out,' Susan said. 'Didn't he say that he could see into Miss Coutts's room from his lodgings?'

'Yes, but–.'

'Then we must go to Stratton Street,' she said suddenly.' That's where she lives, isn't it?' As she spoke, she was peering at him, leaning over to pluck at the buttons on his chest. 'Your waistcoat. There's a shop on the way to Piccadilly.'

Bezer rose sadly from his seat, regretting already the loss of his last piece of respectable clothing - his waistcoat, which, though it was well-worn and a little stained, was about to be exchanged for a meagre shilling.

In fact, the waistcoat rendered them one shilling and sixpence, enough for an omnibus ride to Piccadilly and a muffin and ale in a coffee house on Stratton Street, where they hoped for an encounter with the Irishman. Susan suggested that they should sit and watch for a while, observing the people on the street, and if they had no sighting of the man, then they could make enquiries of the owner and even knock on a few doors nearby. They could see the entrance to Miss Coutts's large four storey house clearly from their vantage point and thus could work out which of the buildings opposite would afford a view into one of her apartments.

After an hour and a half at the table by the window, with the proprietor looking accusingly at them for their lengthy sojourn, Susan nudged Bezer and pointed towards the opposite side of the road. Amongst some pedestrians making their way along the pavement on the opposite side of the street, one figure stood out: tall, black-coated, unmistakably Richard Dunn, striding along in his top hat in a passing imitation of a gentleman.

'There's the blackguard,' whispered Susan, getting to her feet. 'I'll go out and see where he goes. It's best if he doesn't see us together. I don't think he'd recognise me. Meet me in ten minutes at the end of the street.'

Bezer watched her depart. She pulled her hat down over her brow and then disappeared out of sight. Bezer paid the proprietor and engaged him in a little talk that he thought might prove fruitful. He explained his wife's departure by saying that she had gone to purchase a few little items from *Dickens and Smith* on Regent Street before it closed.

'I was wondering,' remarked Bezer, 'if you happened to know an Irishman who lives somewhere in the vicinity.'

'Irishman? Too many of them by half, to my way of thinking,' said the man.

'Ah but this is a gentleman, an acquaintance of mine, a lawyer in fact, an educated man, not one of the riff-raff,' Bezer said.

'A lawyer, eh?'

'Yes, Dunn is his name. Do you happen to know him?'

The man snorted.

'Him? Now you mention it, he owes me half a crown. Said he'd pay me last week for the drinks I'd given him on tick,' said the man stabbing a finger at Bezer. 'So, when you see him, tell him I'm after him for the money and he'll not be welcome here unless he pays up.'

Bezer took a step back. 'Yes, I'll certainly tell him. Now do you happen to know which number he lives at? I forgot to take a note of it when last I saw him.'

The man scratched his head. 'One of those on the left, I reckon. You know, you could honour his debt, as he's a friend of yours. That'll be half a crown, sir.'

Bezer leapt away quickly, hat in hand, sidling to the door and pulling it open.

'No sir, not a friend exactly, an acquaintance as I said. I'm sure it's an oversight on his part.'

Bezer scuttled out and scampered off quickly down the street, casting a glance at the first door on the left. That could be the one, he surmised, then he glimpsed Susan about a hundred yards further down the street looking in a shop window. Richard Dunn must have crossed the road and entered his door without seeing Susan. He waved to his wife, beckoning her to come to him. She bustled up quickly to join him.

'Yes, it's this one,' she said in an undertone. 'I saw him going in. Go on then, knock on the door.'

Bezer hesitated. Now they had successfully tracked the man down, he felt a worrying cold feeling creeping over his body. Was it safe to go after such a one as he? There was something disturbing about his manner, about his obsession with the lady, Miss Coutts. If he had a weapon or if he decided to get violent, they were risking a hurt or worse.

'Dearest one,' Bezer said. 'I would not wish to put you in danger.'

She threw him a look of mild disgust. 'What would you have us do then, forget our money? Anyway, I've had a thought about how we might persuade him.'

'Really?' said Bezer and, as he knocked, he half hoped that there would be no reply.

For some moments it seemed that his wish would be granted. However, Susan stepped forward, pushing him aside and rapped on the door again. There was a voice from inside, a woman's, and the door was opened to them by a middle-aged slatternly creature wearing a blood-stained apron. Her hands were daubed with blood and she held them, fingers upwards, like grotesque bunches of flowers. Bezer let out a gasp and recoiled, but Susan seemed unconcerned and spoke up in the sugary tones she adopted on occasions requiring people to look upon her with favour.

'So sorry to trouble you, Ma'am. I can see you're occupied. But we wish to visit an acquaintance of ours who lives in rooms in your house, we believe, a Mr Richard Dunn.'

The woman gave them each a quick glance, as a powerful smell of something boiling wafted along the passage and out of the house on to the street. Hungry as he was, Bezer was not tempted by this odour. The woman nodded her head in a signal they took to mean they could enter.

'Up there, first floor. Door on the left,' she said. 'And mind you don't make a mess of the stairs. This is a clean house. And don't stay after six o'clock. I don't want no more lodgers.'

Bezer, insulted, was on the point of saying that he would rather sleep on the streets than in this malodorous charnel house, so out of place in this respectable street. He bit back the urge to comment, however, as though it might tempt fate to state such a thing. Also, he knew that where there was blood there were certainly knives. The woman retreated down the passageway towards the place from which the sickening smell had drifted. On the upper landing, they found the door and Susan tapped on it in a more ladylike manner than her attack on the front door. When this produced no result, she thumped it with her fist.

'Mr Dunn, a word if you please,' she said in a hard voice, with her cheek nearly pressed to the door.

Bezer shrank inwardly at the prospect of what might be about to occur. The door flew open and Dunn was standing there with the familiar supercilious look on his face.

'Well, Mr and Mrs Fortescue,' he said with a tight smile. 'And what brings you here? How did you find me?'

Susan took a step towards him. Shamed by her courage, Bezer did the same. They were two after all and they had right on their side.

'You know what we want, Mr Dunn, fair payment for our work. And of course, the agreed share in the fortune when you have it,' Susan said.

Dunn smiled, showing his teeth.

'Ah well,' he said, placing his hand on his hip as though he were engaged in casual talk with one of his cronies. 'The wheels of the banking world move mighty slow. But won't you step inside for a moment, for I'd not be wanting to upset the neighbours.'

Bezer felt he would rather throw himself into the Thames with stones in his pocket than enter those rooms. The outcome of both might well be the same. But Susan had barged in, in a move which shocked Bezer, giving him no option but to follow her. Then he remembered that she had worked out another stratagem. He had no choice but to trust that whatever she had devised would work.

They stood in a narrow hallway off which there appeared to be two rooms. Bezer's heart sank when Dunn closed the door behind him.

'Will you come and take a seat, and we can discuss our business in a civilised manner,' Dunn said.

'We'll stay here, thank you,' Susan replied sharply. 'You owe us money for penning your letter and we've come for it now.'

'Yes, absolutely, now, at this moment. We insist,' added Bezer. 'You gave your word.'

'Och, did I now? I doubt it sir,' said Dunn.

Bezer saw the man's jaw twitch and Susan's colour was deepening.

'If you don't pay us, sir,' she said in her acid voice, 'we shall call upon Miss Coutts, for doesn't she live just across the way? We will confess to our forgery, a terrible sin, which we regret with all our hearts and souls and pray daily for forgiveness. We will say we were driven to it by want, through no fault of our own and in desperation took your offer. But now we are so tortured by guilt we have come to confess all to her and to bring you to justice for your wickedness.'

Bezer caught his breath, watching Dunn's face change horribly.

'You vile old hag,' he said, his face flushing and his eyes fixed in a murderous stare.

Dear God, make him not strike her, Bezer prayed silently. She had gone too far this time. But Susan did not flinch. Instead, she raised her voice.

'And we will tell her that you are a villain who promised us a cut of the fortune you were trying to cheat from her.'

Dunn let out a low roar, then lunged at Bezer, who saw him coming but, paralysed with terror, could not budge. He felt a hand clamp so tightly on his throat that he thought he might faint, while his arms and legs flailed uselessly in a weak struggle to break free.

'I'll kill him, you old bitch,' Dunn growled, looking at Susan and tightening his grip.

He would die at the hand of this madman. This was to be his fate and Susan's probably, after Dunn had dispatched him.

'If you breathe a word of this, I'll hunt you down, both of you and split you both from belly to chin. Aye and I'll keep that promise all right. Now get out of here if you value your miserable lives.'

It was a chilly morning on Bond Street but there was already a bustle of shoppers and workers about the place. An omnibus disgorged a dozen people from its top and lower decks. Steam rose from the horses' flanks into the chilly air. A boy was washing a shop window and another ragged one was swinging a bucket as he approached a pile of horse dung and scooped it neatly up. Several gentlemen were striding along with purpose on their way to business. Two shambling figures, arm in arm, heads bowed, in dirty, ragged clothing moved slowly past the splendid new shop front of *Asprey's* the jewellers until they reached a low parapet outside a tall building set back from the road. Here they sat down to reveal their beggarly state and their intentions for the day ahead.

The man, a stocky individual wore a torn and soiled coat, too small for his girth and a ragged cap on his head. His face was a mass of suppurating scabs. His companion was a woman, her body padded with a multitude of rags over the limp skirt of her gown. On her head was a fraying straw hat.

'Don't lick your scabs,' she said to the man crossly.

'Sorry, my dearest one,' Bezer said, 'but this may be my only source of nourishment today.'

'Don't be so stupid. We're bound to pick up good money today in this place. Most folk'll pay just to keep wide of you,' she said. 'Now watch out for some likely ladies and gents. Take your cap off and get ready.'

Bezer looked up the street at a group of oncoming pedestrians who appeared to be two couples, ladies and gentlemen. He hoisted himself off the wall, pulled off his cap, revealing the tufts of hair, made more beggarly by Susan with the application of a little grease. Bezer tottered unsteadily into the path of the approaching people and held out his cap. Susan had instructed him to say as little as possible, probably, he mused, because she knew that his superior manner of speech would betray his true origins as a cut above and thus evoke less sympathy from the charitable.

The two couples had seen him and the gentlemen had started steering their ladies to the far side of the pavement, away from Bezer. They kept their eyes firmly fixed ahead and one of the ladies held a handkerchief to her nose and mouth.

'Kind sirs and ladies. Can you spare us a penny or two?' Bezer muttered in what he thought was a suitably abject tone.

One of the gentlemen glanced at him.

'Keep away, my man and for goodness' sake take yourself to the infirmary.'

The couples passed by at a quickening pace without looking back. Bezer turned to Susan and then shuffled back to join her on the parapet.

'Can't expect the first ones to bite,' was all she said, as she looked down the street in the opposite direction.

A few moments later, two more ladies

alighted from a hansom cab, a maid accompanying them carrying a basket. They too started walking towards Bezer and Susan.

'My love,' said Bezer forlornly, 'it is I believe your turn. Ladies might look upon you with more bounty.' He felt weakened by his first failure and unable to face another rebuff.

Susan rose from her seat and took a few steps towards the ladies. Maybe, Bezer mused, they should look upon this latest misadventure as a piece of clever play acting. What was an actor after all, but a man assuming a character and wearing suitable clothing upon a stage, appealing to an audience? It was an art, so why should they not try to perfect it? The ladies were coming closer and, to Bezer's joy, not deflecting their eyes from Susan as she held out her hand and muttered some words designed to stir their sympathies. He could only catch a few snippets – my poor husband – a dreadful affliction – lost his job on account of it – too old to take in washing.

The ladies had stopped and were listening, their faces frowning with concern. One had her hand in her reticule and Bezer's heart jolted in his chest. His mouth filled with the anticipation of a pie and gravy, but he saw the lady handing Susan a small piece of paper. Was it a banknote maybe? This kindly lady would be blessed for ever in Bezer's heart as well as in heaven for her generosity. Then the ladies and their maid passed on, after a few more words to Susan, which Bezer couldn't hear, though when he saw Susan's face and her lumbering gait as she returned to him, he hoped that this was her desire to stay within her character rather than another failure of their endeavours.

'Would you credit it?' she said sourly, slumping down beside him and handing him the piece of paper.

Bezer took it. It was a ticket with the familiar message: *Present this to the Society for the Suppression of Mendicity, Lion Square Holborn. Relief offered for the deserving poor.*

'No, no, no,' he moaned and could not prevent the tears from flowing.

'For goodness' sake, be a man,' snapped Susan. 'You'll wash your scabs off.'

By the afternoon, when they had added the last sixpence to their earnings, Bezer had begun to feel better. His weeping had caused the blood and brown sugar mix on his face to form a filthy overall crust, which was in some respects a more shocking sight to beholders. That or a change in their luck and the frequent moves to other pitches had resulted in a decent sum for the day. By now, Bezer's face was beginning to itch badly and he begged Susan to allow them to return home. She agreed, pocketing their gains. They returned to their rooms and she changed quickly back into her former self to go shopping for supper. Bezer collapsed on the bed, ecstatic with joy and relief.

Rousing himself when he heard Susan going out, he plunged his face into a basin of water and scraped off his beggarly disguise, hoping that his wife would buy a good bottle of liquor to reward them for their efforts. They had after all, collected a sum totalling one guinea, which would furnish them well for a number of days. He took off his beggar's clothing and dressed himself in his few remaining more respectable garments. He thanked God that they had not yet had to resort to pawning all of these, though he still regretted the loss of his waistcoat. Perhaps Susan might agree, if things went well at this begging business, that they should redeem it.

The anticipation of Susan's return with food for supper was deeply pleasing to Bezer. However, it could not quite erase his humiliation in receiving a charitable ticket from the very organisation where he had been employed in a professional capacity. Susan did not seem to feel this hurt as deeply as he, but then she had not had his status, his pride in being someone, in working in smart offices in Holborn, having people under him. She had, when he thought about it, been of a somewhat lower rank than he, when they had met, a mere seamstress, although he had to admit that she was clever. Maybe it was his fault for giving her pretensions of living like a lady. Some married women had their own lucrative businesses, supporting themselves and their husbands, managing shops and suchlike, but not Susan. She could have made some sort of living in her former craft when they were most in need. However, he could not imagine a life without her.

After an hour, she returned, promisingly laden with provisions. She pulled out a ham hock, a loaf and a bottle of gin, a pie, potatoes and carrots.

'Well, we shall feast tonight,' she said. 'Didn't I tell you that we would do ourselves proud?'

It was an unfortunate turn of phrase, Bezer thought, but he was starving hungry. Their supper that night was the most delicious that Bezer had ever tasted in his life. The drink on his empty stomach had the most marvellous warming effect and rubbed out of his mind the doubts and discomforts of the day. What they had had to do was worth it. The only niggling, bothersome aspect was that they were going to have to do it all again and again. For now, however, Bezer would not think about this. He poured himself another glass.

'Pass me the bottle,' said Susan, whose face was glowing. She was clearly of the same way of thinking as Bezer.

Drink now. Give no thought to tomorrow. Bezer felt himself drifting into a pleasant dozing state, his eyelids drooping where he sat, his body loosening. He heard Susan's breathy snoring as she slumped in her chair. The peace of their slumber was suddenly and violently broken when a fierce crack sounded at their door, as of a blow with a hard object. Bezer jerked up from his chair, his head swimming.

'What?' he said, stumbling over to Susan and jabbing her in the arm, knowing that any visitation here at this time of night was not likely to be friendly. Whatever it was, he could not face it alone. It couldn't be anyone from the bank, surely. Their aliases and the fact that they had given no address could not have led to a pursuit. Richard Dunn, the evil Irishman was another possibility. He had threatened them with violence and was, Bezer reckoned very capable of carrying out his threat, being deranged in his mind. The knock came again with a rough voice this time. 'Mr Bezer Blundell, open up on the orders of the magistrate.'

Susan, awake now, grabbed Bezer's arm and tugged him towards their bedchamber.

'What can we do?' he blubbered as she towed him after her. 'There's no escape. We're lost, my dearest.'

'Be quiet,' she said, pulling the coverlet from the bed and running with it to the window. But he went to her, held her, knowing that whatever plan she had was foolhardy, impossible, even for her.

'Come, my dear,' he said, holding out his arms to her. 'Let us face them with dignity.'

There was in fact nothing dignified about the way the ruffians who called themselves constables of the law hustled them down the stairs and into the waiting wagon. A few of their neighbours were there, gawping on the steps to witness their arrest, as well as some interested onlookers who had heard the disturbance. Susan and Bezer were pushed into the back of the wagon, along with a large constable wielding a truncheon. Susan was speechless, having offered no resistance to their taking, no more had Bezer. The men had given them no explanation, had answered no questions about the charges, or their accuser or evidence against them. These things, Bezer knew, were necessary in order to apprehend persons deemed to have committed a crime.

The cell was a stinking place, his bed a plank and the snoring of the other three inmates deeply distressing to Bezer. A tin pot in the corner swam with piss and Bezer lay shivering in his clothes, staring at the tiny, high window hour after hour, longing for a sign of daylight. A kind of numbness had taken hold of his body when something rattled, a metallic clang in the door and the voice of a man shouting that it was time to get up. The three other fellows in the cell, malodorous villains, cursed and groaned themselves awake and Bezer wished that he were dead.

'Get out. You're for the beak,' said a warder opening the door and pointing at Bezer. 'Move your arse, then.'

Bezer, sweaty and with his clothes sticking to his skin, his throat sour with dryness and foul breath followed the man along a narrow corridor. He thought of Susan and hoped more than anything that she would join him for whatever ordeal was awaiting. They had been together throughout their troubles and together they would stand in front of those who would judge them and condemn them.

'Where are you taking me?' Bezer asked the

warder.

The man grinned. 'Hangman, where'd you think?'

'No, no,' said Bezer recoiling, only to see the broadening smile of the man's face.

'Nah, keep your shit in your breeches. You and your wife are up before the magistrate. Mind you, there's no saying it won't be the gallows in the end.'

In a narrow corridor leading to the door of the courtroom, Bezer could have wept with relief to see Susan coming along accompanied by a woman warder. The night in the cell did not appear to have reduced her in the way it had done Bezer. There was no warmth nor welcome in her face, however, when she saw him, as though she was somehow blaming him for the situation in which they now found themselves. When he tried to offer her a greeting, the warder rebuked him, ordering silence as they waited. After a tense period, the door opened to admit them.

The large chamber was almost empty, with a cold smell of dust and a handful of people sitting on wooden benches in rows, facing a larger one, where a gentleman sat; a heavy bodied person, in a dark robe. He did not look up as they entered. The two constables who had arrested Bezer and Susan were sitting in the front row and a clerk sat at a side table with a large book, pens and ink pots. The warders pushed Bezer and Susan into the room and positioned them in front of the magistrate.

The magistrate looked up, his eyes drawn down as though by weariness. His whole demeanour was sunken and heavy. He ordered them to give their names, ages, address and occupations, which the clerk wrote down with speedy deliberation in the record book.

'You are accused of making false statements and fraud,' said the magistrate.

Bezer, in spite of the nauseous feeling of dread was a little curious about which particular person would have made this accusation. In his mind he tried to recall all the letters they had written and to whom, but there were so many that in his current state he could not sort them out in his mind.

'You are accused of fabricating false information for your own financial gain. You and your wife have posed as fictitious claimants demanding money from a respected lady. She has reported your falsehood to the Society for the Suppression of Mendicity. These constables were employed by the Society to trace the originators of this false claim.'

'It's not true,' Susan burst out. 'There's nothing on us.'

'Be quiet,' said the magistrate sharply. 'I have not finished. Blundell your record for theft from the Society is now known and the purloining of certain documents from the premises to further your dishonest practices. The complaint received from Miss Coutts has led the trustees to suspect you of the serious criminal acts of fraud and forgery. You and your wife will therefore be committed and tried at the Old Bailey on these charges.'

Chapter 17

Nathan welcomed Mr Joshua Ellacott to the school, introducing him to the assembled children as their new teacher, as Nicholas Greaves had done to him. Nathan was struck by the fact that now he seemed to have assumed the role as master in charge, though he had never sought it out and would not, but for the untimely death of Mr Greaves, have undertaken the role. Marianne and her husband were experienced and educated people, unlike himself. Marianne, however, had seemed glad to defer to Nathan, maybe feeling less sure of taking on the burden of this responsibility as a woman still grieving for her husband. He realised too, that she was a shy woman, capable of quiet resilience and determination but with little desire to wield power or control. When he had asked her once to lead prayers or hymn singing or to read to the boys, she had declined, saying that he could command more fittingly than she. So, here was he, performing duties that he had never imagined himself doing.

The new recruit, who had volunteered for the post, Joshua Ellacott, newly graduated in Divinity from the University of Oxford, was priestly in dress and manner. He had a steady, unwavering gaze and exuded the self-confidence of someone with absolute convictions.

'Boys and girls,' he said with a preacher's heavy emphasis. 'The Lord has brought me to you to do His work. Here in this humble school, you will learn to read the Word of God, to worship and adore Him and our Lord Jesus Christ who died for us all, for all our sins.'

Nathan looked at the children, most of whom were attentively watching the young man, with only a few scratching themselves under their ragged clothes, or picking scabs on their knees. One small boy was asleep against the shoulder of his elder brother. Nathan glanced at Marianne, who was sitting with her group of girls at the edge of the main body of boys. Her eyes met his and for a brief snatch, or maybe it was something Nathan had imagined, exchanged a look of mild amusement. Though still in her widow's black, Marianne looked to Nathan less pale and strained than of late. Her face was softer, more becoming, he had to admit and he found himself drawn to look at her again, though by now her attention was elsewhere.

'We are sinners all before God, subject to the lusts, weaknesses, follies and vices of our nature,' Joshua Ellacott continued, as the children grew more restive, though his voice surged on. 'Here I will teach you to open your hearts, so that our Lord will feed your souls.'

'Feed me belly more like,' said a voice from somewhere in the midst of the boys.

Joshua Ellacott's cheeks coloured and his staring eyes scoured the heads of the boys seeking out the source of this rude interruption. Nathan knew that he would have to step in, though he held back for a moment while considering the best approach. Stepping forward a moment later, he tried to catch the man's eye, but Joshua Ellacott was looking heavenward, beseeching the Almighty directly.

'Thank you, Mr Ellacott. You will lead the prayers later on, but now our lessons must begin,' Nathan said.

Nathan sensed the heat of the new teacher's indignation, but he did not look at him as he gave out instructions to the boys. They clattered noisily into their groups, clustering into the appropriate parts of the schoolroom. Marianne led her girls and gathered up a few of the smaller boys who had come to the school for the first time and were wandering rootlessly about the room.

Nathan then turned to his new colleague.

'Mr Ellacott, would you please take this group of boys to learn their letters,' he said pointing to a clutch of children sitting in the front row.

His colour having returned to normal, Joshua Ellacott looked at Nathan with a disbelieving stare.

'You mean they can't read at all?' he said.

'They have had no schooling until they came to this place. They go mostly hungry and ill-clad. We have to start from where they are.'

Joshua Ellacott looked unconvinced, glanced at the blackboard, which contained the letters of the alphabet and a list of simple three-letter words.

'Very well,' he said with a sour look.

Nathan hoped that there would be sufficient

soup today, as more children had appeared than usual. At noon, large pots were brought in on a cart by two hefty men, courtesy of the Women's Society for the Relief of Paupers. When Joshua Ellacott ordered everyone to wait until he had said grace, the boys were on the point of rioting. However, a compromise rapid prayer was said over their bowls and the young churchman retired into disgruntled acceptance as the boys devoured their soup.

Nathan was glad when it was time to finish for the day. He managed to curtail a lengthy closing sermon from their new colleague by saying that some builders were due to be arriving to discuss the building of a bath house next door. It was partly true, as Miss Coutts had promised to finance such a project, though when it was due to start was not yet fixed.

Nathan stacked up the slates, replaced the furniture and made ready to lock up. He wanted to talk to Marianne, to gauge her opinion of their new colleague, but held back from broaching the subject with her. Joshua Ellacott was a highly educated young man. He came on Miss Coutts's recommendation too, as Nathan had received a note from her to inform him of his imminent arrival. Nathan was sure that Marianne shared some of his reservations about Joshua Ellacott, though out of politeness she might not wish to express them openly.

However, as she was putting on her hat and coat, she turned to Nathan and sighed.

'Where did he come from, this Mr Ellacott?'

she said.

'He is the grandson of a bishop who is an acquaintance of Miss Coutts,' he said. 'He is going as a missionary to the colonies and wishes to acquire some experience of teaching children before he goes. You do not think him – suitable?'

'No, he is not. He is too pious, too rigid and puritanical in his thinking,' she said with unusual force.

Her face was flushed and a note of anger sharpened the usually soft tone of voice.

'My husband would never have tolerated such a man.'

Nathan was shocked at the strength of her reaction and was unsure how to reply. Was this a criticism of him, a lack of the force of leadership to send the man packing?

'Mr Hines,' she said. 'I do not mean to criticise. Far from it. You are tolerant, liberal and can abide the sanctimonious as well as the irreligious, much better than I am able.'

Nathan had never seen the gentle and mild-mannered Marianne Greaves in such a mood and realised that she had been seriously upset by the presence of the man.

'I agree with your opinion of him,' Nathan said, 'I don't think he'll find the rewards he is seeking among these children.'

'And he has some views that are repugnant to me,' she said. 'He told me that he did not approve of women teachers or of girls being educated. Women's constitutions are too weak and girls should be taught domestic skills only, in separate establishments. That's what he said.'

Nathan shook his head, wondering why Miss Coutts had felt moved to recommend such a person for the Ragged School. Her work in providing women and girls with homes, training and the means of supporting themselves was praised in the city.

'But maybe,' Marianne said, 'it is I who is not suited to this work, if it must be tied so closely to religious observance. Nicholas had no time for religion of any sort.'

She hesitated, aware that she may have been speaking too freely.

'Is it safe to tell you this? I do not offend you I hope?' she said, examining his face.

'No, it causes me no offence,' Nathan said, surprised by her candour. 'I had great respect for your husband regardless of his private beliefs. He was a humane and compassionate man.'

'He was also an atheist,' she said, 'though I told him never to declare this. We would never have been appointed to the school. Miss Coutts objects even to non-conformists, so we told her that we were Anglican, which was not a complete lie as we were both baptised into that church.'

'And you, what do you believe?' Nathan said, drawn in by the woman's unexpected revelations.

He moved closer to her and she looked up at him.

'I really don't know,' she said. 'I believe in

upholding Christian virtues and values, though I am not a regular church goer.'

They stood for some moments in silence; these revelations had changed something between them.

'Are you a believer, Mr Hines?' she said.

'I was,' he said, 'and like you have had doubts. I have witnessed things that made me deny the presence of a God, least of all a loving one.'

'You have suffered the loss of someone too,' she said.

He nodded, dismayed but in a strange way glad that she should know this about him.

'My wife and children,' he said.

'Your wife and your children Mr Hines? Forgive me. I didn't mean to renew your grief.'

He shook his head, meaning to dismiss her apology, but found that he had to tell her.

'Kate, my wife, fell ill with the cholera,' he said. 'It came upon her so quickly, the vomiting and diarrhoea. Her body shrank and she was in such pain.'

He could not meet her gaze as he spoke.

'I went for a doctor, leaving my boy Daniel and my girl Rosie with her. The doctor came and bled my wife for hours, until her skin was grey and her fever turned to ice. He said there was nothing he could do, but I would not believe it. I ran for another medical man, one recommended by a neighbour. He brought a substance called Calomel. It is a vicious mix. She was in agony for many hours before she died.'

He heard his voice breaking, felt a lump clogging his throat, but he also felt Marianne's hand on his arm.

'Don't go on, if it is too painful.'

Nathan heard her say this, but he could not stop now. He had told no one, apart from Silas, how they had died and what he had done in the end.

'My children. If my children had not been taken, then maybe I might believe in God's mercy,' he said.

He could not tell her all, not without bringing back the image of his daughter. The man was a quack, a charlatan, but Nathan, desperate and powerless, had told him to name his price, if he could just save his child. The potion the man had brought was a herbal one, infused in creosote which blackened his daughter's mouth and killed her that night. It was torture to him still, to remember how he had paid men to increase the suffering and death of those he had loved most in the world. Yet he regretted kicking the man out of his house, punching his face, pummelling him so that he might have died, had Nathan not remembered his son upstairs, violently sick and calling for him.

He had begged Silas to buy as much laudanum as he could with all the money Nathan had left. So, he had dosed his sick son to ease his pain and his passing in Nathan's arms. Then he had taken all the remaining drug too, cursing God and hoping never to wake again.

Nathan, aware of the tears that had wet his face, was aware too, that Marianne was holding his hand. They sat down side by side and for some time were silent. It was not an awkward but a soothing quietness. At last, she spoke.

'Do you think,' she said, 'that we have spoken too deeply to address each other as polite acquaintances?'

He looked at her, found her gaze on him and nodded.

'Yes, Marianne,' he said, taking her hand in both of his, feeling his heartbeat quicken.

She smiled. 'But Nathan, what are we going to do about Mr Ellacott?'

That evening, Nathan found himself humming as he prepared his supper and he stopped, uneasy at the recognition of his mood. It was not proper to have feelings for Marianne Greaves, though these were surely the mark of friendship, gratitude, of fellow feeling, a mutual respect between them, no more. On that he was decided. He busied himself for the rest of the evening with checking the books, the records that Silas was keeping so meticulously. He examined Silas's entries for the day then checked the storeroom and the unredeemed items that were to be sold. His friend's work was exemplary. Silas was simply better at this business than he. If only his own position was certain and not dependent upon a philanthropic gesture, which he supposed might be withdrawn at any time, he would transfer the business legally to Silas. Nathan was aware, however, that he could never claim to be a genuine schoolmaster; his education was too meagre to pass himself off as any kind of scholar. But for the moment, he realised with some surprise, that he was quite content, a state so unfamiliar to him that he could not entirely believe it.

The next day at school, they had an unexpected visitor, a woman, who seemed to be acquainted with Marianne. Marianne broke off her work with the girls and went to receive her, as Nathan and Joshua Ellacott were occupied with their classes. Joshua's group were repeating after him in low, dull voices the lines of a psalm, while Nathan's class were occupied with copying a text on to their slates. Nathan glanced up at Marianne, who was ushering the woman to join her group of girls. The visitor was a woman of middle years, respectable looking, plainly dressed and who seemed at ease with the girls, sitting among them and engaging them in talk. After an hour, one of Marianne's girls approached Nathan.

'Mistress says would Master come over and meet the visitor, please and thank you,' said the small girl.

Nathan smiled and nodded, instructing one of the older boys to watch the class and in his stern voice telling them to carry on with their work.

'Mr Hines,' said Marianne, 'this is Miss Brennan, the superintendent of St Bridget's Orphanage for Girls. She has three girls whom she would like to send to us.'

Nathan greeted the woman, interested to hear more about them.

'There are three who seem bright and able,' said the woman. 'One can write her name already, though she is a silent little soul.'

'I see no problem with admitting more girls, though it's a decision for Mrs Greaves who takes the girls' class as you see,' said Nathan looking at Marianne.

'Yes, it would be good to have more in our group,' said Marianne. 'Lettie will be leaving soon. She has a place as a kitchen maid and I have hopes of finding work for two of the others.'

So it was arranged that Miss Brennan would return the next day with the three orphan girls. She took her leave, thanking Nathan and Marianne again. At the end of the day, once the children had been dismissed, Joshua Ellacott strode up to Nathan and Marianne.

'What was the purpose of that visitor today?' he said in the tone of one who wished to take charge.

Nathan, angered by his manner explained a little curtly about the new girls who would be attending the school from the next day.

'It is a retrograde step, in my view. Females need to be educated in a separate institution. It is distracting for boys, who cannot hold their minds on learning.'

'That is your view, Mr Ellacott, but I do not share it. Our patrons, I believe, would wish wholeheartedly for girls to have the opportunity to learn to read and write and count. Miss Coutts, as you know is a highly educated lady and supports the training and education of poor girls who seek to better themselves.'

'And I find your remark offensive, Mr Ellacott,' said Marianne sharply, tugging her hat from the peg. 'It is not fitting for a man newly arrived to cast judgement on the management of this school.'

Nathan was surprised to hear Marianne speak with such forthrightness, but could not help being mildly amused by the look of affront on Joshua Ellacott's face. Marianne said nothing further but left the schoolhouse quickly without looking back.

'Well,' said Joshua Ellacott, 'that illustrates exactly the concerns I have about the female sex, their hysterical nature.'

Nathan struggled to keep his temper with the man.

'Mr Ellacott,' he said. 'I suggest that if you are displeased with the conduct of the school, you should take your concerns to Miss Coutts or Mr Dickens.'

'Conduct?' said the man. 'You'd do well to look to your own conduct, Mr Hines. You and that widow woman alone together, it is unseemly, immodest and indecent.'

Nathan's anger was still present when he returned home to the shop. He found a woman customer there at the counter, talking to Silas. Nathan acknowledged them both on his way through to his kitchen at the back. He had noted that their conversation did not appear to relate to the pledging or redeeming of any item. He took off his coat and sat down by the stove, holding his hands in front of it to warm them, with the thoughts of Joshua Ellacott still simmering in his mind. He hated the sanctimonious attitude of the man, but this was not the only thing that had disturbed him. The man's veiled accusation suggested that Nathan had been too open in his regard for Marianne. Had he noticed something pass between them? Nathan didn't think this could be the case, but what dogged him was that he recognised his attraction, his desire for Marianne Greaves. He had felt no stirrings towards her while her husband was alive; it was only recently that he had developed something more than admiration of her qualities. Kate, his wife, he had lusted after wildly from the moment he had met her, but he had been younger then. Now he was no raw youth. He was nearing forty years old and she was a widow of around those years too, he assumed.

He heard Silas taking his leave of the woman, calling her Alice in a tone and manner altogether different from his usual bluntness. Nathan, his curiosity aroused, listened for the sound of the shop door closing then rose and returned to it, to help Silas close up.

'Who was that last customer?' he asked.

Silas gave no immediate reply. He snapped the cash box shut and locked it.

'Fine woman,' he said a moment later, on his way into the storeroom where he started grappling with the window shutter.

Nathan followed him in, determined to draw him out.

'Was she pledging something?'

Silas let go of the shutter.

'Used to. Ladies' handkerchiefs, tablecloths, that kind of stuff. But not any more. In a good way of business now.'

'And so she just called by to pass the time of day, did she?' Nathan said, sensing that Silas, though not given to chatter, had something he wished to reveal.

'She's a craftswoman. Never saw stitching so fine,' Silas said in a peculiarly wistful voice, picking up the shutter again and making his way to the door.

Nathan followed with the second shutter. Silas was busying himself with the padlocks, but suddenly spoke out.

'I'd ask her, but would she say yes? A man like me?'

Nathan was astonished by Silas's revelation, though he found himself a moment later delighting in it.

'If she keeps coming back when she's nothing to pledge and nothing to redeem,' he said, 'it must be for your company, Silas. And if you admire her, love her, then you must act.'

Silas turned to Nathan, looking stunned, as though Nathan had told him he had inherited a fortune.

'Come back in, Silas,' Nathan said. 'Have a

drink with me, then go off and ask her.'

Silas smiled and nodded.

An hour later, Silas had tidied himself up, combed his hair, asked Nathan to approve his appearance and then had gone. In their conversation, they had touched upon matters of the heart in a way they had never done before. Nathan thought of his advice to his friend: 'If you admire her, love her, then you must act.'

The next day, before the start of school, Nathan arrived to witness Joshua Ellacott exchanging words with Marianne. He could tell by the edge in her voice that she was seriously displeased by something he had said. Nathan was glad to see her facing down their new teacher, whose expression was contorted with distaste at being addressed in this way.

'Mr Ellacott, my late husband and I were charged with the duty of managing this school,' Marianne was saying. 'So I think it is not wrong of me to consider myself as its superintendent. I shall write to Miss Coutts to confirm this. You have no authority here to force changes to our practices.'

'I will pray that you will come to recognise the importance of feminine modesty and decorum, madam,' he said stiffly. 'I see little evidence of it now.'

Nathan could stand by no longer.

'Mr Ellacott. I must ask you to leave. You will insult Mrs Greaves no further. And I think you are not suited to this work.'

The man's chest rose in an outraged intake of breath.

'You dare to dismiss me? You are a common shopkeeper, worse, a usurer,' he said, raising a finger and pointing at Nathan as though he were a vision from hell. 'The Scriptures pronounce on you and your kind. "He that lends at interest and takes profit, shall he live? He shall not live. He has done all these abominations; he shall surely die; his blood shall be upon himself." Ezekiel Chapter 18, verse 13.'

Nathan grabbed the ranting man by the scruff of the neck, his grip tightening as he steered him towards the door. Though Joshua Ellacott attempted to struggle free, his flailing arms were ineffectual against Nathan's greater force.

'And I know about her godless husband,' he squealed. 'She's no better than he or you, though she pretends otherwise. Miss Coutts will know of your foulness. You pollute the minds of the young~.'

Nathan pushed him out of the door and closed it firmly, turning and leaning with his back against it, shocked at what he had just done. Marianne was standing watching and Nathan saw a smile forming on her face.

Nathan knew that in all likelihood they had not seen the last of Joshua Ellacott, but he tried to banish any concern he felt about the penalty he might have to pay for his action against the man. There was little time to ponder, as the boys and girls were soon pouring in through the door, clattering, filling the place with noise. Nathan brought them to order quickly, his monitorial system working with reasonable effect now, so that when Miss Brennan from the girls' orphanage arrived with the three children to join Marianne's group, the place had a generally industrious air. Nathan glanced at the new girls who seemed to be around eight or nine years old. They were quiet and subdued and crept past the rows of boys, some of whom looked up and sniggered at each other. The girls were dressed in dull brown dresses with canvas aprons and caps, their regulation wear in the institution. Miss Brennan stayed with them and Marianne, Nathan noted, soon had them at work, copying from the blackboard on their slates.

Nathan was pleased to see Ned's younger brother, a child of only about seven years old, a frail, sickly looking boy with legs like sticks. Nathan enquired of him about Ned's progress in Mr Gladwell's shop. The little boy said his brother liked it and Mr Gladwell said he was a likely lad and gave him an extra penny on his wages. Nathan sat the boy beside a placid older one and forged ahead with the lessons of the day, deciding to forgo scripture in favour of reading another extract from *A Christmas Carol*.

'Where's that horrible vicar?' said one boy, a remark that Nathan thought it wise to ignore.

The orphan girls left first with Miss Brennan and then the rest of the children were dismissed. Nathan, curious about how their day had gone, approached Marianne.

'They were very quiet, the new girls. Tess, Lillian and Belinda are their names. Belinda is the silent one,' said Marianne. 'Miss Brennan has told me that the girl has never been heard to speak a word, though she wrote her name upon a paper. She was brought to the orphanage by a lady who encountered her on the street. It is an odd story. The child Belinda was begging on Regent Street but ran after a couple, attaching herself to the woman, in fact she took hold of the woman's gown and would not let go. She had to be dragged off by the woman's husband and was in such a state of weeping and distress that they took pity on her and brought her to the orphanage. They had no other idea of how to dispose of her, as she would not say who she was or where she came from.'

Marianne paused and looked at him.

'Come, Nathan, and look at this.'

He followed her back to the corner where the girls had been working. She picked up a slate from the top of a pile and handed it to him.

'I did not rub this off. The child has written her name again.'

He looked down at the slate, at the neat but childlike hand and the name 'Belinda Harding', that was chalked upon it.

'Good God,' Nathan said, staring at the name. 'And the gown that the woman was wearing, the gown, what colour was it?'

Marianne looked at him with a puzzled

frown.

'I don't know. Why do you ask?' she said. 'Nathan, what's amiss?'

He shook his head. Could it be true that his search was over, the search that had for a time been his obsession? He told Marianne then all about the unfortunate Selina Harding, her pleading letter to Miss Coutts that he had found in her pawned gown. He related what had occurred on his visit to that lady and how eager she was that the orphaned child should be found. There was also the evidence he had collected from the old woman who had helped Selina Harding, the fact that the woman was gravely ill. He told her also of the mistaken selling of the gown by Silas.

'What if the child saw the woman who had bought the gown?' said Nathan. 'Did she think she had found her mother? Perhaps the child and her mother had been separated somehow.'

Marianne frowned, her curiosity clearly aroused by Nathan's revelations.

'Miss Brennan could give us details of that woman, the one who bought the gown,' she said. 'You must speak to the child, though she has not uttered a word herself. But I know she has understanding and language in some form. She is mute but not deaf.'

'And if she is in fact the woman's child, I'm sure that Miss Coutts would do something to provide for her as the daughter of a former servant. She is a generous and benevolent lady,' Nathan said, looking at Marianne, whose eyes were alight with their shared excitement.

She was standing close to him. He felt the warmth of her presence and would in a second have taken her in his arms, had he not exercised the power of his will to resist, as he knew he must. He took a step back.

'Nathan,' she said, 'you're moved by this, I can see.'

'Yes, I am,' he said, glad of this excuse to cover his discomfiture, and knowing that he must mention the other matter that had dogged him for most of the day. 'There is the business of Mr Ellacott. I should have not acted so rashly. I have not the authority.'

Marianne frowned, thinking for a moment.

'I will send a message to Miss Coutts,' she said. 'She must know of this of course. It can't be hidden, though it may bring censure or worse upon us. I will write it tonight and bring it tomorrow for your approval. I do not think our action was unreasonable, given the slanderous comments he made and his lack of understanding of the circumstances of the children. Don't worry. I will stand by what you did in ejecting him. In fact, I think it was magnificent!'

She smiled and he felt himself colouring, in the foolish manner of a simpleton, a smitten youth. There was so much he wanted to say to her. But he said nothing, as he could not rid himself of the memory of Joshua Ellacott's accusation.

Silas had locked up and left by the time Nathan returned. This was unusual, as Silas usually wanted to share with Nathan the business of the day, show him the books and discuss the takings. He had left a note, however, hastily scribbled. *She said Yes. Supper at The Bell. Join us, Your friend, Silas.* Nathan laughed aloud, rejoicing for his friend, envious too, but with no resentment.

The next day, Marianne was anxious to show Nathan the letter to Miss Coutts. She thrust it before him.

'She must know our side of the story. Mr Ellacott will certainly have given his version to Miss Coutts and probably to his grandfather, the bishop.'

St John Street, Clerkenwell

Dear Miss Coutts,

I write to inform you, as our valued patron at the Ragged School, Field Lane, of a difficulty we have encountered. Your advice and guidance would also be much appreciated.

Mr Nathan Hines and I were very grateful that another teacher, Mr Joshua Ellacott had come forward to offer his services. It was an honour that a man of such educational prowess should have agreed to work with the humblest and most needy children in the city. However, he was, I fear, unprepared for what he would encounter and could not readily reconcile his beliefs about how such a school should be run and the manner in which my late husband and I had established it.

Mr Dickens, on a recent visit, seemed satisfied with the children's learning and our efforts on their behalf, albeit that academic progress is hampered by conditions of life beyond our control. Mr Ellacott's continued presence in the school became impossible when he made slanderous comments about the fitness of myself and Mr Hines to be teachers of the young and our moral characters. Mr Hines, whom I believe you encouraged to take up this position, is a man of strong moral principles and is an exemplary teacher. He is respectful to me at all times and graciously conscious of my state of widowhood. The slights cast by Mr Ellacott are cruel and without justification or truth.

It is my hope that you will understand my strong reservations about Mr Ellacott's suitability to remain in the school. Should you require further clarification of this unfortunate situation, please do not hesitate to send me word.

Yours respectfully
Marianne Greaves

Nathan read the letter, feeling first admiration and gratitude for Marianne's clear statements, but then with a little embarrassment about her comments on his moral rectitude. If she knew what turmoil he trapped inside him, how he suppressed his feelings for her, she might not have made such assertions. The letter showed that their friendship was secure, but also that it could be no more than that. He knew he must never expect more.

'Thank you for your kind remarks,' Nathan said, in a stiffer manner than he had intended.

'I will make sure it is delivered today,' she said, with a look at him that made him turn away and busy himself with preparations for the day.

It was difficult to find an occasion to talk to the child Belinda Harding, but Marianne signalled to Nathan that he might come to her, when the boys were occupied with eating. Nathan found the girl sitting on a form, head down, a slate upon her lap. Miss Brennan had not stayed with the girls that day, though she assured them that she would send a woman at the end of school to accompany them to the orphanage again. Marianne laid a hand on the girl's arm.

'Belinda,' she said. 'Mr Hines would like to talk to you. Will you speak to him?'

The child did not look up, but continued to stare down at the slate, where she had written her name and a short line of scripture.

Nathan crouched down beside her.

'Belinda Harding,' he said, gently. 'Do you remember your mother?'

The girl did not move her head or alter her bowed posture in any way, but Nathan saw that she was weeping, silently. He glanced at Marianne, who took the girl's hand in hers.

'I think your mother might have had a pretty silk gown, green with stripes, cream coloured. Is that right?' he said.

The child turned her head suddenly, gulped and held her hand to her mouth.

'Yes, yes,' she said, in a thin voice that cracked as it came forth. 'I saw it. A lady had it on, but she wasn't my mama.'

Marianne, wide-eyed glanced at Nathan and put her arm around the child, drawing her close, stroking her hair and Nathan knew he need question her no further today. Instead, as soon as he returned home, he penned a letter to Miss Coutts, telling her that Selina Harding's daughter had been found.

Chapter 18

Angela was determined. She would not let the falsehoods of a madman damage her health and disrupt her life. She had had a restful night's sleep and had awakened early with a strong resolve to occupy herself with work. In the light of this new day, the claim that Dunn possessed a letter supposedly written by her seemed utterly preposterous. At her desk in the library, she started on the correspondence of the previous day, which she and Hannah had not had time to tackle.

She dealt quickly with the first few letters, replying to an invitation, setting aside the minutes of a meeting for Hannah to file. It occurred to her, as she sat amidst these papers, that she should engage a secretary. The volume of business was simply too much for Hannah and herself. She had been selfishly myopic too, in not realising this before and the burdens she had been placing on her loyal friend and companion. Her expectation of Hannah's constant presence and companionship was excessive, particularly now that Hannah had the responsibilities of marriage. She would mend her ways and lessen the load on her dear friend. She could ask the Duke or one of her church contacts to recommend a suitable person to take on the role of assistant.

The next letter she picked up appeared to be a particularly wearisome plea from a convict.

Pentonville Gaol

Esteemed Madam,

I pray that you, Miss Coutts, are in good health and are in a state of happiness more favourable than that of the miserable writer of this letter. Life has dealt harshly with me and my unfortunate wife, even as we have striven to overcome those many troubles and obstacles that cruel chance has thrown in our way. But alas, vile temptation driven by need and the prospect of penury led us to choose a sinful path, rejecting the righteous one of virtue...

Angela broke off and rose from the desk with the paper in her hand, ready to toss it into the fire, but glancing again at the rest of the letter, she paused.

Temptation came in the form of one wicked man, a certain Richard Dunn, who I know has been most outrageous in his behaviour towards you. I, dear Madam, bring you the means whereby he will be exposed for the malicious creature that he is and disgraced forever, even as I sacrifice myself and my dear wife in the process for your sake. I confess freely to our sins, driven by the evil promises of the said Mr Dunn.

He came to us and bade us write a letter, purporting to be from you, Miss Coutts, which made false promises of riches beyond that which most men would hardly dare to dream of. He turned us from virtue with promises to earn the wages of sin and so our hunger forced us to comply with his wishes. In stating this truth and signing our names to it, I pray that this villain will receive his punishment. My wife's hand might have penned the letter, but the words and the lying sentiments were solely Mr Dunn's.

We lay ourselves at your feet, dear Madam, in the hope that you may plead for mercy on our behalf and save us from the gallows, stating freely and in shame that I am

Your sinful but repentant servant.

Bezer Blundell
a.k.a. Edward Fortescue,
James Allen,
Reverend Archibald Bracewell,
John Smith, Esq,
Robert West,
Dr Bernard North

Angela sat down, laughing drily and mirthlessly in relief. Everyone had known that the letter was a forgery, but to find the forgers and have them testify would condemn Richard Dunn with absolute certainty. She would write straight away to Mr Marjoribanks and her solicitor to tell them about the extraordinary piece of evidence.

After penning explanatory notes to the two, she dealt quickly and with ease with the remaining letters, which were of a routine, untroubling nature. However, the last one threw up yet another cause for concern.

Hyde Park Gardens

Dear Miss Coutts,

I regret that I am forced to impart some distasteful news to you and I humbly apologise. Duty, however, calls me to proceed. The matter pertains to some disturbing discoveries at the Ragged School in Field Lane where, as you are aware, I have been offering my services.

The two persons currently in charge of the pauper children are unfit for their roles, being grossly indecent in their behaviour and devoid of all the Christian virtues and morals essential for directing and controlling the minds and spirits of the young.

In their acts of lewdness, Mr Hines is more culpable than Mrs Greaves, whose wayward nature has been unleashed by the loss of her husband's authority over her. They must be dismissed, Miss Coutts. I have taken it upon myself to inform the bishop my grandfather of this distressing state of affairs and hope that you and he will act upon this intelligence.

I am your obedient servant,
Joshua Ellacott.

This letter threw Angela's thoughts into confusion, as she simultaneously doubted the truth of the content, but was forced to consider the words of this pious man. She was aware of Mr Joshua Ellacott's credentials as a churchman devoted to the furtherance of Christian education but she had found him, when he had visited her with his grandfather the bishop, to be a stern and humourless young man. The widow, Mrs Greaves, had seemed to Angela a strong, quiet and well-educated woman while her encounters with the pawnbroker Nathan Hines had served only to increase her esteem for the man and remove all the prejudices she had held of a person of his trade. The accusation of lewdness between these two must surely be false. She had heard, however, about men's lustful needs, particularly those with no wives. Her distasteful experience with Richard Dunn had also created in her a suspicion of the motives of some men in their dealings with women. In addition to this, Mr Hines was a handsome and vigorous man and Mrs Greaves was a woman alone. Angela's dilemma now was how to act upon these accusations. She was therefore relieved when Hannah appeared later that morning in the drawing room and she was able to pour out all that she had discovered in these letters.

She told Hannah first about the self-confessed forger, Mr Blundell, and showed her the letter, which delighted her. Then she passed her the one from Joshua Ellacott, allowing her a few minutes to digest its content.

'I cannot believe it of Mr Hines,' said Angela,

'but a bishop's grandson would surely never fabricate such slanders unless there were grounds. In the case of one of these men, I have made an error of judgement, but which?'

Hannah frowned, holding the letters, sighed and looked at the sleeping puppy on Angela's lap. 'What a pity that people are so much more complicated than dogs,' she said, rising from her seat and coming to sit on the sofa with Angela.

'There has been so much trickery and deception, my dear,' Hannah said. 'First you have had to endure the appalling Mr Dunn's false claims, then the fraudulent letter about your father. It is not easy sometimes to tell truth from lies.'

Angela nodded and knew who she could turn to for immediate help.

'I shall send a message to the Duke and ask him to call. He is always willing to advise,' she said.

Angela rang the bell for a maid and requested that a message be sent to the Duke, who lived very close by. Hannah handed the letters back to Angela.

'So, this couple, Mr and Mrs Blundell are to be charged with forgery?' Hannah asked.

'Yes, I think they are in prison awaiting trial,' Angela said with a frown. 'I know they have been wicked, but I must confess that I am grateful to them for coming forward. What do you think their sentence will be?'

'At one time, people were hanged for forgery, but nowadays I think this is not the case.

Transportation is most likely,' Hannah said.

'And for Richard Dunn?'

'I do not know, but the punishment I would wish upon him is not something I dare speak to you. It is not fitting for a Christian,' Hannah said with a smile.

The puppy, waking up, stretched, yawned then sat up. Angela reached for him and hugged him to her, he licking her face. She laughed while Hannah rose and rang the bell to order tea.

With the tea tray, the maid brought another note.

'Oh dear,' said Hannah, 'are we to have no rest from correspondence today?'

She took the note, delivered, according to the maid only half an hour previously by a man who gave his name as Hines.

Hannah and Angela exchanged a look of surprise and Hannah opened up the folded paper.

'Read it to me, Hannah dear,' said Angela languidly. 'I really don't think anything else could shock me today.'

Fleet Street

Dear Miss Coutts,

I have some surprising and happy news to report. I believe that I have found the lost orphan child of Selina Harding, the unfortunate wife of your former coachman. You will recall my visit some months ago and the letter addressed to you, but never delivered. You were concerned at that time as I have been, for the welfare of the child. Now she has appeared at the Ragged School, having been rescued from the streets and is in the care of the St Bridget's Orphanage for Girls.

It is my wish, if you would be kind enough to agree, that I should bring the child to you, so that you may satisfy yourself as to her identity. I should be ready to attend you at the shortest notice should you desire this.

I am yours truly,
Nathan Hines

'This is extraordinary,' said Angela. 'Has he really found the child?'

'I suppose this could be the case,' Hannah said, hesitating, 'but it could also be a fabrication.'

'But why?' Angela said, thinking that if Hannah's suspicions were correct, Nathan Hines was a most plausible and convincing liar.

At that moment, the maid announced the arrival of the Duke, who had clearly hurried to Angela as soon as he had received her message. Her delight and gratitude at the sight of him would have moved her to kiss him, had this been seemly, which it was not. Instead, she thanked him for his prompt response to her request and spilled out the details of the surprising revelations of the day.

'So you see, dear Arthur, it's the dilemma of

Mr Hines that troubles me. Do you think I should see him and this orphan child?'

The Duke, tossing aside the letter from Nathan Hines, cleared his throat.

'My dear Angela, the man is a pawnbroker. Many of these fellows are no better than criminals. How hard would it be to pick up a little beggar child from the street and coach her to play the part of a lost orphan? This is a common strategy for wily beggars. This man would persuade you to part with money for her upkeep, which he would pocket himself, throwing her a few pennies on the way.'

'But if we were to question the child, surely...' Angela said, alarmed at what she could predict the Duke's advice would be.

The Duke snorted.

'The fellow is obviously of bad character and not to be trusted, a personable villain, the worst type. And Ellacott has clearly seen something between him and the widow. These are matters for the police to investigate. I would not have you cheated again.'

Angela looked at the Duke's face and saw there the responsible, experienced expression of a father and protector, not a critic. She remembered too, the distressing fraudulent letter she had received from a low woman purporting to have had her father's illegitimate child. It shocked her that there were so many of a criminal disposition with such cunning means of operating. It was clear that the Duke wished her to harden her heart, not be so susceptible to those who were outwardly plausible. She had thought Richard Dunn an extreme, but perhaps he was one of many who would continue to harass her with ever more subtle strategies to extort money. The Duke was a man more versed in the flaws and foibles of his fellow men. However, in the case of Nathan Hines, did Angela's instinct have no sway?

'Arthur, you are questioning my judgement of Mr Hines's character,' Angela said, unable to conceal the slight his comments had passed on her capacity for independent action.

The Duke frowned.

'I mean no insult to your intelligence and insight, my dear,' he said. 'You know how highly I esteem your goodness, your desire to assist others. It may be that you are correct in your assessment of this pawnbroker fellow. If he is, as you say, blameless, let the authorities reveal as much on an examination of the evidence against him.'

Angela sighed. Though she was uneasy, she had no further energy to resist the guidance of her wise and noble friend.

Chapter 19

'It's the blooming peelers,' one of the boys said in a loud whisper as the school room door opened suddenly.

Two uniformed Metropolitan Police officers stood in the cold draught that had blown in.

All heads were turned and Nathan, who was standing, chalk in hand in front of his group of forty boys, hoped that the men had not come to haul one of them away. It would not have been unexpected.

'Mr Nathan Hines?' said one of the constables.

'Yes?' said Nathan.

'Would you come with us, sir?'

Nathan, aware that the eyes of all were on him, felt the affront of being summonsed in this public manner.

'Now?' he said, trying to let puzzlement hide his anger.

'Yes, now,' said the constable, while his partner stood back at the door.

This constable moved towards Nathan, watched by the boys, some of whom shrank away as the man walked past them.

'What you done, sir?' shouted one of the boys.

Others joined in the jumble of whispered questions and speculation, gabbling, quips and laughter. Nathan squirming inwardly, placed the piece of chalk on the blackboard ledge and glanced quickly at Marianne, who was staring towards the scene, a look of alarm on her face.

'Let me dismiss the pupils first,' Nathan said, taking a step towards the constable, hoping that he would grant him at least this remnant of his authority.

The man shrugged and his partner repositioned himself in front of the door, as though he expected Nathan to make a run for it. Nathan turned back to the class and clapped his hands loudly, calling for a pause in their chatter. The suddenness of their silence seemed to impress even the two constables.

'We will have to finish the lessons for today. Go now and in an orderly manner and we will see you tomorrow,' Nathan said. 'Back row first.'

They departed, strangely subdued and the constables watched them until the last children and Marianne's girls, all except the three from the orphanage, had left.

'What is this all about?' said Marianne to the constable. 'Where are you taking Mr Hines?'

'Bow Street Station, madam,' said the first constable who had taken Nathan by the arm. Nathan's instinct was to throw off his hold, but he knew that this would only lead to greater humiliation.

'Are you arresting me?' he said. 'If so, on what charge?'

'We don't know nothing,' said the first constable. 'Just following orders. Sergeant'll tell you, down the station.'

What use would it have been to object, Nathan thought, to struggle and resist? He could not look at Marianne as he allowed himself to be led away. They marched him to the police headquarters in Bow Street and took him into a room where he was told to sit down. Another officer appeared, senior to the others and told him he had been arrested following allegations of indecency and fraud. Nathan, struggling to control his outrage and puzzlement demanded to know who had brought these charges. The sergeant refused to elaborate, saying that he would be brought before the magistrate the next morning. The first constable led him down a damp-smelling corridor in the station building, off which were several doors to police cells. He pushed Nathan into one of these without a word.

The room contained two wooden benches and rough blankets, but no other inmates, a bucket in the corner and a tiny barred window high up in the wall. This was the only source of light, a greyness that invaded the interior. Nathan sat down on the bench that was to be his bed for the night. His mind was stunned with the shock of what had happened and now he wished that he had put up some kind of fight. It would have been a more manly action, than his sheepish puzzled acceptance. He knew who and what must be behind this charge, Joshua Ellacott. The man had threatened him and clearly had enough influence to lead to the arrest of someone of Nathan's station in life. But fraud? He had no idea how this could have occurred. The accusation of lewdness between himself and Marianne was false at the overt level. They had done nothing improper and Joshua Ellacott could have no evidence of this, unless of course he could have seen into Nathan's mind and discovered the lust, the desire that he had suppressed.

He lay down, helplessness creeping over him. What would become of the school without him? Marianne could not manage on her own. She would not be able to tolerate the return of Joshua Ellacott. What would she do? Would she be dismissed? Nathan was not concerned about his business, which he knew was safe in Silas's hands. But there was the child, Selina Harding's daughter. Marianne knew the whole story and with her friend Miss Brennan might be able to make an appeal to Miss Coutts. He was, he realised, entirely dispensable. Whether he was convicted or not, he would be disgraced. He would in all likelihood not be able to return to the school. It was futile to speculate until he had heard what charges and what evidence had led to this. He thought of Marianne and how she was a woman he could have loved. It mattered little now whether she had any regard for him, though he believed in her friendship, her warmth towards him. He tried to remember what it had been to hold his wife close, to embrace his children, hoping that his imagination was strong enough to conjure up a small scrap of that past happiness.

Nathan did not sleep, rather he turned and turned on the hard bunk as his mind did the same, revisiting events and actions that could have led to the accusations against him. He had, long ago, been guilty of accepting stolen goods, as most in his trade had done. He was not proud, but he had been desperate to pay for medicines for his daughter, who had always been delicate and then when the cholera had come. But after that, he had sworn never to do this knowingly again and had run his business according to the law, in strict observance of the regulations governing pawnbroking. Silas had done the same since he had taken over. Beyond this, he had never violated any law, nor harmed another living soul, unless he considered the suffering his wife and son endured on their deathbeds. This was not by his hand but by his desperation and his misplaced faith in the powers of medicine.

He watched the arrival of dawn, a reflection from the small window as it became gradually lighter. The day would at least bring change, revelation, he hoped, a release from this limbo of unknowing. Someone clanged on the door of the cell, shouting for him to rise and make ready. A short time later, the door was swung open by a constable. Nathan asked the man if he could wash and shave and was told this was not possible.

'Lucky to get before the beak so soon,' said the constable.

The man was holding iron shackles which he locked around Nathan's ankles, ignoring his pleas and assurances that he would not try to escape.

'That's what they all say,' remarked the constable, putting the key in his pocket.

Nathan shuffled after the man back along the stinking corridor, hearing a raucous shouting from one of the other cells.

'Shut your gob,' yelled the constable, banging the door with his truncheon.

They climbed a short stone staircase up to the next level into a lobby where the policeman nudged Nathan towards another door. The policeman opened the door and they entered a large room furnished with several rows like pews in a church facing a large high desk, where the magistrate was to preside, though the place lay empty. Nathan had never been in a courtroom in his life. He glanced at the rows of people and was surprised to see Marianne, sitting next to Miss Brennan and Silas and behind them, the companion to Miss Coutts, Miss Meredith. Further along the front row sat Joshua Ellacott. Nathan found himself held in the man's glare and looked away. If he had not been afflicted by the humiliation of his situation, he might have tried to return that look with one of defiance. He glanced towards Marianne, who nodded to him, with a serious expression. Silas, too, acknowledged him with a slight nod.

The policeman led Nathan to stand before the magistrate's bench. Glad that he had his back to the onlookers, Nathan knew that he must maintain a calm and dispassionate manner. A few moments later, the magistrate arrived - a thin, grey-haired gentleman. He sat down without looking at any in the courtroom and took a pair of wire-rimmed spectacles from a case. A clerk approached Nathan with a Bible and instructed him to take the oath, while the magistrate shuffled some papers that had been placed on the bench. He looked up and peered at Nathan.

'Mr Hines,' said the magistrate. 'There are two accusations made against you by persons in this court. I am here to judge the veracity of these and decide whether there are criminal charges to answer. We will hear from the complainants in the first instance.'

Nathan's stomach sickened as he waited for Joshua Ellacott to rise from his seat and take the oath.

'Your honour, I accuse this man, Nathan Hines of lewd behaviour with a woman, Mrs Marianne Greaves while they were together under the guise of teaching children at the Ragged School in Field Lane.'

He declared this with the same confident, self-satisfied tone that had irked Nathan.

'And were you present to observe this lewdness?' said the magistrate, peering over his spectacles at Joshua Ellacott.

'Yes, I was.'

'And you observed them behaving improperly? Please be specific. In exactly what way was their behaviour improper?'

The magistrate's tone betrayed more than a little irritation.

Joshua Ellacott coughed and shifted on his feet. Was he about to invent sights and actions which never occurred?

'They looked at each other,' he said, though

his voice had lost a little of its conviction. 'They stood close together in a manner that would be likely to suggest lustful intentions and he looked at her, with er–. I can hardly bring myself to voice such indelicacies in this company. He stood with unseemly proximity to the woman and he – smiled at her.'

The magistrate's face changed. There was anger in the pinch of his mouth and his narrowed eyes.

'Sir, you accuse this man of serious misconduct and you can only specify that he looked at a woman and smiled at her?'

The magistrate turned to Nathan.

'Mr Hines, have you ever engaged in acts of lewdness with Mrs Greaves?'

'No sir, never.'

Joshua Ellacott's composure flitted away and his voice became shrill.

'The woman, I believe he corrupted her. She is a widow, susceptible, weak-willed and easily enticed into evil. The pair would lead young minds to destruction.'

He was quivering, his face colouring in anger. 'And he assaulted me with violence.'

'Be quiet, sir!' said the magistrate. 'So now you're accusing this man of attacking you, are you?'

The magistrate looked around the courtroom.

'Mrs Greaves is in court, I believe. Let us hear from her. Sir, be seated.'

Nathan saw the clerk take the Bible to Marianne, heard her rise from her seat and repeat the oath. The man's accusations were correct. He had looked at her with longing, but if that were a crime, then half the men in London would be in the dock.

'Mrs Greaves,' said the magistrate. 'Please tell us what you have to say about these accusations by Mr Ellacott.'

'Sir, Mr Hines has never at any time behaved improperly towards me. He has treated me with the utmost respect, acknowledging with sympathy my state of widowhood. There has been a professional relationship between us, no more.'

Nathan bowed his head, hearing Marianne's clear and convincing delivery, humbled by it.

The magistrate had clearly fixed Marianne with an inquisitorial gaze.

'Then why do you imagine, madam, that this man would invent such slights against you and Mr Hines?'

'I do not know. Only Mr Ellacott knows what drove him to say such things. I can only suppose that his remarks arise from some feelings of resentment against myself and Mr Hines. It is true that Mr Hines and I asked Mr Ellacott to leave the school, as he showed neither understanding of the circumstances of the children, nor kindness towards them.'

Nathan listened to her voice, loving her more for hearing such measured fairness.

'And did you witness Mr Hines attacking Mr Ellacott?' said the magistrate.

'Sir, Mr Ellacott refused to leave the school, so Mr Hines had to escort him to the door,'

Marianne said.

The magistrate, stony faced, turned back to Joshua Ellacott.

'Is it the case, Mr Ellacott, that you harboured personal feelings of antipathy towards Mr Hines?'

'Yes, as any Christian man would against an upstart, a godless pawnbroker who passes himself off as a scholar. I have an Oxford degree, I am fluent in Greek and Latin and have dedicated my life to God and to the furtherance of Christianity. Who is he compared to the likes of me?'

'An honest man,' came a man's voice from the row behind Nathan and he recognised Silas's unmistakable tones.

The magistrate looked disapprovingly in his direction, but turning to Joshua Ellacott, frowned angrily.

'Sir, you have been wasting the court's time. There is no charge to answer here. This is no place to play out acts of personal vengeance.'

'But sir –,' squeaked Joshua Ellacott.

'Be quiet. Leave this court,' snapped the magistrate.

Joshua Ellacott was ushered out by one of the constables and the magistrate, sighing, turned his attention back to Nathan.

'Now, this other charge, Mr Hines, it is of a more serious nature, that of fraud.'

Nathan curious, listened as Hannah Meredith, who was now Mrs Brown, told the magistrate about Nathan's letter to Miss Coutts, delivered only two days previously, informing her of the discovery of Selina Harding's lost daughter. Mrs Brown explained how Miss Coutts had received similar letters, written by tricksters assuming false identities, begging for money on the grounds of some claim for favour from Miss Coutts. She had recently been subject to a gross fraudulent claim of this type. So, her recent anxieties arising from the threats of such a criminal and the possible culpability of Mr Hines had made her wary. Thus, when Mr Hines's letter was received, they had reported the letter to the police in the hope that they would investigate.

'Well, Mr Hines,' said the magistrate. 'How do you answer this charge? Did you write with the purpose of gaining financially from the discovery of this lost child?'

'No sir, I had no such intent. I asked only that Miss Coutts should meet the child and try to verify her true identity, find out if she were in fact the daughter of Miss Coutts's former coachman. There is some evidence that this may be the case,' he said.

Miss Brennan was then questioned by the magistrate, stating categorically that the child had written her name, Belinda Harding, before she ever went to the Ragged School and met Mr Hines. Silas testified that he had sold the gown in which the letter had been found by Mr Hines when it had been pawned.

'And where is this letter now, Mr Hines?' said the magistrate.

'Unfortunately, it was taken from me when I was attacked one night and my clothes stolen.

I had a handkerchief embroidered with Mrs Harding's initials too. I kept this in my pocket, as I would regularly try to find out if anyone knew of Mrs Harding and her daughter. I hoped it might help in my search.

The magistrate pursed his lips. 'That's an unfortunate mischance and are there any witnesses who can testify to the truth of what you are saying?'

'I can, sir,' said Silas.

'You again?' said the magistrate. 'Very well, let us hear what you have to say. This is becoming quite a tediously complicated case.'

Silas declared that he had treated Nathan for wounds sustained when he was attacked and stripped of his coat and shoes one night. He had been searching for the woman and the child when he had been beaten, given a bloody nose and robbed for his pains. He also declared that Nathan was an upright and honest man of integrity and virtue. He had been moved by the desperation of the woman whose letter he had found.

'Well,' said the magistrate wearily. 'Mrs Brown, do you want to press ahead with the charge of fraud?'

'No, indeed I don't sir, nor would Miss Coutts,' said the woman earnestly. 'Miss Coutts did receive a letter from Mrs Greaves stating the reasons for Mr Ellacott's antagonism towards Mr Hines and herself. Unfortunately, this letter was overlooked by Miss Coutts's maid and it has only just come to light. If the letter had been read previously,

313

it is likely that Miss Coutts would not have wished to press any charges whatsoever.'

Mrs Brown bowed her head, then looked up at the judge.

'I believe that we, Miss Coutts and I, have been in error and I apologise to Mr Hines and to the court.'

The magistrate dismissed them all and Nathan, numb with relief, was released. When he stepped out of the police station, he found Silas and Marianne waiting for him. He shook Silas by the hand, thanking him sincerely for his words.

'Thank this lady,' said Silas indicating Marianne. 'She came to me, told me what was afoot.'

Nathan looked at Marianne, wishing to take her hand in his, but holding back with the bitter memory of the accusations against him. He must not let anything of that nature be said again.

'I am grateful, Mrs Greaves, for your testimony today,' he said in an uncomfortable formal tone.

Her face was solemn as she acknowledged his thanks. Did he detect a signal from her, too, that there must now be a gulf between them?

Early the next morning, Nathan, having slept poorly, was awake when a messenger called at the shop. Nathan opened the door to receive a letter thrust into his hand.

1 Stratton Street, Piccadilly

Dear Mr Hines,

In the light of recent events, relating to the child, who may be the daughter of James Harding, it is Miss Coutts's wish that you should attend her, along with this child and another female person as companion.

We shall expect to see you at 2 o'clock in the afternoon on Saturday.

Yours truly
Mrs Hannah Brown

The tone of the note told Nathan that the two ladies were still uncertain about the identity of the girl, Belinda Harding. Though he knew that they no longer suspected his motives or thought that he was engaged in some subterfuge, there was still in their minds the possibility that the girl was an imposter. Nathan knew that he would have to provide more evidence alongside the child's patchy testimony. Yet, the poor child's mind and spirit had been lashed by fear, the roughness of her time on the streets, near starvation and God knows what else before her rescue. She was still hesitant of speech, though it was clear that she was coming to trust Miss Brennan, Marianne and - he hoped - himself. One day, he would surely discover from her what had happened to the mother.

Miss Brennan, though on the surface a

strict superintendent, was at heart sympathetic and betrayed an interest in the mute child who had been placed in her institution. She had coaxed Belinda to write her name and had tried to persuade her to speak. Marianne was now, in her patient, gentle way, making progress in this regard and rewarded the child for each small spoken utterance.

Thoughts of Marianne and the distance he was obliged to keep from her made him ache with disappointment and longing. They had resumed their duties at school and the children had seemed almost oblivious to the interruption which had closed it for two days. He knew he must accustom himself to this loss of closeness and abandon all the hope he had of winning her affection or aspiring to a union with her. He could not pursue her now, as this would simply raise suspicions that the accusations made by Joshua Ellacott had been correct and that his own denials were lies. Miss Coutts would hear of it and he would be dismissed from the school. He felt fortunate, however, that his arrest had had no direct consequences in terms of his continuation at the Ragged School.

His summons to appear before Miss Coutts produced in him some apprehension, although this time the subject of the interrogation was to be the girl, Belinda Harding. He hoped that today he might persuade her to disclose more about her mother or memories of her father that would convince Miss Coutts. For this purpose, Nathan approached Marianne and asked if Belinda could stay a little longer after school was over.

'I should like to tell her about the visit to Miss Coutts,' Nathan said.

'Yes, I will ask Miss Brennan if she can stay awhile. I can give her other girls some plain sewing to keep them occupied while we talk.'

He thanked her and turned to go back to this class, but felt Marianne's touch on his arm.

'Nathan, are you quite well?' she said and for a second, he could not turn to face her.

'Yes, thank you,' he said, with a quick glance at her.

She was frowning with concern and must have noted the coolness of his awkward manner.

'You seem downcast,' she said. 'Your wrongful arrest has disturbed you, I think.'

'Yes, that's true. But I shall soon be myself again,' he said with an attempt at a smile.

Her compassion was almost more than he could bear. Fortunately, the demands of managing the boys drew all of his attention and energy for the rest of the day, leaving no leisure for reflection.

A dusty silence descended on the schoolroom after the departure of the children. Only Marianne and the three orphan girls remained in the corner, quietly sewing. Nathan watched them for a moment, wishing that he could share their quiet company. A few moments later, Miss Brennan arrived. Nathan

317

explained his intention and she nodded, bringing Belinda to him, leaving Marianne in the corner with the two other girls.

'Belinda,' said Miss Brennan, 'come and sit here on this stool. Mr Hines has something he has to tell you.'

They sat down in a small circle together, the child fixing Nathan with her dark, solemn eyes. She was a pretty child, thin and undersized for a nine-year-old, Nathan thought, but he was pleased to have seen a change in her in the short time she had been attending the Ragged School. Her cheeks had a little more colour, but her hand still fretted at the edge of her apron as she listened to Nathan speak.

'There is a lady,' Nathan said, 'who knew your father and mother, in fact your father used to work for her family. She would like to meet you, so that you could tell her about them.'

Belinda stared at Nathan. 'A lady?' she said in the small voice.

'Yes, your father was the lady's coachman and groom in a big house where he worked. Do you remember that?'

Belinda nodded slowly, still staring at Nathan.

'Can you tell us about your pa, my dear?' said Miss Brennan.

Belinda frowned, hesitating and then told them that they used to live in a cottage with trees all around and her father went up the drive every day to the big stables with so many horses and ponies. As she spoke, greater fluency came along with her recollections.

'We used to go with him sometimes, me and Geoffrey and Fran. But the baby didn't come. He was at home with...'

'Geoffrey and Fran?' Nathan said. 'Are they your brother and sister?'

Belinda's eyes darkened.

'They're not here anymore,' she said. 'They died. They all died and Pa died too.'

Miss Brennan glanced at Nathan. He did not want to ask more of the child and she, by the look in her eye, seemed to agree.

'They're all together in heaven now, my dear,' said Miss Brennan.

Belinda was weeping now and Nathan wished that he could take her in his arms and comfort her. His own daughter was always calmed by this in her times of sickness, until the end. However, Belinda wiped her eyes and Miss Brennan said they would go home now and would see Mr Hines the next day. He hoped that the child's description of her earlier childhood days would be sufficient for Miss Coutts. Belinda had never spoken of her mother and Miss Brennan had told him that every attempt to discover anything of her had provoked no response from the child, no tears, no words, no expression of any feeling. This surprised Nathan now that he had witnessed the effect of her recollection of the dead brothers and sister and her father. Why no mention of her mother? Could it be that the woman was still alive? He remembered the words of the old woman with whom Belinda and her mother had lodged, that Selina Harding was gravely ill when she left to seek help. Her mother's gown had certainly triggered a reaction from her, a startling one when she had seen another woman wearing it in the street.

As he bade goodbye to Miss Brennan and Belinda and the other girls, he had a sudden but foolhardy idea; he could go to the woman who bought the dress and buy it back from her. It would give the child comfort at least to have the garment, even if no one was ever to discover what had happened to the wearer and how she had been parted from it. He remembered, too, that Silas kept very detailed records not only of the people who pledged their goods in the shop and then returned to redeem them, but also of those who purchased unclaimed items. Silas was insistent on doing this, though Nathan himself had been lax in this regard. It would be important in the event of stolen goods having been illicitly pawned, to help track down the lawbreakers. Silas was right of course, and his punctiliousness in this case would prove advantageous. So Nathan hurried to give Marianne the schoolroom keys and rushed off, telling her that he had to go back to the shop on an urgent matter.

Silas was sorting out the storeroom when Nathan arrived back at the shop. He was whistling happily to himself and greeted Nathan.

'Been running, have you? Peelers after you again?' he said with a grin.

Nathan pulled out a handkerchief, wiped his brow and smiled. 'That's an ill joke. No, listen, I need to look at your record of purchasers.'

He explained to Silas about his plan to retrieve Selina Harding's gown.

'Let me look,' said Silas, opening up a large ledger on the counter, with the list of buyers.

'I know it may be a foolish idea, but maybe it might help the child,' Nathan said, scanning the names.

'Trying to be a saint, are you?' said Silas with a grin.

Nathan shook his head.

'No mortal man can be a saint, least of all me.'

Silas stared at him for a moment, then leaned over the book and pointed with his finger on one of the names.

'There, Stanley, Mrs Letitia, 25 Carter Lane,' he said.

'Excellent,' said Nathan, taking up a piece of scrap paper and dipping a pen into the inkpot on the counter.

'Not a saint, but good enough, best I can get,' said Silas cryptically as Nathan wrote on the paper.

Nathan looked up at him puzzled.

'Need a best man. You willing?'

Nathan clapped his friend on the back, delighted to hear the good news that Silas had so obliquely conveyed. Silas told him with glee that the wedding was to be in a month's time and Nathan agreed wholeheartedly to be his best man. He apologised for not having time to drink a glass to celebrate, but promised that the next day they should do so. Leaving his friend, who was whistling contentedly again, Nathan hurried out.

The address was not in a prosperous area, but neither was it a slum. Number 25, a tall brick building, was divided into apartments, Mr and Mrs Stanley living on the first floor. The couple were suspicious at first of Nathan's explanation. It was clear that they were not well off and the woman was reluctant to part with the gown, as she explained sadly that it was the best she had ever owned.

'But I will pay you well for it,' Nathan said, feeling reckless, knowing that he was about to offer her enough to have a new one made.

He took out two guineas and watched her face change.

'That's a very generous offer, Letty,' said her husband standing by.

She went to collect it from the bedroom and returned with it, folded into a bundle.

'And what's become of that poor little girl?' said Mrs Stanley. 'Is she all right in the head now?'

Nathan assured her that Belinda was recovering well and that the gown would be the only thing of her mother's that she might ever have. The woman looked at him a little shamefaced.

'I ought to have given it her, shouldn't I?' she said.

'No,' said Nathan. 'You bought it in good faith. Don't give it another thought.'

Back home, Nathan hung the gown in the wardrobe in his room. He would not give it to Belinda until after the visit to Miss Coutts as the child might be too moved by it to speak clearly to the lady. As arranged, he met Miss Brennan and Belinda at the orphanage and they made their way to Piccadilly on an omnibus, which the child found exciting. Sitting on the top deck, Nathan felt her small form pressing against his, saw for the first time a smile on her face as she looked down on the people and traffic below.

'Look Mr Hines,' she said. 'That man has a little monkey.'

Nathan smiled at her and Miss Brennan was eager to share her excitement and curiosity at the sight of an organ grinder down on the pavement, churning out his music to the passersby.

Belinda fell silent, however, when they climbed down from the omnibus and walked to Stratton Street.

'The ladies are kind,' Nathan said to the child, aware of her trepidation. 'Don't be afraid, Belinda.'

Remembering his previous visit to Miss Coutts, Nathan led Miss Brennan and Belinda down a passage at the side of the building to the servants' entrance where a maid let them in. She conducted them upstairs, first to a wide entrance hall and thence up a carpeted staircase to the reception rooms above. Opening a door on the left of the landing, she ushered them into a drawing room, with two tall windows overlooking the street below.

A surprising sight drew Nathan's and the others' gaze to the window, in front of which sat a large grey bird in a cage. It swayed from foot to foot on its perch and turning its head, it greeted the new arrivals.

'What a shocking bad hat!' screeched the parrot.

Belinda who was hanging close to Miss Brennan's side stared in silent awe, then Nathan heard her giggling quietly. The two ladies were sitting at either end of a large sofa on the left opposite a marble fireplace where a glowing fire warmed the room. They smiled in welcome and amusement as a small dog bounded up to Belinda.

'Good afternoon, Mr Hines and Miss Brennan, I believe,' said Miss Coutts, 'and this is the child. I see my little Wellington likes her.'

Belinda, having overcome her initial astonishment, had bent down to pet the little dog, who licked her hand enthusiastically. 'You had better make a fuss of him now before Fan wakes up,' said Miss Coutts.

It was only then that Nathan noticed another dog asleep at the side of the sofa.

'Miss Coutts is very fond of all in the animal kingdom, as you can see,' said Mrs Brown, with a smile, 'as well as the human one, of course.'

The parrot squawked as though to disagree and everyone laughed. Nathan was glad and grateful for the mildly eccentric Miss Coutts and her companion for permitting such a pleasant and informal reception.

Miss Coutts then fixed her gaze on Belinda, who had now stood up facing the ladies, the little dog having trotted back to its mistress and jumped on to the sofa beside her.

'Now Belinda,' she said, 'Mrs Brown and I would like to talk to you about your Papa. You remember him, don't you?'

'Yes, Ma'am,' Belinda said in a small but audible voice.

'Can you remember where you used to live, the estate where your father worked?'

Belinda paused, twisting her fingers together, her face colouring. Nathan feared that the situation had been too much for the child and that she might retreat to her former mute state again. She spoke up, however, faltering a little as she started, but growing in confidence and fluency.

'I mostly remember the big stables. There were horses for the coach and for the gentlemen and ladies and there were ponies too, that belonged to the young ladies. There was one with a spotted face.'

Mrs Brown glanced at Miss Coutts, who gave a slight nod of approval.

'And do you remember the pony's name?' said Mrs Brown.

'Yes, he was called Pepper. Pa said he was Miss Angela's pony when she was a little girl and he was very old. He was too small for her to ride, so Pa let me and my brother ride him sometimes. Pa said Miss Angela wouldn't mind.'

Miss Coutts looked at Nathan with a serious expression.

'Mr Hines, I owe you a sincere apology.'

Chapter 20

'No, I regret I can be of no help to you, man,' said O'Rourke, 'for haven't you brought this upon yourself, with all your chasing after the woman?'

Richard Dunn would have punched the impudent fellow in the face, had he not had need of his favour. In his fallen state, he would have to accept any who would be willing to spend time with him. There was a servant girl, a scullion, Sal, plain as a porker but she'd take messages for him, in return for a few flattering phrases. In the Fleet prison there was plenty of waiting to do and too much time for reflection on life, friendship, fidelity and treachery too.

'So the trial's started, has it?' said O'Rourke casually, as though he were idly passing the time of day strolling in the park.

Dunn felt his blood stirring, to think that the man was coming here under the guise of offering sympathy and help. The truth was that he'd come to crow and gloat over Dunn's misfortune.

'Aye, and it's all to do tomorrow,' Dunn replied grimly.

'Och you'll accept my apologies for not being there at the beginning of the proceedings. It must have slipped my mind. I've so much to do these days.'

Dunn could not stomach much more of this.

'Well, if you've no food, drink nor comfort to offer, you should be departing,' he said sourly.

O'Rourke recoiled in surprise.

'Dear God, man, if I'd known you were wanting anything I'd have brought it. What is it you'd be after having? Name it and I'll bring it, though it'll maybe be next week or even the next before I can be back.'

'You think I'll be here next week? You think I'll be condemned, do you?'

'Ah well, there's no knowing is there, with the strange workings of the law,' said O'Rourke, gazing around the cell. 'And by the way, Dunn, I'd remind you there's that small matter of the bet. You owe me five guineas, I think you'll recall. Didn't you wager that you'd be in Miss Coutts's bed by the year's end?'

'Damn your soul to hell, O'Rourke,' shouted Dunn, lurching towards him. 'Get out!'

O'Rourke leapt back and scrambled for the door.

'Steady on, there's a good fellow,' he said, calling for a warder. 'Hey, hey, visit over, if you please.'

Dunn laughed to see the cringing coward in fear of a beating. He was a miserable worm of a creature, not worth dirtying a fist upon. 'Rot in hell, will you,' was Dunn's last words to his one-time friend, who scurried out like a rat.

He sat down on the stool, staring at the dirt on the flagstone floor. They thought they had him beaten, the bastards, but he'd rise again and smack them in their faces with his triumph. He was strong and he knew the law, too. He would not to be cowed by the callousness of others. With pride in himself and dignity, he would field whatever slanders might be thrown at him in court. In any case, wasn't it a victory on his part to have forced the woman Coutts to face him in court? That was a thing and a half. Her influential friends and her riches couldn't get her out of that one.

In addition, the case was by no means theirs. No one could prove that she hadn't written the letter. They might get a dozen snivelling bank clerks from Coutts Bank to swear the letter was not in her hand, but that would not be impartial testimony. The fact was that it was simply his word against hers that the letter was forged. His landlady would testify quite truthfully that she had seen him with his injured right hand, the bandage up to his elbow and him completely incapacitated by it. How could a man in that state write anything, let alone forge a letter? They could not bring the charge of forgery against him, though that devil Thesiger, who fancied himself as the greatest lawyer in town, was prosecutor.

Dunn suddenly remembered that he'd got the pig-faced girl to launder his shirt for tomorrow's court appearance. He'd shout for the warder to make sure he had it. It was important to cut a respectable figure.

There she was, all demure and modest, coming in with her witchy companion, her familiar, and the courtroom was full to see the playing out of the drama. Well, he'd give them their two half pence worth of entertainment when they saw their heroine, the virtuous Miss Coutts, for the dishonest ruthless villainess that she was. He was well used to courts of law, having been bred to it. He was no powerless ignorant criminal, like most of the guttersnipes who turned up here. He knew his rights. Wilful and corrupt perjury, that was the charge. They'd never make it stick.

He took his place in the dock and looked out at them all, fearlessly. He eyed Miss Coutts, though she of course could not meet his gaze. To think that he had once imagined he loved her for her enticing looks, that he had been bewitched by her sly little smiles and invitations. What he saw now was a woman who had wilfully and cruelly wronged him. Two witnesses were required to prove perjury and there was only one, the supposedly saintly Miss Coutts. He, by contrast, had his own word, the power of his testimony, which he had rehearsed in his mind many times, and the evidence of his landlady.

The murmuring in the court ceased when the judge arrived and started proceedings. The first witness Dunn saw, to his delight, was his landlady, who did a pretty good job of convincing them all that he was sorely disabled and incapable of writing. But then the prosecution called another witness to the stand, a convict, no less, with his shackles about his wrists. What was afoot?

The man looked familiar somehow, and slowly, as he was sworn in upon the witness stand, Dunn realised who he was, Fortescue, the forger, the one whose wife wrote the letter. Except his name, he declared, was Blundell.

This was a blow he had not foreseen, that this pathetic petty criminal would come forth and reveal how the letter had come about. But the man was a convict. A jury would surely not be swayed by the testimony of a liar and a cheat. Where was the wife? Dunn felt the sweat prickle on his brow as the prosecutor, that puffed up peacock Thesiger swaggered towards the witness.

'Tell the court, Mr Blundell,' he said, 'how you and your wife came to meet Mr Dunn.'

The man cleared his throat with a cough. Prison had clearly not agreed too well with him, his drooping face and his clothes hanging from his body like wet washing.

'Sir,' said the man, 'I am ashamed to say it is to my eternal regret and miserable admittance of guilt that I met Mr Dunn in a public house. Here he engaged my services to write a letter. Would to God that I had listened to the voice of my conscience.'

The wretch was drawing himself up now, playing up to an audience like some cheap conjuror.

'I was, you understand, offering a business, a legitimate one, of course,' he went on, 'scribing letters for those unfortunates who do not have the precious gifts of literary talent as I have.'

Dunn squirmed at the words of this pontificating windbag.

'I was, for convenience, going by the name of Fortescue,' said the blackguard Blundell, 'to avoid those who might pursue me for some irregularities in the past. But sir, I and my poor wife had fallen upon terrible times, through ill-fortune and the blasts of fate, and we were forced to take a course in life, which though we knew was sinful, was the only one to keep us from starvation.'

The man was an insufferable, garrulous bore, trying to ingratiate himself to lessen his sentence, thought Dunn. There was hope that the jury would all nod off during this self-pitying diatribe. Even Thesiger was impatient.

'Yes, yes, your motives were no doubt driven by financial considerations, but we need to hear how the letter was written.'

Blundell or Fortescue sighed and dabbed his eyes with his cuff.

'Pardon me, sir,' he mumbled. 'Yes, Mr Dunn dictated word for word the letter, which I took down in my own hand for speediness. Then I passed it to my wife, as she had a model for the hand of the lady, Miss Coutts to be precise. My wife is a gifted scribe, sir.'

'And what did your wife have that provided her with Miss Coutts's written hand?'

'It was a notebook, sir, which Mr Dunn had upon his person and which he confessed to us he had taken from her house.'

A shocked gasp followed by a gush of whispering passed through the courtroom. They could gossip all they wished, thought Dunn, but he had the notebook safely secreted where no one would find it.

'And you have presented both of these documents as proof?'

'Yes sir, I reported the exact expression of the letter in my hand, and a page from Miss Coutts's notebook, which my wife removed, for surety you understand, during her writing.'

Dunn's stomach turned. The scheming bastards. They'd torn out a page. Worse still, the woman was called to the stand. Brazen old bitch that she was, she had lost none of the flesh of her husband. No doubt she had set herself up in a good way of business in the gaol, duping poor devils into giving up their food. There she was declaring that she'd always suspected Dunn of being a madman. So too, did the sly Miss Coutts, all dainty and refined as she gave her testimony, only she used the word 'deranged', being an educated lady, damn her soul. Then came that snake from Coutts Bank, Majoribanks, then her solicitor all peddling the same stuff against him, toadies all, in the pocket of their rich mistress. By the time the prosecution had rested their case, it was his turn to defend himself, but he found that the excitement, the appetite, the hunger for the success that he thought would be his, had all but fled.

He had one last chance maybe and the skill of a professional to aid him, the professional being himself. He knew how to play this one.

'Gentlemen of the jury, you have all made mistakes in your lives, I don't doubt if you're honest men that you would admit this,' he began, in a suitably confessional tone. 'I confess myself to have made several, through the natural weakness of a man and my trust in

333

my judgement of a lady. I fell in love, painfully, sincerely, heart and soul with that lady you see in court today, Miss Angela Coutts. Through the travails of my courtship, which cost me dear, ruined me in body, spirit and purse, I ended up a bankrupt.'

The attentive silence, the faces of the crowd in court stirred up a little of his confidence. Did he detect a spark of sympathy somewhere amongst them? He went on to tell them how he knew now that Miss Coutts, in a wicked plot to incriminate him and rid herself of his suit, had worked with the two convicted forgers. But was there some restlessness amongst the listeners, a shuffling and whispering?

'Yes, gentlemen of the jury, she had them copy my name upon a sworn affidavit,' he said, hearing an unfortunate quavering in his voice.

He cleared his throat. His leg was shuddering as he stood, but he plunged on.

'Heartlessly, and knowing the dire consequences of her trickery,' he said, though his body felt as though he were sliding down a cliff, losing his grip on the crumbling rock that might save him.

'Yes, erm, she had her forgers sign that affidavit with my name, a document swearing that Miss Coutts was indebted to me to the sum of £100,000. All those who testified today, liars all, who say I claimed this sum will be damned forever in hellfire!'

Was that laughter in the court? A current of sniggering amongst the onlookers shocked him, their grinning faces were more than he could bear. The judge silenced them, but Dunn, having no more to give, shrank down into his seat.

Guilty of wilful and corrupt perjury. Eighteen months in prison and two fines to pay before his release. Dunn lay down on the bench in his cell and closed his eyes. Already the sting of his hurt and rage was fading a little. It could have been worse after all, he mused. Aye, and weren't there always more fish in the sea worth catching?

Chapter 21

Bezer felt his body lurching with exhaustion, but his legs were driven on and on, as though controlled by a force beyond himself. The man beside him was wheezing noisily, his head bobbing up and down as he tramped the steps.

'Halt!' shouted a warder and Bezer tried to obey, though his body, now part of the machine, was not so quick to oblige. The wheel was still turning but slowing down and the man beside him suddenly flipped backwards, falling and hitting the ground behind the platform with a heavy thump.

'Off! Next lot!' yelled the warder again and Bezer, with shaking legs, tottered down the steps and collapsed a few yards from the wooden platform. The lifeless man who had toiled beside him on the treadmill was dragged away by two warders as the next shift shuffled towards the contraption and climbed up the steps to begin. A warder prodded Bezer away with his truncheon and he staggered to his feet.

'No more, I beg you,' Bezer groaned. 'I am an educated man. I can't do the work of an ox. Have pity.'

The response from the warder was a harder shove in his back in the direction of the wall, where other wrecked men were leaning or lying. They would be allowed an hour's rest before they had to take over again. Bezer, aching in every shred of his body, could no more stop his tears from flowing than he could hold back the tides on the Thames. He sank down on the ground, burying his face in his arms.

'First time inside?' said a voice beside him.

Bezer, embarrassed and surprised to be addressed by a fellow inmate, sniffed, rubbed his nose on his sleeve and raised his head. The speaker was a small man, skinny and rat-like, one of the lowest sort that infested this place.

'Yes,' Bezer mumbled, pulling himself up a little in a weak attempt to restore a little dignity in his bearing. 'Fortune has not treated me kindly. There are many far greater villains walking freely abroad than I.'

The rat man grinned showing a few brown teeth.

'True,' he said, 'wiles and luck are what'll stop you getting nicked.'

'You're right,' Bezer said, impressed by the man's analysis. 'And how did it happen to you?'

'Got grassed up,' he said. 'Can't do nothing about that.'

'And what was your sentence?' Bezer asked preferring to know this rather than the nature of the man's crime, though he looked small to be a murderer or someone who would present a particular physical threat.

'Transported.'

Bezer, mildly glad to have found another who was to share the same fate, nodded sympathetically. 'I too and my poor wife will suffer the same dire penalty, sent to a savage land on the other side of the world.'

The man scratched at a scab on his wrist and coughed for some moments, with a sound like cartwheels on gravel.

'Get out of it, if you play your cards right,' said the man. 'I did last time.'

Bezer, sat up straight. 'How?' he said.

'Go all meek and holy. Swear on the Bible, a bit of weeping and wailing and promising that you'll go straight till you die.'

'And you did this?'

The man nodded.

'Yes, two years hard labour they gave me instead.'

Bezer pondered on the possibility, thinking that hard labour in his own country might be preferable to the torment of a voyage that could kill him. Even if they made it to Australia, he and Susan would have to live among criminals and savages and never walk the streets of London as free citizens ever again. He would try and speak to the minister or vicar or whoever came to give them their dose of religion.

Transportation for twenty years. When the judge had passed sentence upon him and Susan for ten counts of forgery and deception, Bezer had nearly fainted. The judge's words had hit him like a blow to the chest. He had not breathed for some moments and Susan, at his side, had cried out. Their hope of greater leniency, because of their testimony against Richard Dunn, had been dashed. Worse still, the villain himself had been sentenced to a mere eighteen months, along with certain financial sureties. So before they were transported, they were to be sent for a spell in the huge Millbank Penitentiary. It was a castle-like building, with towers and walls like battlements on the banks of the Thames, that housed hundreds of prisoners - women and men. This new information, that the sentence of transportation could be reduced, gave Bezer a scrap of hope and the idea took a strong hold of him.

The next morning, the prisoners were herded into the central yard of their hexagon shaped block, formed of a continuous corridor of cells. In the centre, stood a brick watch tower with a warder positioned aloft. Others with their weapons of choice, heavy batons, flanked the prisoners as they stood listening to the sermon. It was being delivered by a young man with mad, staring eyes, more the red glare of the devil than that of a man of the cloth. If Bezer was hoping for mercy or at least sympathy from this one, he looked set for disappointment.

'Repent therefore and turn again, that your sins may be blotted out!' raged the youthful minister at them, in a tone like a strangled cat. 'God said, "Those whom I love, I reprove and discipline," and so you sinners who have violated the laws of man and of God, must suffer the punishments from both.'

Bezer, as he stood amidst the stinking, flea-ridden men, tried to dream of what might be. He had travelled from the extremes of despair to delirious fancies of his release under the influence of the benevolent Miss Coutts. However, he could not forget that she had been one of the victims of their attempts to gain money and favours. He thought fondly of the clever plans that he and Susan had formulated. He longed for her now, and supposed that she must be incarcerated in the women's wing of the prison. Even a gifted woman like herself would be hard-pressed to get them out of this fix. They were truly doomed this time.

The minister had worked himself into a state of frenzy judging by the colour of his face, but this was having little effect on most of the listeners. In fact, the tight-packed grouping facilitated the passing of messages and contraband between the inmates. A few of the more fearful or devout were clasping their hands together and with eyes towards heaven, were muttering amen and other such devotions. Bezer closed his eyes and made an attempt to pray. It would be a form of preparation for when he met the minister or the governor and tried to show that he was fully redeemable. He would solemnly promise to toil in honest labours and for the rest of his waking hours beg forgiveness of God. Having thought this, however, it all seemed such a miserable prospect, like spending the rest of his life on the treadmill.

'Come, merciful death,' he silently prayed. 'Take me, quickly and peacefully, not with the torments some of the inmates suffered, vomiting, diarrhoea, blackened faces, skeletal corpses loaded on to wagons bound for the graveyard outside the prison walls. With hands pressed together in front of his chest and eyes squeezed shut, he was incapable of making more effort to get his message across to his maker. He heard the minister saying a final prayer and then the warders growling orders to move. Bezer, however, stuck to the spot, on his knees, hoping that his devotions would draw the attention of the minister.

'Get a move on,' called a warder from somewhere on his left-hand side.

Bezer cracked open one eye and saw the threat advancing, but then, as he was about to cringe under the blow, he heard another voice.

'Hold your hand,' said the minister. 'This man is still at prayer.'

Bezer kept his eyes pressed shut though he would dearly have loved to see whether the minister was coming nearer and whether there might be a chance of submitting his pleas.

'Filthy sinner that I am, cleanse my soul, oh Lord,' Bezer said aloud. 'I have lived a life full of abominations, but here in this place I have seen your light shine upon my black soul.'

He heard the minister exchange a few words with the warder.

'Five minutes, that's all,' the warder was saying and Bezer inwardly rejoiced.

He opened his eyes, gratified that his rhetorical powers had not completely deserted him.

'Sir, your sermon touched my spirit and I

felt God's presence here, even in this terrible place,' Bezer said to the young minister. 'Now I know there is hope of redemption. Can it be true, sir that I could be cleansed?'

The minister's eyes seemed to flame with excitement as he stared at Bezer.

'The Lord's heart is always open to those who truly repent,' he said.

Bezer felt that this was the most promising five minutes he had spent in all his time in this hideous place. He explained to the minister how he, Bezer Blundell, wished to be considered for a lesser sentence, along with his wife Susan Blundell, who had always been more devout than he, until he saw the light. He begged the minister to intervene on their behalf, to have the sentence of transportation reduced to redemptive toil in his native land. He prostrated himself at the man's feet and listed the sins for which he humbly and sincerely repented. He made all the promises that he could think were required of a truly virtuous life, and begged to know the name of the minister of God who had brought such a vision to him. The Reverend Joshua Ellacott seemed gratified to give Bezer his name.

The young churchman then embarked upon a long and tedious diatribe, punctuated frequently by what Bezer assumed were biblical quotations. Bezer's knees ached and the prayerful posture he was having to sustain was causing his body to quiver, as his muscles threatened to snap with the tension.

'Sir, sir,' he bleated in a short pause in the

minister's sermon. 'Will you speak for us?'

Joshua Ellacott stared at him with unforgiving eyes.

'I am merely God's weak instrument,' he intoned. 'You must bear the punishment meted out to you. Only by the suffering and trials most hard and distasteful to you will you have any hope of entering the Kingdom of God. Only then will you be truly repentant.'

Chapter 22

1 Stratton Street, Piccadilly

Dear Mr Hines,

Your visit with the orphan girl touched me profoundly. I am greatly comforted to know that she has been found and must commend you for your part in the saving of this child from destitution. In memory of a steady and hard-working servant, her father, it is my intention to pay for the girl's education and training into some suitable employment, until she is of the age for marriage or is required to support herself through honest labour.

To this end, I wish to enquire whether you would be prepared to act as her legal guardian. You are, I believe, a person of honesty and benevolence and would provide the child with appropriate protection. If you are willing, I would ask you to present yourself to my solicitor, Mr Warner who will prepare the documentation. You will then be able to draw a sum of £50 per annum for the upkeep of the child and her education.

Please notify me at your earliest convenience as to whether you agree to these arrangements.

Yours sincerely
Angela Burdett-Coutts

Nathan read the letter a second time. The

gladness that he felt on behalf of the child Belinda was tempered by surprise at Miss Coutts's proposal to him. To be the girl's guardian, to take charge of her life until she was grown was to act as a parent. Could he bear the worry and the pain of such a role again? To watch vulnerable young lives for which he was responsible cut off, threatened by sickness, was something he shrank from. The other lingering thought would always be that her mother might still be alive, somewhere. Until he knew her fate, it would be something that would trouble him. And what of her kin? Might there be a relative who by reasons of blood and obligation would wish to raise the child? Yet, the suggestion by Miss Coutts had shocked him into a realisation of his growing affection for the child.

Before the trouble with Joshua Ellacott, Nathan would have gone to Marianne for advice, but now with his self-imposed distance from her, he could not think of approaching her with this. Miss Coutts thought him a principled and morally upright man, a suitable guardian for an orphan child. For Belinda's sake, he must live according to that flattering definition of himself. He surely must not manifest his feelings for Marianne; any covert or open show would simply confirm the basis of Joshua Ellacott's accusations. Nathan wondered where that pious young man had gone and in what branch of God's business he was now engaged. His way was a pitiless path to faith or redemption. Marianne's by contrast employed compassion without judgement. If he could maintain a professional stance with her, a discussion about the welfare of the child, what harm could it do? He resolved in the end to speak to her. He also needed Marianne to be there when he gave Belinda her mother's gown. The girl was clearly fond of her teacher and appeared to trust her.

Nathan folded the gown carefully and placed it in a cloth bag, remembering something important he wished to say to Silas before he left for the school. Silas was already busy in the shop when Nathan approached him on his way out.

'I've been thinking,' Nathan said, 'now you're to be a married man with extra responsibilities, whether you would like to be a partner in the business. I'd sign it over to you entirely, if I had the means, but my fee at the school is not enough to live on. A share in the shop would suffice for me however, if you were willing. Think about it. We'll talk on it later.'

Nathan left Silas silent and open-mouthed and made his way to the school.

At the sight of Marianne and her cautiously welcoming smile, his doubts disappeared. He knew that she would be glad to hear of Miss Coutts's generosity to Belinda and he told her of the proposal that he should become the child's guardian. Marianne smiled.

'I can think of no one more fitting, Nathan,' she said. 'You will do it, won't you?'

He glanced away for a moment, unable to meet her gaze, remembering his previous resolve.

'Yes,' he said. 'I will take her out of the orphanage to come and live with me. I have an extra room above the shop. And of course, she can come to school each day.'

He stopped himself, sensing that the strength of his desire for this to happen was too keenly expressed.

'I will write to Miss Coutts straight away. But I have something else to tell you. I have the gown, Belinda's mother's.'

Marianne gasped. 'May I see it?' she said.

He held up the bag to her and she pulled out the garment, shaking it free of its folds.

'It is an attractive gown. I'm so glad that you found it again,' she said, then frowned slightly and looked at him. 'But we must be prepared for tears when Belinda sees it. She has never spoken of her mother.'

Marianne folded the dress again, replaced it in the bag which she took to a small wooden cupboard in the corner and unlocking it, placed it on the bottom shelf.

'Tell her later that you are to be her guardian. It may overwhelm the child to hear of that too.'

'Yes, of course,' Nathan said, rejoicing that the barrier that he had created between them had been broken down. Now it might be possible for him to maintain a friendship with this woman with whom he had once wished for a stronger bond.

The children arrived, including the usual new ones, small and hungry, in want of food.

Some of the regular ones were missing, however, no doubt sent on errands or jobs of work, or caring for younger children. Nathan was accustomed to this reality now and tried to provide for all who attended, no matter their level. His best monitor, Saul, a bright Jewish boy, was absent and there were no other boys with the same presence and ability to command others. However, the day went remarkably well; some children read haltingly aloud and others listened with admiration for their achievement. Maybe, Nathan thought, these little steps were significant.

A servant from the orphanage arrived at the appointed time, at the close of the school, to accompany the girls home. Nathan waited, watching while the servant sat down with the girls and Marianne went to the cupboard to retrieve the bag, then beckoned to Belinda to come with her.

'We have something to show you, Belinda,' Nathan said, as they sat down together in the opposite corner of the schoolroom.

The child's eyes were wide, as though she imagined something fearful or hideous that was to be revealed to her. Marianne, sitting close to the girl, pulled out the gown and spread it across their laps. Belinda said nothing, but touched the fabric gently, her fingers moving along the velvet trim of the neckline and collar. Nathan exchanged a look with Marianne and saw in her expression that they must wait and be patient. After some moments, Belinda looked up at Nathan, then at Marianne.

'Mama's best dress,' Belinda said. 'She looked very pretty in it. They took if from her. I said no, but they took it.'

She clutched the bodice of the dress and pulled it to her, hugging it to her chest. Her tears had started, noiselessly, her head bent over the garment. Nathan and Marianne sat silently waiting until Belinda lifted her head to him again.

'A lady had it, Mama's dress. She was wearing it and I asked but she wouldn't give it.'

'I know,' said Nathan, 'but the lady didn't know that it was your Mama's. She bought it in a shop.'

Belinda frowned. 'But how did you –'

'I bought it back from the lady for you.'

She stared back at him, glancing at Marianne as though to verify the truth of what she had heard.

'To keep?' she said.

'Of course.'

Marianne reached for Belinda's hand.

'Can you tell us what happened to your Mama?' she said gently.

At first Belinda shook her head, weeping, but then her tale flooded rapidly from her.

'She was very sick and we couldn't stay in our room any more so we went to an old woman who helped us. Mama said she could get money and get food, so we had to be tidy and go and Mama put on her dress and said I mustn't worry, but she couldn't walk very well and then she fell down.'

The child's voice had become hoarse and dry. Marianne put her arm around her shoulders and pulled her into an embrace as her muffled sobs continued. Nathan listened to the story that he had longed to know, but now found himself sickening to hear from this child.

'She fell down in an alleyway,' Belinda sobbed. 'She didn't move. Her hands were cold and I couldn't make them warm. I tried to make them warm.'

Nathan could see the scene in his mind and he could not banish the sight for some moments. The woman had died in the street with her child at her side.

'Then some boys and girls came and they said she had a fever, so they took her dress off to cool her, but I said no, no, don't it's my Mama's.'

Her words tumbled out through her tears. 'But they wouldn't listen. They ran away and I ran after them, but they went and I couldn't find them and then I was lost and then –'

Marianne held her in her arms, rocking her gently, whispering to her that her Mama was at peace now in heaven and that she was safe. Nathan thought of the young girl who had brought him the gown, one of a gang of thieves who had stripped a dead woman in front of her child and then had pawned her gown. Selina Harding's body would have been removed, like the corpses found daily floating in the river, and with no means of identification would have been buried by the parish in a pauper's grave.

The servant woman and the other two girls had heard Belinda's sobs and sat silently watching. The child had at last exhausted herself to silence still in Marianne's arms. Nathan saw that Marianne, too, had been weeping, but she spoke softly to Belinda.

'Will you help me fold your Mama's gown?' she said. 'You must take it with you. Your Mama would want you to have it.'

Belinda took the bag calmly from Marianne and with the others, left the school. Nathan and Marianne stood side by side watching them depart. There was, he felt, a sense of exhausted relief, a slackening of the air between them. He couldn't speak yet of the effect of Belinda's story and had seen how it had moved Marianne. He reached for her hand. She returned his gentle pressure, though they did not look at one another. They stood for some time before Marianne finally spoke.

'Nathan, we should beware. This may be seen as an act of lewdness.'

He knew by her voice and then by her smile as he turned to her that this was no pious expression or warning. At this he knew that nothing could hold him back and that she would not resist him. He lifted her hand to his lips and kissed it, then slipping his arms around her waist embraced her, her body softening against his.

Chapter 23

Two years later

Though Angela was always in a state of happy anticipation at the prospect of a visit from her dear Arthur, today she felt a greater surge of joy. She would confess to the dear man what was in her heart, ignoring what people might think of her, of their disapproval, their condemnation, their gossip. If he were to agree to her proposal, she would be happier than ever in her life. Her projects at home and abroad were flourishing. The time was right for her to be bold. She would also be able to share with the Duke that morning the very interesting news she had received in her correspondence.

Geoffrey, Angela's secretary, had developed an efficient system for sifting and sorting her mail. The correspondence and papers requiring her attention were placed carefully upon the table in the window of the drawing room. She preferred to look at them there, as the light was better and she had Cocky, her white cockatoo as cheerful company, since the demise of the Duchess's old grey parrot. The volume of letters seemed to be building every day, which was not surprising, given the number of projects she was currently managing. Geoffrey designated different piles, which he labelled appropriately. But this morning, Geoffrey had left a folded newspaper on top of the letters, which she had read with some astonishment and a measure of relief.

MORNING HERALD **1843**

Mr Dunn's conviction for wilful endangerment of Princess Mary
Court of Queen's Bench – Saturday
Before Lord Denman and a special Jury

The indictment charged the accused Mr Richard Dunn with persistent harassment and wilful endangerment of the royal person of Princess Mary. The prosecution presented evidence of Mr Dunn's unlawful entry to the Princess's private house, his scandalous letter, his open pursuit of the lady, while she was engaged in public affairs...

Angela, having scanned the lengthy account of the trial, found her own name mentioned as a previous victim and read with some surprise that Dunn had been sentenced to transportation, to a penal colony for life.

The sentence of the judge concluded that the safety and security of a royal person, and indeed any lady of wealth, could not be assured unless this man were removed from the country and closely confined.

Justice, Angela thought, was sometimes a long time in coming. She laid the paper down and noted that there were two letters marked by Geoffrey 'From Foreign Lands'.

The first, she noted, was from Van Diemen's Land, an island of the antipodes which housed a penal colony. The letter was densely written in a neat but florid hand.

Sullivan's Cove
Van Diemen's Land

Esteemed Madam,

Though I and my dear wife are persons sunk so low in the ranks of society and to you, honourable lady, merely insignificant, I entreat, however, you to recollect a small service we once rendered you. We played a vital part in the conviction of the reprobate Mr Richard Dunn. Though now we dwell in chains of bondage in a far off savage land, we have accepted our punishment as our due for our sins against others, committed through want and poor judgement of a character bent on leading us astray.

In our repentant state, we are determined to set for ourselves a new course in life, once we have had our freedom restored to us. It is our fervent wish, for which we pray to God for strength and fortitude, that we should take up honest and worthy toil. To this end, my wife, who is a seamstress by profession, or couturier as the French would have it, along with her many other qualities and skills, has suggested that we should establish a business together. I have considerable knowledge of the world of commerce and finance and it is thus our plan to create an enterprise in the trade of ladies' apparel. This country, crude and uncultivated, is sorely in need of models of civilisation upon which to build society. You, honourable lady, seek to civilise savages via the Christian message. We would seek to offer the same service via ladies' accoutrements. Even the humblest and lowest of the low require respectable attire for their Sunday worship, while those of higher rank can, in their finer apparel, praise and glorify God with more magnificence and splendour.

So, with this aim in mind, esteemed Miss Coutts, we appeal to you most respectfully to consider providing us with sufficient monies to build and furnish our establishment. By these means, we seek to bring civilisation to a desert and redeem our souls by wholesome labour. Each month of our long servitude will now be spent with hopes and prayers for your benevolent and merciful response to our plea.

I am your humble and penitent servant,
Bezer Blundell

Angela laid the letter aside with a sensation of amused incredulity. In spite of herself she could not help admiring the resilience of this man Bezer Blundell and his wife. Would it be completely foolish on her part to gift them money? She would have to take advice about how she might ensure the lawful use of any investment.

She picked up the second letter, noting with pleasure, the identity of the writer.

Adelaide, South Australia

Dear Miss Coutts,

My husband and I send you our warmest greetings and hope that this letter finds you well. Nathan, Belinda and I are all in good health and spirits and are now much more accustomed to our new country. It has been strange at times, dealing with the unfamiliar and sometimes difficult conditions, but we have made good progress with our plans, of which I hope you will approve.

Our school is now well established, though it is a modest two roomed wooden cabin amidst a forest of gum trees. We already have fifteen pupils, the children of labourers and artisans mainly, who have been settling in our small town in greater numbers. They are, like children all around the world I imagine, lively and energetic with a great capacity for learning. Most have mastered the rudiments of reading and Nathan is impressed by their progress in arithmetic and mathematical principles. The textbooks, reading books and Bibles are heavily used each day. We also teach needlework, woodwork and cooking when we have the opportunity. Belinda, who we love as our daughter, is a most capable pupil/teacher too and is a great help to us.

We rejoice, too, that our family has increased with the arrival of our twin sons. We feel blessed with good fortune, and grateful, too, that your generosity and kindness has enabled us to provide a sound start for children in this new country, which they will help to build. Although the children do not know their benefactress personally, their lives are touched each day by what your generosity has afforded them, as ours are too. Without your bounteous financial support this venture would not have been possible and it is our hope that expansion of the town and of our school will soon lead to self-sufficiency through the charging of modest school fees.

I will write to inform you of our further progress and development at the year's end, in the expectation that our pupils' success will be a fitting testament to the value of what you have helped us achieve through your beneficence.

I am yours truly
Marianne Hines

Author's Note

Although *The Pawnbroker's Pledge* is a work of fiction, it draws strongly upon aspects of the lives of real people in 19th century London, most notably the banking heiress Angela Burdett-Coutts and her relentless stalker, Richard Dunn. The outrageous behaviour of Dunn, a dangerous fantasist, and the subsequent legal action against him, are well documented in contemporary newspaper accounts. Likewise, the enormous wealth of Miss Coutts and her determined and pious commitment to philanthropic works, in particular the relief of the poor, made her a reluctant celebrity at the time. Other significant people in the life of Miss Coutts also make appearances in the novel: Hannah Meredith, Miss Coutts's constant companion and friend, Charles Dickens and the Duke of Wellington.

As with much historical fiction, the imaginative re-creation of the past leads to the selection of particular factual material and the manipulation of known facts and chronologies, to suit the purposes of the narrative. Thus, for example, I have treated the character of Bezer Blundell, a real person with a splendidly Dickensian name, and the organisation for which he worked, 'The London Society for the Suppression of Mendicity'.

My exploration of the period and setting, through characters from all social strata, including beggars, impoverished workers, fraudsters and those striving to improve the lives of others, has highlighted many parallels with modern society. Nearly 200 years later, we still witness the gulf between rich and poor, the desperate circumstances that lead people to beg and live on the streets, the efforts of those with compassion and moral responsibility to alleviate poverty and compensate for the economic and social structures that maintain inequalities.

About The Author

Clare Hawkins was born and brought up in the west of Scotland and is a graduate of the universities of Edinburgh and Sheffield. After many years working in different sectors of education and when her two daughters left home, Clare embarked on a short distance-learning course on novel writing. What started as an experiment quickly became an enjoyable obsession with writing historical novels.

Inspiration for plots and settings derives from her fascination with British social history and her background and experiences of living in various different regions in England. Her second novel *The Bookbinder's Daughter* was short-listed for the Historical Novel Society's International Award 2012/13. Since then some of her other novels have been short and long-listed in various competitions: The Mslexia Novel Competition, The Yeovil Literary Award, The Exeter Novel Competition. She published her Civil War novel *Lament for a Siege Town* for a local interest market and her short stories have appeared in Sundial Magazine and The Copperfield Review.

Clare lives with her husband in Essex and is a doting grandmother of four, a volunteer in community education, a keen allotment gardener, cyclist, and musician of very modest ability.

www.blossomspringpublishing.com

Printed in Great Britain
by Amazon

25586701R00209